I T is for you—a gift," the old woman said.

"A gift?" Persis echoed.

"A gift of blood. To your hand only will it go. And in your hand it will bring life—and death. *She* wished it so."

"She—?"

Askra was already shuffling toward the outer door.

Persis plucked gingerly at the box, not liking the feel against her fingers. It unrolled slowly and then she saw the fan. There was no mistaking the opal-eyed cats carved upon it.

She slammed the lid back on the box. She did not believe in witches or curses, but that did not matter. *She knew that what she now held in her hand was an instrument of evil. . . .*

the opal-eyed fan

Andre Norton

FAWCETT CREST • NEW YORK

THE OPAL-EYED FAN

THIS BOOK CONTAINS THE COMPLETE TEXT OF THE
ORIGINAL HARDCOVER EDITION.

Published by Fawcett Crest Books, a unit of CBS
Publications, the Consumer Publishing Division of CBS Inc.,
by arrangement with E. P. Dutton, a division of
Sequoia-Elsevier Publishing Company, Inc.

ISBN: 0-449-23814-8

Printed in the United States of America

10 9 8 7 6 5 4 3 2 1

Though Lost Lady Key does not exist, features of two coastal islands and one key are combined to furnish its checkered history. On Sanibel a mysterious race built a city of canals and mounds composed of shells and rammed earth, as well as shell-paved roads. These unknown people are rumored to have been exterminated by an uneasy combination of Spaniards and imported Seminoles, leaving only evidences of a civilization somehow linked with that of the Mayans of South America.

Captiva, Sanibel's twin island, is supposed to have served as a prison for women taken during the pirate raids of the late seventeenth and early eighteenth centuries.

But Indian Key provided the house with its escape route through the sea turtle pens, its master who refused to acknowledge the power of Key West, and its doctor who pioneered in growing tropical fruits in Florida. An Indian massacre in the middle 1800s brought an abrupt end to this small empire—the fabulous house (known for its luxury, up and down the coast) was burned. A pall fell over the site and no attempt was made to rebuild or reuse the land.

1

The room was dusky dark, but it was quiet. Where was the wind—that threatening, screaming wind which had engulfed the whole world, whipped the sea mountain high?

Persis Rooke turned her head slightly, though she did not yet open her eyes. Here was no musty odor underlaid with the stench of bilges. Rather, a faintly spicy fragrance. Her mind seemed as sluggish as her body, and the latter bore painful bruises that made her wince as she shifted position a little.

She stretched out her hands. Under them was the smoothness of linen. Was this a dream? She did not want to open her eyes and find herself once more wedged into the narrow ship's bunk. She lay still, grateful for the silence, the feel of the linen, and tried to remember as she slowly, at last, opened her eyes.

This was—a room! Not the tiny stifling cabin into which she had barely been able to squeeze herself and her belongings. She lay on a real bed—she must be in a house—on *land*!

A drapery of netting hung about the bed, making the rest of the room dim and misty looking in the morning light. Solemnly, as she had sometimes done as a child, she gave the skin on her right wrist a sharp pinch. The resulting pain was reassuring. She *was* awake. Now Persis braced herself up on the wide expanse of the bed to look around. Her head whirled a little and she fought that giddiness stoutly.

She must remember— She had been on a ship, there had been a grating crash as the *Arrow* had brought bow up on a reef. Then—

The wrecker!

Persis shook her head in spite of the giddiness that it caused. She felt the warmth of the returning outrage. That—that pirate! The one who had loomed out of the storm to where she clung to a rail, had shouted some incomprehensible words at her, and then carried her, in spite of her screams and her attempts to fight free, to toss her down into the small boat below, her hair streaming about her, the protests battered out of her by the wind along with the air from her lungs. She had been so angry at his high-handedness that she had almost lost her fear. But after she was in the boat—

Persis shut her eyes again. No, it was very queer. She thought she would never, never forget that pirate's face, his treatment of her as if she were a bale of goods. But later—there was just nothing.

Uncle Augustin!

What had happened to Uncle Augustin?

Persis, now thoroughly aroused, slid to the edge of the bed, hooked fingers in the netting, and jerked it along until she could find an opening in it. That sense of duty long drilled into her was completely awake. She hardly glanced about the shadowy room where only an edging of light showed around the massively shuttered windows. She must find her uncle. He had been only a feeble shadow of himself before the storm. Perhaps—

She looked around a little wildly; she simply could not go charging out of this room wearing only her night rail. And that, she noted now, was not one of her own fine lawn ones, but a garment too big and of coarser stuff. Where was her clothing?

At least that wind was gone. But under her feet the floor still seemed to sway as if it were the deck of the lost *Arrow*. She made her way to the nearest window by holding on to the edge of the bed as a support.

To throw open the shutters was a task she fumbled over, though she was usually quick with her fingers. Then she looked out into a still morning. At first nothing was visible but the crowns of palms. Then, by leaning forward on the broad windowsill, she discovered that she was on the second story of a house which had been, in turn, erected on a mound of—shells? Could they be *shells*? How could so substantial a dwelling have been placed on a foundation of *shells*?

There was water below, and a wharf on which were piled boxes and barrels and—yes—her very own trunk!

Also, there were people. Persis watched three dark-skinned men trundle a large box by wheelbarrow back toward a building of which she could see only a bit of roof. The three wore breeches cut off at the knees, leaving their brown legs bare, and their shirts were much patched, faded, and salt stained.

Wreckers—like that brute aboard the *Arrow*.

Persis felt distaste and a touch of fear. Though Uncle Augustin had said that the wreckers of the Keys saved lives and goods, she remembered talk in New York of their greediness, tales of conspiracy between some captains and the Key men to lose ships on marked reefs. They were certainly not very far removed from the pirates who had earlier made these same waters their own and had had hiding places hereabouts.

But what had happened to Uncle Augustin?

Now that there was more light, Persis saw a wrapper lying across a chair by the bureau. As she snatched that up, she caught a glimpse of herself in the mirror on the wall. It was a very ornate mirror, perhaps better suited for a formal parlor, deeply framed in gilt which was a little dimmed. But the dimming had not extended to the glass.

What a miserable sight she was!

No neat braided knot to top off her coiffure, no carefully disciplined bunches of side curls, just a mass of tangled brown hair sticky and matted, as she discovered when she poked and pulled at it. She looked like one of those noisome hags illustrating one of Mrs. Radcliffe's weird stories. Persis was no beauty, but she had never allowed herself to be untidy. Now her reflection appalled her. She was startled by a tap at the door and whirled about to call:

"Come!" Then she added, "Molly!" with deep relief, running to throw her arms about the woman who entered, a liberty Molly would never have allowed normally. For she was as set in her idea of the perfect lady's maid as Persis was schooled to be the lady in charge of Uncle Augustin's household.

"Miss Persis, you'll catch your death!" Molly freed

herself and shook out a light cloak from the bundle she carried, putting it around the girl's shoulders. "It's a mercy we ain't all at the bottom of that there sea, so it is!"

"Where's Uncle Augustin?"

"Now you have no call to fret, Miss Persis. He's as snug set as a baby in a hearth cradle. Shubal has took him some soup and he swallowed near all of it. That the good Lord brought us safe to land is a mighty mercy—"

"But where *are* we?"

"This is Lost Lady Key, leastways that is what they call it. And you've been sleeping right in Captain Leverett's own bed. This is his house."

"Who is Captain Leverett?" Persis' head ached. If Uncle Augustin had his faithful Shubal in attendance, she need not worry about him for the moment. Molly's calm had its effect, for she was acting as if it were the most natural thing in the world for Persis Rooke, a most respectable lady, to wake up in the bed of an unknown captain in a house she did not even remember entering.

"Why he's the one who rescued us. It was he as got you into the boat so his men could bring us ashore. Don't you remember that, Miss Persis?"

The pirate—oh, she remembered all right! Persis set her teeth. It was not likely she'd ever forget being thrown about. Molly could talk of being saved, but surely one did not have to be treated like *that*!

"It was a bad reef the *Arrow* got hooked on," Molly continued. "Though Captain Leverett thinks they might be able to pull the ship off once she's lightened of cargo. They've been bringing in stuff out of the hold since last night."

"Wreckers!" Persis sniffed.

"We was right glad to see them, Miss Persis. It's these wreckers as save ships, lives, too. And Captain Leverett, he's a proper gentleman. Gave orders to get the doctor for Mr. Augustin. There's a real doctor living here, though he don't do much doctoring anymore. Seems he's more interested in planting things to watch 'em grow, or so Mrs. Pryor says. But he ain't forgot his doctoring when there's a need for it. He said as how Mr. Augustin has had a bad shock, and the wetting didn't do him no good neither. He looked at you, too, Miss Persis. Seems like when you fell into the boat you got a knock on the head. But he said that was no great matter—just to let you sleep it off."

"I—" Persis pushed impatiently at her tangled hair. The past few days had been a bad dream. First the awful seasickness which had kept her captive in her cabin in spite of all her will to conquer it—then the terror of being tossed about in the storm—the final shuddering crash—

"You'll be all right, Miss Persis. And Miss Lydia, the Captain's own sister, is lending you some clothes. I'll go and get 'em. That there dress you had on is ruined. But first—" Molly went out to get a tray on which was a mug, with a saucer set on top of it, and alongside a respectable silver spoon.

"They've a real good cook here," the maid announced. There was satisfaction in her praise, for Molly and Uncle Augustin's cook were old enemies, enjoying a feud Persis sometimes suspected was highly satisfactory to both. "This broth has real body to it. You get that inside you, Miss Persis, and you'll feel a lot better. You look washed out."

Persis averted her eyes from the mirror. Washed out was a very mild term for what she saw there now.

"I look worse than that," she agreed with dismal

frankness as she picked up the spoon. The liquid in the mug did smell good and, for the first time in days, she felt hungry instead of squeamish.

"My trunk is down there—" she gestured to the window. "Can you get them to bring it up? I'd rather wear my own things."

She had fretted so over those dresses since Uncle Augustin had suddenly decided to make this trip to the Bahamas where it was supposed to be so very much warmer, that the heavy silks and woolens one needed in New York would not be proper. She had had such a difficulty shopping for muslins, a light silk or two at the beginning of the fall season. The whole contents of that trunk were the result of much time and effort. And she had had to be very careful in the cost of her selections because Uncle Augustin's affairs were in such a muddle after the disastrous fire last year when half of the city had gone up in flames.

"Them things'll all need washing and tendin' to," Molly announced. "So you'll have to wait on wearin' 'em." She eyed her mistress measuringly. "Miss Lydia, now, she's a might fuller at the waist—for all her lacing—but not too much."

Persis sighed; now she was going to hear Molly's standard comments on her own deficiencies.

"I know I'm as thin as a rail. But I'm just made that way, Molly, no matter how much I eat. All right—it's plain I'll have to wear something and if Miss Leverett is kind enough to offer, I must be gracious enough to accept."

But she was not. Persis hated the thought of wearing someone else's clothing. Such a small thing to trouble her when she ought just to be glad they were safe. One thing she was sure of—to go to sea again (*if* the *Arrow* was ever patched up or they were offered

13

other transportation) was going to require all the fortitude she could summon.

Two hours later she was more at ease with herself and her world. A slim black girl brought in cans of hot water and Molly had washed all the salt stickiness out of her hair, brushing and toweling it dry. She was laced into a muslin far more elaborate in trimming than any from her own trunk. In fact, suited for at least a formal tea drinking.

The gown was lemon colored (to compliment her own brown hair and rather sallow skin) with the fashionable full sleeves, tight from shoulder to elbow and then billowing out in twin puffs of undersleeves of lace. A cobweb-fine lace edged the cape-wide bertha. And the neckline had a turndown collar finished off with a bow. There was even an apron of sheer muslin with a deeply ruched border.

Molly had skillfully braided her hair into the upstanding loops on the top of her head, though her side curls in this humid damp were more flyaway wisps than proper ringlets. Yet this time Persis faced the mirror with hardly any more assurance. She did not think all these frills became her. Her face was too thin, her high-bridged nose too sharp. Yes, she had the look —the slight look—of a schoolmarm.

"Uncle Augustin—" Duty nipped her again.

"Still sleepin', Miss Persis. Shubal is sittin' there right beside him should anything be needed. But no harm your lookin' in on him."

Molly opened the door of the chamber and pointed to another directly across the hall.

"Miss Lydia and Mrs. Pryor—they are down on the veranda. You go down them stairs and straight ahead —"

Persis nodded, tapped lightly on her uncle's door.

14

Shubal peered out at her, his gray whiskers a disorderly fringe about his meager face. He waved her in, but set his finger to his lips in warning.

Here was another huge bed with netting falling from the tester above. Against the pillows which supported his head and shoulders (her uncle had to sleep nearly upright since his illness) the old man's face was clay-white. His thin hair stood up like the crest of one of those strange birds sailors sometimes brought home, and his mouth hung open a little as he breathed in shallow puffs. His eyes were closed.

And it was the eyes which had and did make Uncle Augustin so alive as a person. Their bright, inquiring blue had been the first thing Persis had noticed when he had brought her to live with him after he retired from traveling in foreign parts.

Somehow she had never thought of him as being old, though he had been the eldest of a long family and her father was the youngest of the lot. Now when she looked at that pinched and weary face, the eyes shut, a stab of fear chilled her. She could not believe in a future which did not include Uncle Augustin—his wry humor, his keen wit, and his always interested mind. Though he had also had a reserve, so that her affection was born of duty and appreciation, not love.

Not many men of his age would have taken an orphaned niece of eight into their house. He had given her every comfort but had always kept her at a distance, forging a barrier Persis never tried to pierce.

However, her situation was hardly different from that of Sally Madison or Caroline Briggs, who had shared her studies at Miss Pickett's Academy for Young Ladies and had been her closest friends. For both Sally and Caroline seemed to fear their fathers and hold all older gentlemen in awe.

But Uncle Augustin, as remote as he was, was always *there*. He shared no confidences, of course. She had been astounded when he had first told her of his decision to sail to the Bahamas. Though she had guessed that the situation of Rooke and Company, as a result of the fire, had been a worry which had brought on his first attack.

He had appeared to recover so well from that. Then he said a voyage to a warmer climate was all he needed to put him on his feet again. Persis suspected that more than his health had occupied his mind during the past few months. Mr. Hogue, the lawyer, had come so many times to the house.

And there had been that hunt through the attic storeroom for a certain box. Which, when found, contained little more than a packet of old letters. Yet Uncle Augustin had been delighted with those.

Shubal touched her arm and motioned to the door. She nodded and went out, the manservant following her. He had always been as silent as Uncle Augustin, but his lips were trembling now and he kept glancing back, which added to Persis' uneasiness.

"He—he looks worse!" she blurted out.

"It's the Lord's good mercy he ain't dead!" Shubal's voice quavered. "His heart—the doctor fears for him—I know it. Though he said naught to me. You must speak with him, Miss Persis. Perhaps he'll tell you the truth."

"I will." The truth they must certainly have. This doctor might be the best they had on the island. But surely Key West might house a better one. How far were they now from that port? Could Uncle Augustin be taken there—or could a doctor be summoned here? Persis shivered, remembering the fury of the storm. To go to sea again—

16

"Thank you, Miss." Shubal's hand shook as he reached for the door latch. He must care a lot for Uncle Augustin, they had been together for years and years. Now the signs of his caring made her feel guilty. Uncle Augustin really meant more to Shubal than he did to her. Yet he had given her so much. Everything, another part of her mind whispered—but himself.

"Miss Rooke—"

Startled, Persis looked to the head of the stairs. There stood a woman of the same sturdy build as Molly, but clad with far more elegance in a gray muslin, a ribboned cap on her gray-brown hair which was dressed high in the manner of a much earlier time. Yet this style became her round, rather highly colored face better than the modern curls. She had the air of one used to giving orders and now offered her hand with assurance.

"I am Mrs. Pryor."

A housekeeper perhaps, but no servant, not even what might be deemed an "upper" one, Persis deduced.

The girl curtsied as she would to the mother of one of her friends.

"Please, can you tell me how my uncle is?" If the doctor had shared the truth with anyone of this household, it must have been with the very competent appearing Mrs. Pryor.

For a moment she was eyed measuringly, and then the answer came:

"He is an old man, and one in a perilous state of health. The storm and the wreck—well, they have not been good for him. But I have seen many recoveries which were unexpected. One does not go until one's time comes, and he is fighting—" Her words were far from reassuring.

"The doctor—he—?" Persis did not know how to put into plain language a question concerning his competence.

But Mrs. Pryor seemed to divine what she could not bring herself to ask.

"Dr. Veering is a very good physician. Having a tendency toward lung disorder, as a young man he went to stay several years in Panama. Some time ago he came here and began to experiment with plants, to see how many of the useful tropical ones could be grown this far north. Captain Leverett has fostered his project and given him Verde Key for his garden. But he lives on Lost Lady, and we are lucky. You can accept that he knows his calling well."

"Thank you—" Persis was a little subdued. Mrs. Pryor's unassailable dignity was having the same quelling effect on her as Miss Pickett's had had—reducing one to the status of a schoolgirl. This state of affairs she began to resent.

"Now, my dear Miss Rooke—" The housekeeper became as brisk as Miss Pickett when she was about to order someone to do something for "her own good." "Why not go down to the veranda—there is luncheon waiting. And since the storm has blown itself out, it is quite pleasant there."

Persis' inner reaction was the same as it had been to Miss Pickett's suggestions—to do just the opposite. But that was only silly childishness. So she went.

Her journey, short as it was, through the lower floor of the house proved (to her surprise) that Captain Leverett's residence could match any in the better part of New York. A wealth of furnishings, and the thick carpets were outstanding. Wrecker's loot, Persis thought disdainfully, though she looked about with a curiosity she could not control.

18

Since her knowledge of what went on in the Keys (rank piracy, some of the shipowners her uncle had known wrathfully termed it) was founded mainly on their conversation, she had little liking for what she saw. It was true that a wrecker must be licensed by the government, that he must agree on rescue fees with the captain of the unfortunate vessel he boarded, and he was further bound by the law to hold legal auction of the cargo. But the fact remained that he prospered from the ill luck of others—richly, if this house was any indication.

At least the wreckers now operated under American law, and those from the Bahamas (about whom there were some dark stories) were forbidden these waters. Though there were always rumors of lure lights and the like to bring ships into danger.

Persis went out on the veranda and stopped short. She had forgotten the mound foundation of the house she had sighted from her chamber window. Now she seemed to be on a hill from which one could look down on a sea of green growth and white, shell-strewn sand.

Several chairs made of cane stood by a table on which the dishes were covered by a netting not unlike that used to curtain the beds. And seated on one of those chairs was a young girl who stared at Persis with something near to open rudeness.

Her hair, of a very pale shade of gold, was very elaborately dressed, the upper knot based by a band of flowers. And her complexion had manifestly been well guarded from the glare of the southern sun. But her brows and lashes were dark, giving an arresting vividness to her features which Persis thought a little bold. There was very little color in her cheeks, but her small mouth, with its pouting lower lip, was moistly red as if she had been recently sucking a cinnamon sweetmeat.

19

Now she smiled, her beflowered head a little atilt, her dark-fringed eyes narrowed.

"I never did like that gown. The color is certainly more yours than mine." Her frank appraisal was delivered in a way which suggested there might be something just a little common in being able to wear lemon muslin to any advantage.

"I have to thank you very much for the loan of it," Persis returned with the same briskness. She must watch her tongue. However, she did not greatly warm to Miss Lydia Leverett, even on this very short acquaintance. And it was not like her to take such an instant aversion to anyone.

"Welcome to Lost Lady Key—" Lydia waved a hand to the chair opposite her own. "At least the storm is over. If you sit here, you will have your back to the sea. Doubtless you have seen enough of that for the present!"

There was something about Miss Leverett's disregard of all social formalities and niceties which seemed to put Persis on the defensive.

"Such an odd name—Lost Lady." She seized upon the first subject she could think of, not wishing to discuss the wreck.

"Not when you know the story. There was a lady and she was lost—or disappeared," Lydia returned. "She is our ghost now. Be warned. Some say she brings ill luck to those natives unfortunate enough to meet her.

"This was a pirate hold a hundred years ago. In fact, the foundation of this house was part of a fort built by Satin-shirt Jack. And before him there was the mound— that was made by the Old Ones." Lydia was watching her guest, a queer little quirk about her lips
20

as she paused. "Some of the islanders tell tales about *them*—all blood and sacrifice. They were supposed to be giants able to shoot one of their arrows straight through a Spaniard's breastplate.

"But the Spanish finally killed them all—unless that dirty old witch, Askra, is really one of them. She looks as if she is old enough to be so, goodness knows. Then the pirates under Jack raided the Spanish and killed all of *them*—except the lady. She was the Commandant's wife or daughter or something like that, so Jack claimed her as part of his share. Until he was found dead and she was gone—

"The Spanish came back again—or so it went. Do I frighten you, Miss Rooke, with all these bloody tales? This *is* a place which should be haunted—enough has happened here. And the islanders swear that the ghosts do walk."

Persis smiled. If Lydia thought such childish stories were in the least alarming, she must have a very low impression of Persis' intelligence. "Many old places have odd stories about them," she answered composedly. "Even in New York."

"New York!" Lydia sat up straighter. "How I would like to go back to New York! Indeed, visit almost any place apart from this one!" She arose abruptly and went to stand by the rail of the veranda, looking frowningly out over Lost Lady Key.

2

"Have you been to New York then?" Persis eyed her hostess with some impatience. She was hungry, but it was not polite to help herself without invitation.

Lydia's full skirts swirled out as she turned abruptly. "Me—in New York?" She laughed angrily. "I have been to school in Charlestown, and to Key West, and that is all—since Crewe chose to come here. But I was born in New York—only now I can't remember it at all."

She came back to the table and twitched away the net with a vigor which matched her sharp tone.

"To be imprisoned here—it is enough to make one see ghosts—and have all sorts of strange fancies when one is bored."

She ate only a few mouthfuls of bread spread with a

thick conserve. But Persis made a healthy meal of biscuits, some fruit that was strange to her, and several slices of ham cut paper thin but nonetheless tasty. There was a custard, too, which had an unfamiliar flavor but which she relished.

Lydia put her elbows on the table, supported her chin on her clasped hands, and fastened her gaze on Persis.

"Tell me about New York," she commanded.

Persis had just started to speak when she was interrupted by a loud braying noise. In a second Lydia was on her feet, heading for the door of the house.

"Ship sighted—" She gave only that small bit of information as she darted within.

Catching some of her hostess' excitement, Persis followed. Lydia was already near the top of the stairs, her skirts gathered up in both hands so she could climb faster.

Three flights they climbed, the third much narrower and more steep—to emerge on a flat space open to the roof, railed about. Lydia jerked a spyglass out of a box fastened against that rail. With it to one eye she peered seaward.

"He dared it!" her voice was high with excitement. "That's the *Stormy Luck* coming in, it is!" She was smiling now. "Oh, won't Crewe be furious! I can hardly wait to see his face when he finds her here."

"Is that your brother's ship—?" Persis was puzzled.

"No. His is the *Nonpareil*. They're trying to get the *Arrow* off that reef. This is Ralph's ship—Ralph Grillon. He's from the Bahamas."

"But I thought," Persis shaded her eyes, but without the aid of a glass all she could make out was a distant shadow, "that the Bahama wreckers did not come into these waters—"

Lydia made an impatient sound. "The sea isn't fenced in like a field. And the Bahama men were here long before us. They have their rights, even though people like Crewe are too high-handed to credit them with such. Ralph takes the *Stormy Luck* where he wants—and it can show its stern well away from any cutter out of Key West that tries to make trouble. Anyway, Ralph—" now her smile was both amused and sly, "has a special reason for coming here." Without offering the glass to Persis she fitted it back in its case.

"But even he can't make the wind stronger," she continued. "It may be several hours before—" Then she paused, looking no longer to the sea but down to what lay immediately below the house. And her smile vanished in a distinct scowl.

Persis followed the other's gaze. The mound on which the house had been erected might be ground linked with the rest of the key on the opposite side, but here water lapped at its foot and there was a channel, leading straight out to sea. The channel opening was flanked by the wharf still piled high with bales and boxes.

A small boat had been launched from the wharf, two men at its oars, and it was at that Lydia stared. She made a fist which she brought down with some force on the railing.

"Johnny Mason!" she spat the name. "He heard the conch horn and he's off to tell Crewe, the meddler!" She shrugged. "Let him. It won't profit him—or Crewe any."

Lydia whisked to the top of the ladderlike stairs which Persis had not noticed were so very steep when she had climbed them. Now she descended with caution, guessing Lydia to be lost in her own thoughts and forgetful of her. However, in the upper hall, the other girl paused to look over her shoulder.

That look of discontent, faint as it had been, was gone. Her smile no longer was either angry or sly.

"You asked about the Lost Lady," she dismissed the subject of the *Stormy Luck* and its captain, rather to Persis' bewilderment. "I'll have time to show you the fan—the ghost fan itself."

Now she linked arms with Persis—as if they were the best and closest of friends, leaving Persis a little disturbed at this swift change—and drew her into a bedroom which flanked the stair at the head of the hall.

"Sukie," Lydia spoke impatiently to the black maid who was folding body linen away in the drawers of a magnificently carved chest, "you can leave that. Go tell Mam Rose that we'll have company for dinner, special company. We want the Napoleon china and the best of silver. Mind now!"

"Yes'm." Sukie disappeared, leaving some disorder in the room which, Persis suspicioned, was of Lydia's initial making. Her hostess was rummaging in what looked to be an old sea chest, talking as she hunted:

"You won't get any of the islanders to touch the thing; they all say it's the worst kind of luck. Crewe found it in this—" she prodded the side of the chest with her toe, "all buried under some rocks—what was left of the old pirate fort. I begged him for it. Sukie and the rest know I have it. They think I can ill-wish them or some such foolishness, so they step carefully when I give the orders. It's a handy thing. Ah, here it is!"

She came into the full light of an open window carrying a carved box which she opened to take out a fan, spreading its sticks to their fullest extent in the sunlight.

Persis had seen the brisé fans of intricately carved

ivory which the China merchants sometimes offered for sale. And those made in the same fashion of pierced sandalwood, to be used in summer—the perfume of the wood was supposed to be restorative on a very warm day. But this was like and yet unlike either. It was made of carved sticks strung together with ribbon, yes. But the wood of the sticks was dead black. And the heavier end pieces each bore the head of a cat in high relief, the eyes of which were fashioned of shimmering dark blue stones. While the inner carving was again that of cats stalking among grasses, sleeping, sitting.

"Those are what they call black opals," Lydia indicated the eye stones. "There was a jeweler in Key West who told Crewe that. And he thinks this may be near two or three hundred years old—but he was not sure whether it was made in China or Italy. But it's magic—the Lost Lady is supposed to have used it to kill Satin-shirt Jack, and then fanned herself out of existence afterward." Lydia laughed. "Go ahead, take it; these cats neither scratch nor bite—at least they never have me!"

Persis put out her hand with some reluctance. The fan was strange, even though it was beautiful. But it gave her an uncanny feeling—even though she did not believe in its supposed ill luck. She held it close to study the cats. They had—she searched for the right term—a rather unnatural look. In fact, as she held the fan open she had an odd fancy that they were all staring at her measuringly. Quickly she closed the fan and handed it back to Lydia.

"It is indeed unusual," she commented and knew that Lydia was watching her closely as if expecting some reaction to mark Persis as superstitious as the islanders.

"Yes," Lydia dropped it back in its box and, returning that to the chest, made no move to pick up the garments she had spilled out during her search. "Oddly enough, even though this is always here, when she walks the ghost holds it in her hand. I find the idea of a ghost fan amusing. Now, I must find Mrs. Pryor. If I don't coax her a bit, she won't bring out the best wine — Come along if you like."

Persis shook her head. "I must see about my uncle. Thank you."

When she tapped on the door of that chamber Shubal opened it instantly, as if he had been anxiously awaiting her.

"Miss Persis—please—the master is awake. And he's asking for you."

She should have been here earlier. Why had she let Lydia interfere with her sense of duty? Persis hurried to the side of the bed. It was strange to be looking down instead of up into those wide eyes. For even in his old age, Uncle Augustin was a tall man who, until his illness, had held himself confidently straight.

"I am here, sir. I am sorry I was not earlier—"

He raised a hand as if by great effort. "No matter—" His voice, though hoarse, still had its remote, courteous tone.

"There is something I must explain to you, Persis." He stopped between words to draw puffing breaths she felt uneasy hearing. "We are always vain of our strength, unconsidering of our weakness. I—perhaps I have made a mistake in undertaking this, even a grievous error. Yet looking back I cannot see how I might have chosen differently.

"You know that the failure of Rooke and Company seriously compromised those funds which are our support. I might have been able to redeem those losses had not time been my enemy. I am too old, which is a hard thing to admit."

His straight gaze dared her to make any comment of sympathy.

"Three months ago—" he paused and coughed. Shubal nearly elbowed Persis aside, then that hand raised again to wave the servant away with such vigor that he drew back. "I received a communication of some import. We have, as do all families, our secrets. Doubtless you have never heard of Amos Rooke." He did not wait for any answer from her.

"During the days of our Revolution, my father had a younger brother, Amos. He sought out strange company, mingling with the young British officers who were on duty in occupied New York. In other words, he declared himself a 'loyalist.' When the British army at last evacuated the city, he gathered together quite a sum in funds, some of it stolen from his own countrymen. With this he sailed to the West Indies.

"However, a certain portion of those funds did not come from traitorous dealings with the enemy; rather, they had been entrusted to him by his widowed mother, meant to be the marriage portion of his sister and for her own support in her declining years.

"When he fled New York he left no accounting of these monies. It was my father and later my brother Julian and I who supported my grandmother. We learned that Amos had established himself well in the Bahamas where he built and crewed two wreckers. In time he married a widow and had one son. But that son was lost at sea. Therefore, Amos had no legal heirs. He left his estate when he died to his widow, a woman of prudence and frugality and, as some of the ladies of the islands, also holding shares in wrecking ships. But in addition, she was also a very honest female.

28

"It was while she was dealing with her husband's estate that she came upon letters written by my grandmother urging Amos to return her funds; letters which, incidentally, he had never answered. His widow at once wrote to New York and offered to make up the sum in question. At that time I was our representative in London and so out of touch. Julian, my grandmother, and my Aunt Eleanor, all died within two weeks of each other of yellow fever which struck hard that summer. I was summoned home but the letter was delayed in reaching me and it was some months before I found that from Amos' widow.

"At that time I was engrossed by the company affairs and, since the debt was owed to my grandmother, I thanked Madam Rooke by letter but said that I considered the debt discharged by the deaths of those concerned. I did not think of this again for years.

"However, shortly before the fire which reduced our circumstances so greatly, I received word from an attorney in the islands that Madam Rooke, who had lived to a great age, was lately dead. And her will had left all her extensive property to be equally divided between my grandmother's kin and certain charities. The sum willed to us amounted to a sizable one.

"Thus I gathered the letters and papers in that case —" He made a slight gesture to the bedside table where lay a small, locked portfolio. "Those prove the validity of our claim."

His face was near gray though he spoke clearly and with his usual deliberate spacing of words. Now he paused and Shubal pushed past the girl to hold a small glass to his master's bluish lips. Uncle Augustin sipped, then raised his head slowly once more. His eyes did not dismiss Persis. Rather there was a fierce determination in them which spread to his drawn face.

"You"—shallow gusts of hardly drawn breath punctuated his sentence—"must remember!"

"I will, Uncle Augustin."

Now his eyes closed and Shubal waved her back without speaking. The servant followed her to the door as if he must make very sure she would go. But his attention was fixed on the man in the bed.

Persis returned to the chamber across the hall. So there had been a real reason for this voyage to the islands, more than just the quest for the health that Uncle Augustin would never find again. She stood by the window which looked down on the wharf.

There were no men busy there now, though boxes and bales remained. Perhaps their warehouse had been filled. A bird with vividly colored wings and a harsh cry swept past, to be lost in the thick green rimming the pool and the canal. Seaward, that smudge Lydia had named a ship was taking on more visible outlines.

But closer there was a craft making its way up the canal. And this was no ship's boat; rather a narrow, battered looking canoe made of a single huge log hollowed out, in which sat a single paddler. It advanced at a sluggish pace in spite of the efforts of the paddler who headed straight for a small wharf at the foot of the mound on which the house stood. Catching hold of one of the stakes there, the paddler—now obviously a woman— scrambled out, to stand erect, winding a twist of rope around the stake to anchor the strange vessel.

A fringed skirt of tanned hide flapped about her legs and a wide-brimmed hat woven of some reed or frond covered her head, so that Persis, from this higher level, could see nothing of the newcomer's face. The stranger stooped to pick up a hide-wrapped bundle and, settling this on one bony hip, started to the house, climbing a series of hardly noticeable notches in the hillside to disappear around the side of the outer wall.

The canoe bobbed lazily at the post. Farther out, the ship which had so excited Lydia was entering the anchorage by the reef. Men gathered on the larger wharf, watching it. There was something about their attitude which suggested no good will toward the intruder—even as if they were about to consider defense against an invasion.

Persis remembered tales that the Bahama wreckers and those from the Keys had been, not too long ago either, bitter enemies. And there had been hints of secret battles fought far away enough so that no neutral watchers had witnessed such.

Though the law had now settled boundaries and many of the Bahamians and their families moved to the Keys rather than lose their livelihood, old jealousy and hatred might still smolder under the surface. Certainly what Lydia had said suggested that Captain Leverett held little or no liking for the master of the vessel now coming to anchor in a domain he had made his own.

Persis moved away from the window. Lydia seemed very sure of herself, preparing to give this Captain Ralph Grillon the welcome of an honored guest. But—once more her own single vivid memory of those last moments on board the *Arrow* when the master of this Key had dumped her into his boat like a bale of goods, made Persis wonder a little at the other girl's defiance. The impression which remained in her own mind of Captain Leverett was that he was certainly a man to be reckoned with.

So perhaps there were storm clouds of another kind ahead. But that was none of her concern. More important than any arrivals by canoe or ship, arrivals which had nothing to do with her affairs, was Uncle Augustin's story.

He must feel—her breath caught a little—he must feel very ill. He, who had always been so self-sufficient and the master of his destiny, and of hers too, who had waved aside that earlier offer of repayments—must now face dire necessity to make this trip to claim funds from a stranger. And now to tell her about it. Funds tainted with dishonest dealing. Uncle Augustin was a truly honorable man. Was he entirely ruined then?

A tap on the door interrupted her unpleasant chain of thought. She lifted the latch to find Molly outside, and behind her two of the island men carrying Persis' trunk between them. Molly waved them in, her round face one determined scowl. After they had set down their burden and were gone, the maid sniffed.

"Fees indeed!" She snapped at the door closing behind them. "They dare to talk about fees, do they—?"

"What fees?"

Hands on her hips, her face flushed, Molly fronted the girl.

"Seems like those rescued by these seagoin' varmints are supposed to fee them for not being left to drown! Never did I hear such un-Christian talk! Wasn't my own father one of them at the Cape who went out in the boats when there was a ship a-reef at home? And there was no talk then of fees—that I'll give oath on!"

Persis' own indignation arose. All of a piece—this wrecking. You rescued a ship, or at least its cargo, and settled with the Captain for either a fee or else the goods to be auctioned. So of course it would naturally follow that the passengers, also saved, had to fee the
32

wreckers in turn. But she fully agreed with Molly's outraged feelings.

"Did they quote you a sum?" She strove to control her anger. Certainly Uncle Augustin was *not* going to be bothered by this! Though what she could do, except ask Captain Leverett for a reasonable time to pay, Persis did not guess. The more she thought of this system, the hotter her anger grew.

"I did not ask," Molly returned. "Knowin' as how this was yours I just told them straight out to bring it here. Might be all in it is ruined by water anyway. Then that there big Irishman, him who bosses the wharf crew, said as how this couldn't be moved 'cause it was cargo. I give him the sharp of my tongue about that, I can tell you! Cargo, eh! And I had some things to say about this fee business that one won't be forgettin' in a hurry.

"I told him the master was sick abed and not likely to be able to talk fees. And that he wasn't to bother you with such foolish wickedness neither. I don't think," Molly ended on a note of satisfaction, "we'll hear any more about it—not from that one anyway."

So they were not really guests, Persis thought. Captain Leverett's house might as well be an inn, in spite of all its luxury. Mrs. Pryor ought to be able to straighten out the status of such uninvited intruders. Of all under this roof, Persis believed Mrs. Pryor the best to question frankly. And it was up to her to do it.

She had no idea of what funds Uncle Augustin carried—whether they could so meet their "ransom" when this pirate wrecker demanded it. But if she could gain some idea of the sum— They must be able to pay the doctor also. And there would be their passage on to Key West, and from there to the Bahamas. She, who had never handled more than the household accounts in her life, was more than a little disturbed.

Molly was busy with the trunk. Perhaps Persis could find Mrs. Pryor and get it settled about their status under this roof as soon as possible. Murmuring that she had an errand, Persis went back into the hall and down the front stairs. Raised voices drew her to the back part of the house.

"You know, Miss Lydia, what the Captain would say—and do, if he were home."

"Yes, but he isn't. And if he can open his precious house to these people he dragged off the *Arrow*—then I can entertain a friend. *My* friend. And I'm not asking any leave of Crewe, which I couldn't anyway—since he is *not* at home. Mam Rose and Sukie are to do just as I told them—the best china and linen and good food. Ralph Grillon is no seagoing trash. He has every bit as much authority in the islands as Crewe assumes here. And I am not going to be ashamed of this house when he visits. I saw Mason go off to warn Crewe, but it'll be hours, if ever, before he has that wreck off the reef and ready to bring in. I heard him say so. In the meantime, I am entertaining a gentleman and giving him such hospitality as we are noted for—" Her voice rose higher with every vehement word.

Persis, embarrassed, wanting to be away from her involuntary eavesdropping, took several steps backward. So when she bumped into someone who must have entered very quietly indeed, it gave her such a start she nearly lost her balance. A hand fell on her arm, grasping her firmly, and she turned to look over her shoulder up into the sun-and-sea-browned face of a stranger.

"Steady as you go, ma'am!" The laughter in his eyes

matched the curve of his lips. "Never thought I'd be a reef to bring up short such a pretty craft—"

His eyes were not only laughing, but bold. Persis stiffened, not caring for the way he deliberately looked her up and down. As if she *were* a ship and he was considering purchasing her.

He wore a blue jacket with brass buttons which the sea air had not been allowed to tarnish, and his hair curled about his forehead, for his head was bare though he held an officer's cap in one hand. She had to look well up, for in height he matched Uncle Augustin's inches. But he was sparkling alive, having none of her uncle's aloof reserve.

Persis flushed, realizing she had been staring at him almost as boldly as he had eyed her. Now, dropping his hand from her arm, he bowed.

"Ralph Grillon, at your service, ma'am," he introduced himself. There was the faintest of accents in his voice. She found it interesting. "Very much at your service."

She thought he accented that "your" and blushed a little deeper as with a cry of "Ralph!" Lydia came running down the hall, both hands outstretched in very open and informal greeting.

3
_____

Persis had no chance to confer with Mrs. Pryor over the vexing questions concerning fees. Everything now centered about the very dashing Captain Grillon as Lydia made very sure it must. It was apparent that she was completely captivated by her guest, her demeanor far from proper when she showed such a marked preference. Persis, so carefully schooled in the restraint of Uncle Augustin's household, so well taught in the manners of Miss Pickett's Academy, was embarrassed by Lydia's exuberance. And then troubled somewhat on her own account when she became aware that Captain Grillon was making a determined effort to include her in their company, in spite of Lydia's beginning frowns.

That the Captain was handsome Persis admitted,

against her better judgment, for he was too handsome somehow. And she found his familiar way of addressing both her and Lydia increasingly disturbing. Finally she made an excuse of the necessity of attending on her uncle and managed to reach the chamber which had been given her. There she found Molly shaking her head over the creased and dampened contents of the trunk.

"Just look at this!" The maid held up a flounced dress of pale-green spotted muslin. But there were other spots on it now and the ruffles hung damply limp. "I'll wash and iron them. But, Miss Persis, some of these ain't never goin' to look nice and fresh again—I'll give you my word on that!"

Perhaps an hour ago the implied destruction of her wardrobe might have been a catastrophe for Persis. But now, though she did not in the least want to continue wearing the charity of Lydia Leverett, she had more important matters on her mind.

"Molly!" She raised her voice, lacing it with authority to get her companion's full attention. "Is there a way you can arrange for me to speak privately with Mrs. Pryor?"

"Now there's one with her head firmly on her shoulders," commented the maid. "She runs this house, for all the show of Miss Lydia being mistress. She had a boarding house down in Key West 'til the Captain got her to take over here. A widow woman who—"

"Molly!" Persis' voice became even more crisp. "I don't care about her history. I just want to talk with her. Miss Lydia is entertaining a guest and I do not care to journey about the house, hunting her—"

"You wouldn't find her if you did, Miss Persis. Not right now. She took off with that old witch who came up to the kitchen door. Cook and the maids let out

37

such a screech when that happened m'heart fair stopped a beat. I wonder that you didn't hear them, Miss Persis—them screaming so. None of them would go near the old hag, but Mrs. Pryor just took up a basket and filled it right up with bread and cheese and good thick slices off a cold roast. Then she and that witch took off together. Strangest thing I ever did see —Mrs. Pryor, she being so proper and neat, and that other one—" Molly sniffed disparagingly.

Persis was interested in spite of herself. "What do you mean by a witch, Molly?"

"She sure looked like one, Miss Persis. Got a face on her 'bout a hundred years old, nose and chin coming as near one another as the parts of a nutcracker, and her eyes all sunk in. But she isn't blind—she could see good enough with them eyes. I wouldn't want to have her overlookin' me with 'em—not if she took some sort of a spite to me.

"After they were gone, cook tells me as how this witch woman has powers all right. Indian she is, but not like the rest of the Indians hereabouts. They're all afraid of her, too. She speaks as good as a Christian if she wants to and she has healing powers. She brings Mrs. Pryor leaves and herbs and such things for nursing. Mrs. Pryor is well known for a nurse. Did all the doctoring on the Key before the real doctor came.

"And the Captain, he lets this old witch come around and gives her what she wants—'cause of those other Indians—the raiding ones. As long as this here Askra is friendly, then maybe they won't try to move in. They say as how it was her people who lived here a long time ago, and built their houses on mounds. Askra, she comes to talk to the ghosts of the Old Ones. Leastways that is what they say in the kitchen. Sounds like a lot of real nonsense, only when you see
38

them eyes of hers lookin' you over you begin to wonder a little."

Persis was amazed at the new angle of life on Lost Lady Key. The figure she had seen disembark from the canoe, that must have been Askra. And that the very correct Mrs. Pryor would accompany such a visitor anywhere was another surprise.

"They're talking about trouble comin', them in the kitchen. More than just this witch." Molly dearly loved to gossip, but it was seldom she had such unusual material to work with. "They don't take kindly to that ship out there," she gestured to the window. "One of the men has gone to warn the Captain about it. Seems like the Captain don't want to be neighborly with this Grillon. They had a run-in 'bout six months back over some wrecking business. Grillon, he has no right in these waters and the Captain warned him off. But Miss Lydia took a shine to the man and if he comes courtin' she's partial to it. Now this Grillon says as how he needs fresh water, his casks got stove up and stalted in the storm. So he comes here. But they think downstairs as how he really came to spark Miss Lydia, knowing somehow that the Captain ain't here."

Persis went back to the window. Yes, there was now a long boat midway between the *Stormy Luck* and the wharf, near enough for her to see it carried some barrels. Water was scarce in the Keys, even Key West had to be supplied by shipped-in water when their rain-filled storage tanks began to fail. But Lost Lady was unique (which probably accounted for its long habitation by different peoples) in that it had a spring of fresh water, jealously cherished by the islanders, as the captain of the *Arrow* had told them one night.

"All this is none of our business, Molly."

"Maybe so, Miss Persis. But when Captain Leverett gets back there is goin' to be such a rumpus—if this Grillon is still here—as will make you think you are back in a storm again. Now, I'll just take these and see what can be done to freshen them up." She scooped up an armload of dresses, petticoats, and underlinen and went out.

Persis settled on a chair by the window. When Captain Leverett returned—yes, she could well imagine that that great giant who had seized her so roughly would not take easily to having his orders disobeyed. This was his room, too, and she had no right here. If Uncle Augustin were only as well as he had been when they left New York. But she was sure she dared not suggest transporting him now, unless there came a sudden change for the better in his condition. She watched the wharf and the incoming boat. Her fingers nervously pleating the edge of her apron. What should she do?

Life in New York had never been this complicated. It had revolved with slow and undisturbed dignity (if a little dully at times) about Uncle Augustin's routine, so regularly kept that Persis could chart her employment for hours ahead. Then she had been bored. Now she wished herself back in that snug safety where there were no storms, either human or natural, and all the rest which seemed about to beset this house.

Finally she arose and went to her uncle's chamber, tapping softly. The door opened and she faced Shubal who looked even more worried and shrunken. His finger was at his lips, already urging silence as she squeezed through the small space he did not quite dare bar. He hissed at her in a half whisper:

"He's asleep, Miss Persis. But I don't like the look of him at all, no I don't." He shook his gray head. "I wish that our Dr. Lawson could see him. He knows the master, all about what ails him—"

"I am told that the doctor here is very good."

Shubal shrugged. "That is as may be, Miss. But he ain't knowed the master for years, like Dr. Lawson. And the master—he's worse than he'll let on. Seems like he called on all his strength to make this here trip and now that's giving out on him—fast. He won't take no more food. Just tells me not to bother him when I bring it. But how can he keep up his strength when he won't eat?"

There was a querulous note in Shubal's voice. He twisted the fingers of one vein-ridged hand in the other. During the years he had been with Uncle Augustin, his master had been the true center of his life.

"When he awakes, Shubal, let me talk with him. I know you are doing all that you can, but maybe he might listen a little to me." Persis was not sure of that, but she had to answer the pleading in the old man's eyes.

"Miss Persis, I think—" Shubal's quavering voice broke and his eyes dropped. Once more Persis felt that stab of fear. She knew very well what Shubal feared. It lay like a cloud over her mind also. And Uncle Augustin had never meant as much to her as he did to Shubal.

"We must keep from such thinking," she said gently, "we must just hope. After all, wasn't he much worse right after the first attack, Shubal? And then he surprised even Dr. Lawson when he made such a good recovery."

"He was in his own home then, Miss Persis—and—" Shubal's thin old voice cracked as he went to the foot of the bed.

Persis stood by the door. Her first fear was blossoming into a panic she fought against. She would have to, for she would be the one to make decisions now, take the responsibility. And she shrank from that. Going back to her own chamber she sat once more in the chair by the wide window. The wind blew steadily and cleanly from the sea, cooling her flushed face. There she sat and tried to think of the future.

Uncle Augustin must now believe that he would never reach the Bahamas. He was a man who never before had discussed any such affairs with her, who had shut her out from this family secret. He had told her because he believed she would now be the one to carry on.

And here she had no Mr. Hogue to depend upon. None save herself. Shubal, Molly—they would look to her, not she to them. She felt very young and frightened. But she was not stupid. A long buried core of stubbornness arose in her to give resolution. There were men of law in Key West, and she could ask that one of honesty and integrity be named to aid her.

The thought of going back to New York crossed her mind, fleetingly—to be discarded at once. What would face her there but broken fortunes, a future so dark it had driven Uncle Augustin to make this trip, and he was not a man to be frightened by shadows. So if there was this estate waiting in the Bahamas, then it would be up to her to claim it.

Persis drew a deep breath. She did not like what she thought might lie ahead, and she longed for someone to depend upon for advice. But if that was the way the future was going to be, she must be prepared to face it.

Decisions could be made, but the means of carrying such out was another matter. She had no idea what funds Uncle Augustin could control now. There was this matter of the wrecker's fee for example—

Persis looked around the room. She did not even have as much right here as she would in an inn chamber. It was manifest that Uncle Augustin could not travel, even if the *Arrow* could be made seaworthy again. Perhaps if Captain Leverett went to Key West — But he might not take them now. Her suggestion of a headache grew worse and she longed to throw herself on the bed and just forget about everything. Except that she could not do.

Now she was startled again by that queer moaning sound which had first so excited Lydia and sent her racing to the roof walk. Another ship was edging along beyond the *Stormy Luck*, in fact two ships, the first having the second in tow. Captain Leverett bringing in the *Arrow*?

Men gathered on the wharf, one was holding a huge shell into which he blew as if it were a trumpet—producing that wailing moan. Persis arose hastily. If the master of this house was returning she had no wish to be discovered in his bedchamber.

As she hurried out into the hall she heard voices below, but not clearly enough to distinguish the words. With the *Stormy Luck* at anchor and her captain perhaps in this house, some of that trouble prophesied by the servants might well speedily develop now.

She hesitated uncertainly at the head of the stairs. To remain in the Captain's room was unthinkable. To descend and perhaps walk straight into a family dispute was even worse. But at last she crept down the stairs, alert to any sound which would mean she might again be an unwilling eavesdropper.

However, it seemed Persis was too foreboding. As she went out on the veranda, she caught the sound of a voice from around the corner.

"—a good catch." Grillon stood at the corner, holding to one eye a glass much like that Lydia had used on the roof.

"Give the devil his due." The Bahamian captain continued, "If I were to be reefbound in these waters I'd be glad to know Leverett was on the prowl. That ship lists— but she's still afloat."

"You're more generous than he is." Lydia moved into view, her wide skirts brushing provocatively against Grillon. "You wouldn't hear him say the same about you, you know."

"Oh, I know how I stand with Crewe Leverett, m'dear." His drawl was lazy, a little amused. "But because we bristle up every time we face one another is no reason not to respect the man's seamanship. He's a good wreck-master. I'll grant him that. Only he's too free with that tongue of his. As he's going to find out someday." There was no disguising a note of satisfaction as he put down the spyglass and smiled at Lydia in a way which somehow made Persis a little uneasy.

"Nothing can disturb Crewe," his sister snapped pettishly. "He'll always go his own way! Just as he always has—no matter who suffers by it."

"As you believe that you do, my sweet?" Grillon was still smiling. "Fie, now, that's cutting a little thick, ain't it? I don't see you've wanted for much—"

"How can you say that, Ralph?" Her delicate face was flushed, her plump hands balled into fists as if she would like to batter him. "Doesn't he keep me penned up here—on this god-forsaken island—where nothing ever happens. I've begged even to go to Key West. Marcie Daw is willing to have me stay with her. And her father's the Commandant of the base. Crewe can't believe they aren't proper people to visit."

"Ah, but he knows that the *Stormy Luck* makes port

44

there regularly," Grillon laughed. "I don't think he trusts either of us overmuch, m'dear."

Once more Persis was an eavesdropper and was ready to tiptoe back into the hall when shouts from the wharf startled her into looking seaward. Without realizing what she did, she moved closer to the pair at the other end of the veranda to see the better.

"Behold, the master arrives!" Grillon commented. Now his smile had a wry edge to it. "Well, m'dear, perhaps we had better prepare for rockets. Maybe you'd better get out of their range."

Lydia grabbed his jacket in a tight grip, her chin was up and her jawline stubborn.

"I won't! Crewe may give orders here, but about this he doesn't give them to me! Just let him try it!"

Grillon laughed. "That's my Lydia. But, m'dear, this has to be settled between Crewe and me, no petticoats about." He set down the spyglass and rested his hands lightly on the girl's shoulders. "It has to be that way and no other, girl." Then he set her aside as if she weighed nothing at all.

"What are you going to do?" she demanded.

"I don't propose to meet Crewe Leverett under his own roof," Grillon returned. "Best we meet eye to eye out there."

Persis had taken two quick steps backward so she stood within the doorway. She was ashamed she had not once made her presence clear, but now she spoke.

"Miss Leverett—"

Lydia looked over her shoulder. Her expression was hardly a welcoming one.

"I understand," Persis plunged on, "that I have been given Captain Leverett's own chamber. Of course that is not right now that he is returning—"

Grillon laughed again, lounging back against the

rail of the veranda. But Lydia's frown deepened.

"What does all this have to do with me?" she demanded impatiently.

"Why, you're mistress here, ain't you, sweet?" observed the Bahamian. "The young lady rightly wants to know what you decide. Quite properly I would say. It's plain she *and* Crewe can't—"

Lydia jerked away from him. "Leave it to Mrs. Pryor. Her word carries more weight here than mine, always has." She turned her back on Persis and looked out toward the wharf.

Grillon winked at Persis and nodded.

"I saw Mrs. Pryor just a few minutes ago," he said as Lydia continued to ignore the other girl. "I think you may find her in the kitchen, Miss Rooke."

Persis managed a "thank you" and then fled. Did Grillon suspect she had overheard much of their conversation? She fully deserved the feeling of guilt she carried with her.

A door at the other end of the hall opened on three steps down into what was plainly the kitchen. There was an open fireplace with old-fashioned spits and chains, and an oven built inside it. The heat, even though an outside door stood wide open, was enough to make Persis feel as if she had walked into a fire.

A small black woman, her thin chemise blouse plastered to her shoulders in wet patches, her full red skirt only partially covered by a coarse apron bearing the stains left by her work, was thumping out pastry on a board with the vigor of one battling a long-sought enemy. Sukie and another maid were washing vegetables and cutting them up.

Persis' entrance brought a sudden silence, though the cook continued her energetic thumping. Her eyes were not on the girl rather than the task before her.

"Mrs. Pryor, where is she?" Persis addressed them all. For a long moment she thought no one was going to answer. They merely stared as if she were an apparition which they had never expected to see. Then the cook raised a floury hand and pointed to the outer door. She said something but in a thick dialect Persis could not understand.

So the girl brushed past the table and went on into the open. Mrs. Pryor was there, superintending the stretching of a line across a portion of the mound top uncovered by the house, two boys making it tight. She glanced around as Persis' slippers crunched on the layers of broken clam shells which seemed to cover most of the ground.

"It's a good day for drying, Miss Rooke. Your maid will not have to wait long before she can put iron to your things."

"Please," Persis had only one thought in mind now. "Captain Leverett—I was told I have his bedchamber — which was most generous of him. But now that he is returning—"

"You may have no worries, Miss Rooke. The Captain will stay on the *Nonpareil*, of course. He spends many of his nights there when it is in harbor. It is he who gave the orders that you were to have his chamber."

Persis found the other's calmness somehow a little irritating.

"I understand that there is also a matter of rescue fees. Since my uncle is at present unable to discuss the matter, I do not want to trouble him. Can you explain just what is expected of us?"

She saw Mrs. Pryor's lips tighten. "I do not know where you have heard such nonsense, Miss Rooke. Of course there are no fees. What you must have thought of us! There is a hotel down the Key built by Captain Leverett's orders to house the crews of wrecked vessels, if their ships cannot be made seaworthy again, until they can take passage to Key West. And oftentimes there are more passengers than we are able to shelter here. But you and Mr. Rooke are the Captain's guests. Please understand that he would be greatly offended if you believed otherwise."

There was no possibility of questioning further that emphatic statement, Persis decided. Perhaps Molly had misunderstood the man on the wharf or he had been teasing her.

"Thank you for explaining," she said contritely. "But I still feel it improper to keep the master of the house out of his own—"

"Nonsense!" Mrs. Pryor was brisk. "*He* would feel it improper to have it otherwise. You can hear it from his own lips, if necessary." There was a shadowing of offense in that which Persis was quick to note.

"No, your word is quite enough, Mrs. Pryor. And I thank you for it."

The lady, who had been somewhat on her dignity, relaxed a little.

"You are very welcome, I am sure. By the way, Dr. Veering is to see your uncle this afternoon. If you have any questions to ask him, that will be an excellent time to do so."

But those questions were never to be asked. For when Persis reentered the house it was to hear Shubal's thin old voice raised loud enough to echo through the hallways.

"Miss Persis, oh, Miss Persis!"

She ran for the stairs, one hand on the banister to drag herself up there faster. The old servant stood in
48

the door of her uncle's room, his face gray-white with fear.

"Miss Persis—he—he—"

She pushed past Shubal. Her uncle rested half off the bed, his face as blanched as Shubal's. One hand clutched the netting, which had torn in his grip. He looked at her, his eyes wild as she had never seen them before.

"Amos—traitor—Amos—!"

"I went for some water." Shubal shuffled along to join her. "He was just lying quiet. I thought he was asleep. But—Miss Persis—he must have tried to get up—to get to the window—see?"

He pointed to a bedside table now tipped over on the floor, the candlestick hurled by the fall nearly into the middle of the room.

"Why would he get up, Miss Persis? What did he want?"

"I don't know. He must be delirious. Shubal, go down to Mrs. Pryor, ask her to send for the doctor at once. No, first, let's get him back into bed."

As thin as Uncle Augustin had become, it took the two of them to settle him back on his pillows again, and his breathing was very slow and shallow.

"He must have heard them," Shubal said in a half whisper, motioning toward the window. "Loud talk down there. Two men were quarreling. I heard only a few words when I came back and found him so. He—he kept saying that Amos was back—that he had come to kill him!"

"It's all right now, Shubal. You go, I'll stay with him."

Persis gently freed the hand clawing at the bed netting and held it between hers.

"It's all right, Uncle Augustin. There is no one here.

Don't you remember—Amos died a long time ago. Don't you remember telling me that? He can't be here."

He stared at her blindly. There was a gathering of white froth at one corner of his mouth and he still struggled to get up, but such was his weakness she was able to keep him in bed.

"Amos traitor—said—murder— I never murdered—" Then his body went limp and his hand relaxed in her grasp. For the last time those vivid blue eyes closed.

4

Through the dark of the night the wind whispered in a way Persis had never before been aware of hearing. From her unbarred window she saw only a faint glimmer which must be a lantern on the wharf. But she did not focus on that, rather her eyes turned inward on pictures her memory presented.

Uncle Augustin was—gone.

And, to her dull surprise, his death had left a bigger void in her life than she would have guessed possible. She knew now his will had ruled her days, so much so that she could not think of life going on without him.

Slowly she stepped back from the window. Within the room only a single candle battled the shadows. Persis felt a flash of anger. Why had she been left in so much ignorance by Uncle Augustin? She was neither

51

foolish nor flighty, but neither had she ever been allowed to think for herself.

Shubal had gone to pieces and she had taken enough initiative to order him to bed. Dr. Veering had given the old man a sleeping draft at her request. But that was all she had been able to do.

For Captain Leverett had simply taken command. In a way, he had acted as high-handedly as when he had swept her off the deck of the *Arrow,* displaying a little of the same impatience—or so she thought. Distraught as she had been at her uncle's final collapse, she had not been a hysterical female, though one would have believed so the way *he* had given orders right and left.

There was lacking in him that reckless air which Ralph Grillon showed. The Captain might be only a little older than the Bahamian, but his self-confidence was so complete that he was as impervious as Uncle Augustin to the will or desires of others.

He—

Persis tensed. How could she have forgotten! The portfolio which had been Uncle Augustin's last charge to her! Hours ago she had sent Molly off to bed, and promised to sleep herself. Only sleep had not come; her mind kept reenacting that last scene when her uncle had called in fear the name of a man long dead.

What had moved him to talk of murder? Persis shivered, drawing her shawl closer about her. The story he had told her about the Rooke who was a Tory—was there more to it than what Uncle Augustin had chosen to say? Had he known Amos Rooke as more than just an infamous family legend?

Uncle Augustin had reached the age of seventy-five and this was 1837. Persis made some hazy calculations. Why, he must have been at least in his early twenties at the time of the British evacuation of New York. And, though the part of the family that had backed the Revolutionary cause had withdrawn from the city several years earlier, he would have been old enough to have known Amos Rooke, even hated him for his betrayal of both family and country.

Yet he had spoken to her as if Amos Rooke were a stranger, as if he himself had had no direct knowledge of the man. Then why—why had he died denying that Augustin was a murderer—in fear of another dead man?

Persis resolutely took up the candle and lifted the latch of the door. In the portfolio which had been entrusted to her, she might find an answer. Though she had to force herself into the dark of the upper hall, shielding her candle with one hand against any puff of air, Persis could hardly bring herself to lay a hand on the latch of her uncle's chamber. And, as she stood there, she heard the faintest of sounds.

Frozen, she glanced toward the head of the stairs. There was no breeze blowing here, that was no rustle of leaf or scrape of branch she heard. Yet she was not mistaken, there came a sound—and from the stairs. Not a footfall, rather something far less defined. Like —like the brush of a skirt edge against the banisters.

Lydia—Mrs. Pryor—? Why should either move through the night without a candle? The maids would use the other flight at the rear of the house. And they were not supposed to be here at all either, but in their cabins beyond the mound. Only Molly and Shubal had been housed in small chambers on the third floor, rooms intended really for an overflow of guests.

Persis strained to catch the faintest creak. No, she was not imagining this. There was someone coming up the front stairs. With one hand against the wall as a

53

support (as if the paneling under her fingertips tied her to reality), the girl advanced, step by cautious step, to the head of the flight.

A moment later she could have cried out at her own stupidity. The candle she carried must show as clearly as a beacon, already giving her away to whoever moved so stealthily through the dark.

She stopped short. What had she to be afraid of? She had a perfect right to collect her uncle's possession, confided to her care. But, as those sounds grew nearer—

Nothing—nothing to see. Only the whisper sounded louder. Fear caught her in an icy vise. She leaned back, pressing herself against the wall, closing her eyes. She refused to look. She would not! Still she was aware of a— For a moment her disturbed mind could not even find a word to cover the sensation which possessed her—she was blind, near dumb with panic—but there was a *presence*—

Persis knew that she must open her eyes. If she did not, this fear would fill her and she would scream mindlessly. That scream already arose painfully in her throat. But if she screamed she also knew, but not how she knew, she would be utterly lost.

The hall was cold, so very cold. Yet just moments before she had felt her shawl too heavy. So cold! Persis forced open her eyes. Her candle was burning steadily, but it showed only emptiness. No, that was not quite so!

There was a glint, as if the limited radiance was caught for a second by something from which it was reflected. And that glitter moved, languidly, slowly, back and forth in the air about the height of her own breast.

Had those spots of light been at floor level, she could

have told herself they marked the eyes of some animal. But these were in midair.

Voiceless, unable to move, Persis watched those small glints pass—until the dark at the other end of the hall swallowed them up. They had *not* been born of her imagination! And she would take oath that something had gone by her unseen, perhaps unseeing, in the hallway.

Shivering, but able now to move again, she slipped along, her shoulders scraping the wall. She would have to cross the open where that *thing* had passed, in order to reach her own door. For the present she could not bring herself to do that.

Her free hand caught on the latch of Uncle Augustin's door. Still facing outward, for she could not yet turn her back on the hall, she lifted that latch, felt the door open behind her. Then she whipped inside, shutting the door with the last remnant of her strength.

Once that was closed, Persis stood, her breath ragged, hearing in her ears the pounding of her own heart. Logic and common sense began to war with her fear. The strange cold was gone, also the sound, and certainly she no longer saw those—eyes—eyes?

All houses had noises peculiar to themselves which were produced during the silences of the night. As for the glints—could those not be something like the lightning bugs she had so often seen in the dusk at her own home? Finding themselves trapped inside a house, they had risen to a higher level seeking freedom.

Yet all the time Persis fought to satisfy herself with such explanations, she knew that she was merely tamping down tightly such a fear as she had never known before. Now, resolutely, she turned away from the door. The portfolio had been on the bedside table.

55

She held the candle a little higher. Yes, it was still there.

The bed was smooth of cover. There was nothing here save that which she had come for. After the fashion of the South, Uncle Augustin had been already encoffined, and the sealed coffin waited in the parlor below. In the morning he would be laid to rest—far from all he had ever known, in a place where the island dead slept peacefully.

Persis, the portfolio in hand, crept back to the door. To open that again required every bit of confidence she could summon. Then, with it open, she looked up and down the hall, listened, until she could force herself to make the short journey to her own chamber.

There she latched the door quickly, threw the portfolio on the bed, and set about moving the heaviest chair in the room to blockade the entrance. Only when that was done, still breathing fast, she put the portfolio for safekeeping beneath her pillow, and blew out the candle, creeping into the wide bed, and letting the ghostly veil of the insect netting fall about her. This, gauze though it was, she welcomed now as a kind of barrier against the rest of the Leverett house.

Sheer fatigue overcame her at last and she slept uneasily, with dreams she could not remember after. A pounding awoke her abruptly. It was light and the chair she had used for a barrier was shaking as the door was shoved impatiently against its back.

"Miss Persis—!"

Molly! And what would she think about that chair? The sunlight from the window, Molly's voice, banished the last of the night's fears—or at least pushed them too deep into her mind to matter now.

Persis struggled through the netting, tugged the

chair away in haste. But Molly's expression of surprise made her aware explanations were necessary.

"Miss Persis—whatever—?"

"I had a nightmare, Molly. When I woke up—in the middle of the night—I thought I heard something moving out in the hall."

"Heard something? Well, I never!" Molly set down with a decided thump the small tray she was carrying. "Miss Persis, what has gotten into you? You were never one for such fancies. I guess," she nodded, "it is this house, what with all them stories about it. I'll be thankful when we can pack up and go back to a proper town where there ain't this whispering 'bout witches and haunts and such. Stay here long enough and we'll all be believin' in them. Now you drink up this chocolate. This is going to be a hard day and you'll need somethin' sustainin' to weather it."

Thus, delicately, she hinted of the funeral.

"Seein' as how there's no decent black for mourning, Miss Persis," she continued briskly as Persis sat down and obediently drank the lukewarm contents of the cup Molly had brought her, "I made out with some changes for your white cambric. There's a black sash for that, and black gloves. It will just have to do."

"Thank you, Molly." The need for proper mourning had escaped Persis until this moment, but it would never have escaped Molly who prided herself on having things properly done.

"Since you are family and a female," the maid continued with her usual competence, "you won't be expected to show yourself until the service. That Sukie will bring you breakfast, and the Captain said, if you favored it, they would hold the service at nine. Seems like they have no proper preacher here," Molly sniffed. "The Captain, he'll read the service himself. He does it, they say for all them that are drowned and come ashore. Miss Persis—"

She stopped her bustling about and faced her mistress squarely. "I—" she began and then paused as if not quite sure of her words, then she hurried on, "Shubal, that poor old man's clean tuckered out. Seems like now he's decided he's nothing to live for, him always havin' been so close to Mr. Augustin. But, Miss Persis, what are we all goin' to do?"

Persis set the chocolate cup carefully on its saucer. There was only one thing they could do, they must go ahead with Uncle Augustin's plan to claim the estate in the Bahamas. Only she did not in the least have any idea of how to go about that.

Perhaps some lawyer in Key West would. She drew a deep breath. Molly, Shubal—neither one had lived since youth outside Uncle Augustin's service. It was only right they should look to her now for answers. The trouble was, she did not have much of one—yet.

"We must go on to Key West as soon as possible," she made herself say firmly. "I have Uncle Augustin's papers. He explained to me—" she told Molly as simply as possible the tangle of family history which had brought them south.

"Amos Rooke!" an exclamation from Molly interrupted her in midsentence.

"What do you know about him?" Persis asked avidly.

The maid pursed her lips as she could do on occasion. "Well, it's another old story, Miss Persis. You know that the master had three privateers out in 1812. He did right well with them, too. He always had a hate for the British —seeing his grandfather died in a British prison of fever and his father was killed in the war. So whenever he could, he took his revenge on them.
58

"They did say as how one of the ships which was took by the privateer *Eagle* came from the Bahamas and belonged to some kinfolk of his. And that Amos Rooke's son was killed when it was taken. It was just a story, mind you, no proof of it that I knew. Nor did the master ever have anything to do with it personally. He never even knew about it 'til months later. Men are killed when they go out fightin', and it ain't no fault but their own for being there."

Persis was startled. If Uncle Augustin was even so remotely concerned in the death of Amos' son—could that explain his dying cry that he was no murderer? And it might be the reason why he would not accept the first offer from Amos' widow—though it was all so many years ago. It had nothing to do with her now, except that she was a Rooke also, and would profit by the fact that those deaths had occurred. But it made her uneasy and unhappy.

Molly seemed to sense those feelings for she said quickly:

"Now don't you fret none 'bout claimin' this money, Miss Persis. The old lady wouldn't have left it in her will did she feel hard against the master. You do just what your uncle wanted. But 'bout goin' to Key West—"

"I know—that will mean going to sea again." Persis believed she could understand a protest against that. She did not want to think of it herself.

"Not just that, Miss Persis—though I ain't sayin' as how I'd relish that too much. But they do say as how the *Arrow* ain't goin' to be able to go on. Not unless they do a lot of work on her which ain't possible right here. And the mailboat—that don't come too often."

"But Captain Leverett's ship must certainly go to Key West—"

"That's just it, Miss Persis. Right now the Captain is havin' hard words with the Key West people. Leastwise that was what Mr. Hawkins was sayin' only this mornin' when he came out to the kitchen to get himself a snack. Mr. Hawkins, he's bosun on the *Nonpareil* and a mighty knowledgeable man. Why, just think, Miss Persis, it turned out he was born up on the Cape not far from my pa's place. 'Course he went to the sea when he was twelve and ain't never been back, no more'n I have. But we know a lot of the same people.

"Well, Mr. Hawkins says that those folks down at Key West don't take kindly to the Captain setting up his own place hereabouts. Takes away some of their trade. They've been tryin' to get him into court about it. But there ain't nothin' they can do—seein' as how he bought the whole Key fair and square, and has his license for wrecking. Only when he goes to Key West they always try to start some kind of trouble to make him mad and start a fight so he don't go there regular."

"Then we'll have to trust to luck," Persis said resignedly. She shrugged on the waist of the white muslin gown. "Captain Pettigrew will have to go somewhere to see about the *Arrow*. If he can't take us with him, perhaps he will take a letter to Key West. We shall have to find a lawyer there to advise us."

She pulled the portfolio from beneath her pillow, fingering the lock doubtfully. Sooner or later she would have to open this with the small key Uncle Augustin had always worn on his watch fob. But she shrank from that task at present.

"Put this in the trunk please, Molly, down at the bottom. It is full of important papers."

"Yes, Miss Persis."

Then Sukie came in with a breakfast tray and Persis ate as much as she could. She was perfectly willing to accept Molly's dictates as to what was acceptable conduct for the newly bereaved. But as she settled on a chair by the window, she tried to make a few plans.

It would seem that the best she would do was to ask her host frankly for assistance—much as she disliked the thought of that. She, Shubal, and Molly could certainly not remain here as uninvited guests, perhaps for weeks. There must be *some* way of reaching Key West or the outside world.

The *Arrow* was in the sheltered portion near the dock now. But it was plain even to a landswoman that the ship listed badly and rode ominously deep in the water. Beyond it was the *Nonpareil*. But the *Stormy Luck* was nowhere to be seen. Persis guessed that Grillon's interview with the master of the Key had been such as sent him speedily back to sea.

Captain Leverett—since she had to depend upon his good will she must master that dislike which arose in her every time she remembered his roughness on board the *Arrow*. Maybe, she reluctantly admitted now, he had done his best to save her life.

But he was a wrecker and even (according to Molly) one his own kind did not accept. This pretentious house of his was filled with loot from lost ships. What kind of a man was he really?

She combed her memory for a picture of the man who had left bruises on her arms when he had torn her loose from her hold to throw her—as she believed at the time—straight into the sea. He was tall, her head had topped his shoulder by very little. And his wind-tossed hair had been streaked by the rain and so plastered to his skull she could not say whether he was fair or dark. At the time she had been only cowed by his

61

complete assumption of authority over everything and everyone in sight. She could not even guess at his age. But she fully believed he was not a man one could warm to, even if met under less tumultuous circumstances.

She had seen him again last night when he had once more assumed full command, but she could remember very little indeed of that second meeting. Except he had not roared at her as he had the first time, but rather spoke in a dry, matter-of-fact voice which she only partially heard. That he was such a man as Uncle Augustin—though perhaps less polished—she could well believe. ✓

And—Persis sighed—he would be the only one who could advise her now, much as she disliked admitting that. If he could not, or dared not visit Key West, certainly he would know what arrangements she must make to go there—or to whom to apply for legal aid. There must be a will among Uncle Augustin's papers—he was too good a man of business not to leave such.

Again Persis sighed. She felt almost as tired and beaten as she had upon her first awakening in this room when she had not been sure of where she was. She was sorry for Uncle Augustin, in a vague way. But until his illness and the loss of the company, she was sure he had been happy in his own remote fashion. Somehow she was sorrier now for Shubal, and a little for herself—as well as uneasy. This was rather like having a secure and sturdy house fall away brick by brick.

At a tap at the door she started up, breathing a little faster.

"Miss Rooke?"

Persis' breathing steadied. It was Mrs. Pryor. Why had she expected somehow to hear that deeper voice of authority? She went out into the hall where the housekeeper waited.

"Miss Rooke—" The repetition of her name sounded as if the formidable Mrs. Pryor was disconcerted in some way.

"I know," Persis summoned her own courage. "Thank you, Mrs. Pryor. In the parlor, I believe?"

"Miss Persis," Molly puffed in her haste, coming up the back stairs to catch up with Persis. In her hands she carried a tight bunch of flowers, as bright and varied in color as those pieces of patchwork she delighted in. Persis accepted the roughly made bouquet thankfully. Though she had never associated Uncle Augustin with flowers, certainly not ones of such violent hues.

The service was strange to her and she found herself shaken, moved by the loneliness of death in this far place where there was nothing of the world Uncle Augustin had always known. She found herself crying for the man she had never understood, but who had been kind to her in his remote fashion. Somehow she was glad that the words said for him were those chosen for other strangers who had also met death far from home.

She watched Captain Leverett read from a small, well-worn Bible. Yes, he was tall, and his now dry hair was sun bleached to a shade even lighter than his sister's, showing near white against the dark tan of his skin. His eyes were a piercing gray-blue—with something about them which reminded her of Uncle Augustin. They appeared to see directly into a person, as if to read the very thoughts of one's mind. He was not a handsome man, she decided, yet in any assembly he would be a notable one. She was grateful to him as she had not thought to be.

Just as she was grateful to those others gathered here. Dr. Veering in his rumpled white linen suit, but wearing a black stock, Lydia and Mrs. Pryor, Shubal and Molly, between whom she stood.

"Ahhh—" there was a sigh which was nearly a groan.

Shubal, his thin old hands pressing against his breast, wavered on his feet. Persis caught his shoulder, tried to steady him. Then Dr. Veering moved swiftly in and took most of the weight of the man's frail body.

"He would come," Molly said. "But he ain't fit to be out of bed, he ain't!"

Dr. Veering gestured and two of the servants waiting discreetly at the parlor door came to carry Shubal back. Persis was aware of Captain Leverett moving to join her. She spoke without looking up at him.

"They were together ever since they both were young. I—"

A hand caught hers, drew her fingers up to lie on a strong supporting arm.

"Your uncle must have been a very good master to win such devotion. Do not worry about his man; Veering will see to him."

"I—" Persis' sight suddenly blurred with tears. She stumbled forward to lay Molly's flowers on the top of the coffin.

Captain Leverett did not leave her. The floor seemed to sway under her like the deck of the *Arrow* and she found herself clinging desperately to that strong arm as if it were the only promise of safety. All safe and normal life had been torn asunder. Shubal's collapse had made her completely aware of that.

5

Persis' straightly stiff back was a credit to the drilling Miss Pickett had imposed upon her young ladies. Her hands, primly folded, rested on the still locked portfolio on her knees. But she watched very closely the man standing near the hearthside, nor did she miss the fact that his frown was growing deeper.

"I agree, Miss Rooke, that legal assistance is necessary in this matter. Unfortunately, there is none to be had nearer than Key West, and as to when you can journey on there—"

"I understand, sir," she said firmly, "that there is a mail packet visiting here at intervals." Her chin rose a fraction of an inch; she would not beg for help, if that was what he was waiting for.

"At intervals is right—long ones," Captain Leverett

returned. "Also, the quarters aboard the packet are very cramped. And, if they have already picked up other passengers, they would refuse you room. But perhaps something else may be done, Miss Rooke. I shall give the matter my fullest consideration."

"Thank you, sir." He was almost as formidable here in this room as he had been on board the *Arrow*. She could imagine him sweeping her off again to suit his own plans. It was plain to her that she presented a problem and one he wished were absent. Now she arose.

"We are most grateful for your hospitality, sir. The care for my uncle, and now for Shubal, has been all one could desire, even from a close kinsman. And Shubal cannot travel, ill as he now is. But certainly we have no right to continue to intrude upon your home. I have been told that there is a hotel for shipwrecked travelers, perhaps it would be better for us to move there—"

Now he was positively scowling. "Certainly not! Oh, it is not too uncomfortable, I grant you. But it is not for a lady, especially one now alone."

"Sir, it is time I must learn to manage for myself. And with Molly, I am certainly not alone!"

He was halfway to the door as if he could spare her and her concerns no more time. But he spoke over his shoulder.

"Let me hear no more of such a scheme, Miss Rooke. You will remain under this roof until we can make acceptable travel arrangements for you."

Persis almost gasped. Such brusqueness was sheer rudeness and her resentment awoke at once. This Captain Leverett had no control over her. Yet it seemed he expected her to meekly accept his orders, as if he were her guardian.

She clasped the portfolio tighter. It was true that she lacked some months yet of being legally of age. But her uncle had never mentioned to her that he had made provision for any guardian. Perhaps some stranger might take over, and she would not be even allowed to go on to the islands.

Would any lawyer in Key West be empowered under the circumstances to act for her on her own will? She had not thought of that before. If she only knew what the law might be in her case—not yet of age and without a guardian.

She went to look out of the window at the late afternoon scene. The heat was heavy, for the earlier sea breeze had died away. And she began to understand Lydia's feeling that the Key was a prison. But she would not allow herself to be trapped! Surely Captain Leverett must be as glad to see the last of her as she would of him.

Persis returned to her chamber. The portfolio was still to be gone through, and on the chest in her room lay the watch with the key attached to its fob. Seating herself, she unlocked the case and shook out on the bed a number of documents. Two, fastened together with tape, she recognized as letters from those in the attic box. Then there was a long, thrice-folded sheet bearing an impressive seal and in fancy script at the top the words *Last Will and Testament*.

Persis scanned the strange formal language of that. A pension for Shubal, and one for Molly, as well as a bequest to Mrs. Robison, the cook who had ruled their New York kitchen. Mention of some books to go to Mr. Hogue, and arrangements for a funeral which had been decided upon as decorous before Augustin Rooke had made his decision to come south.

Last of all—"the remainder of my estate and properties to my niece, Persis Rooke." No mention of
guardianship. Clearly Uncle Augustin had never
thought he would die before she came of age. But he
had known his health was precarious before he started—or perhaps he would not admit that to himself.

She read some letters—the most recent one first. It
was from a lawyer—a Mr. Lampson Brown in the Bahamas—urging Uncle Augustin to either come or send
some reliable agent for the settling of Madam Rooke's
estate. Though he mentioned no sums in the letter, it
was plain that the inheritance was enough to warrant
concern.

The taped letters were much older, of course, time-
browned. Persis spread out the first—the ink was very
faded. She looked to the window—it was not only that
her eyes were unaccustomed to the crabbed writing,
but the light had begun to fail swiftly. Clouds were
gathering, and again the wind was rising. Such gusts
followed that the curtains were blown out into the
room and she hurried to close them, securing the shutters when she saw the whipping of the fronds on the
palms below. Was a second storm on the way?

Lighting the bedside candle she held the letter page
close to that to be able to read at all.

The subject matter was what Uncle Augustin had
told her. And the hand was that of an educated person, the contents much to the point. Papers had been
found after the death of Amos Rooke which made it
clear he was in debt to his New York kin. The writer
offered to send the sum so long owed. Her expression
was stiff and Persis thought she was unhappy to admit
the cupidity of her dead husband, but honesty had
won out. The page was signed "Caroline Rooke."

But the second letter contained information Uncle Augustin had not mentioned. It was longer than the first and the hand was shaky, though when Persis compared the dates of the two it had been written only four years after the first.

"'To Augustin Rooke, Esquire,'" she read in a half whisper as she struggled to distinguish the words—

I have to ask of you a very great favor, but it is necessary for my own peace of mind that this be done. As you know my late husband had a son born of an irregular union before our own marriage. However, he acknowledged this boy openly and made him his legal heir, since it was clear that at our time of life we would have no children.

Unfortunately this boy, James Rooke (his name assured to him by adoption) was of a wayward and passionate temper. He quarreled continually with his father, took up with bad company, and was a constant source of unhappiness and disgrace for my husband—though he gave James many chances to reform.

When the sea war broke out again with your country, James, much against his father's wishes, sailed on a privateer fitted out here in the islands. This was later captured by one flying the American flag. We have heard nothing from him since— save a rumor that he was killed during a boarding action. Yet until his death my husband clung to the hope that James might still be alive. This, I will admit, I fostered, since it relieved his mind during his long illness.

I made private inquiries which stated that James was seen to fall wounded on boarding the deck. This has been since accepted by our courts to mean death, so his father's estates were passed to me.

But very recently I heard another tale—that James, though wounded, escaped, and since has not been seen. I have traced the ship which fought with the *Heron* and discovered that, by some strange twist of fate, it was owned by you. Since it was not lost, and you may be able to find some of those who served on board—can you supply me with any information they may have about this affair?

James was twenty years of age, of a brown complexion, with dark hair. He had a sword scar across the back of his left hand and was of a reckless spirit.

I await, sir, your reply, since this is a matter of grave importance.

Persis' first conclusion was Amos' wife must have hated James. The fact came through plainly that she had only put up with him for the sake of her husband. And she dreaded James' turning up to claim the estate. How had Uncle Augustin answered this? Persis searched among the papers on the bed.

There was another legal looking document which she puzzled through—a deposition—or the copy of one (for it had *copy* written across the back) taken from two men. A Captain Willard Owens—

Why, she knew Captain Owens. He had retired, but twice he had visited her uncle in New York.

The other was a Patrick Conner and had the word *Bosun* written in beside it. Both men swore on oath that they had seen such a man as was described in the letter, that he had been wounded, and had died of his wounds the same night—to be buried at sea.

So. Persis laid down that paper. Madam Rooke had more than one reason to be grateful to Uncle Augustin. He had refused the repayment she had offered him, and then he had assured her inheritance. Now she could better understand why Madam Rooke, in turn, had passed a goodly amount of that inheritance over to the older branch of her husband's family. Certainly she had not held the death of her trying stepson against the New York Rookes.

The girl made a neat pack of the letters and papers, relocked them into the portfolio. The key she put away in her small jewel box. But had Uncle Augustin blamed himself for James' death? He certainly had died with a troubled mind.

As she replaced the portfolio in her trunk, Persis was even more keenly aware of the wind now buffeting the house. Some of that fear born in the last hours on the *Arrow* moved her. But she was safely on land now, not out on the open sea.

Then a sound arose above the wailing of the wind, a sound eerie enough to startle her. It stirred in her again that other fear, the one which had gripped her last night when she had stood in the hall sure that a "presence" had passed her by. Shivering, she picked up the candle and went to the door.

According to Uncle Augustin's watch it was only near twilight. Yet night had fallen very quickly. She wanted to be with someone, the memory of those moments of sheer terror during which she had been frozen against the wall growing in her.

She heard a bustle below, a slamming of shutters being barred against the outer world. The door to the

71

veranda was also slammed. Another storm! Persis thanked fate that she was not at sea for this one. Vigorous as wind and wave were, the key was safer than a ship.

Lydia came out of a nearby chamber, also holding a candle.

"This will be a bad one. Do you have a waterproof cape?" she asked.

"No." Persis was bewildered. Was Lydia suggesting they go *out* into the rising fury of the wind?

"A pity. Hold this, will you." Lydia gave her the candlestick she was carrying and proceeded to shake out a gray bundle she had folded under one arm. It was a cape provided with a hood. She shrugged the folds of cloth over her shoulders, pulled the hood over her head with little regret for the elaborate arrangement of her fair hair.

"I'm going up on the lookout," she stated.

Persis thought of that narrow, railed walk on the roof. What could Lydia mean? The gusting wind might well tear her off that perch. Her consternation must have been mirrored on her face for the other girl laughed.

"Oh, there's no danger really. Henderson, my brother's lookout, is already there. And he will have rigged ropes to hold on to. Just as Mason is waiting below ready to carry a message should a distress rocket be sighted."

"Captain Leverett would take his ship out in a storm— ?"

"How else did he reach the *Arrow*? He is pledged to do so by his license. The *Nonpareil* has even weathered a hurricane. Yes, Crewe is waiting for any signal."

She took back her candle and flitted to that other
72

steep stair. Persis hesitatingly went in the opposite direction, slowly descending step by step into the dim, shuttered gloom of the first floor. To go out in a frail ship braving the very teeth of the storm—yes, the man she had known on the wave-washed deck of the *Arrow* could and would do that. He could not be denied the virtue of courage, no matter what other flaws of character he might have.

Mrs. Pryor was busy in the parlor, checking the windows and shutters. She turned to Persis with an abrupt question:

"Are the shutters in your chamber well secured, Miss Rooke?"

"Yes. Will this be a very bad storm?" It seemed to the girl that the house, sturdy as it appeared, was beginning to shudder under the steady blows of this wind.

"It would seem so. And we are, in a manner, vulnerable here. Though the house is set on stakes and so yields a little to the wind. Otherwise it might, in the worst blows, be pounded off the mound. All the fires are out in the kitchen; we shall have only cold food until this has safely passed."

Now she had to raise her voice to be heard over the outside shriek. How could Lydia be out in this—up on the roof? Persis marveled at the girl's recklessness.

"Lydia went up to the lookout," Persis blurted out. She had no control over her hostess' actions, but perhaps Mrs. Pryor could do something.

Mrs. Pryor shrugged. "She and her brother—it is in their blood. And she knows the dangers, though they have plenty of lifelines fastened there. What she will get out of it, save thoroughly wet clothes—" Again the housekeeper shrugged. "And the Captain has already put to sea."

"I don't see how he could—" Persis ventured.

"Best ride out a blow at sea than have his ship torn from its mooring and perhaps beached." The housekeeper made sure of the last fastenings. "Laws, now, just look at that!" She gestured to water seeping in under the closed window. "We'll have to plug that before it reaches the carpet!"

Persis trailed behind as Mrs. Pryor purposefully hurried toward the kitchen. Mam Rose, Sukie, and the other maid crouched on the edge of the hearth as if they were chilled, and a fire still flamed there. Molly stood by the big table, both hands over her ears, her eyes squeezed shut as if she could so deny the fury of the wild elements without.

"Get up!" Mrs. Pryor advanced on the group by the hearth. "Water is seeping in the parlor. And perhaps other places along the east walls. Find the rags, the old towels, and get ready to mop up."

"Water done come in plenty, Miz Pryor." Mam Rose made no attempt to move, as she screeched her answer. "It'll git in through de turtle pen iffen it rise some more."

Mrs. Pryor marched across the floor of the kitchen, stooped to pull up a trapdoor. Flinging it full back she picked up a storm lantern and lowered it, focusing its gleam downward. Mam Rose and the two maids edged reluctantly away from the fireplace to gather up mops and armloads of strips of cloth out of a bin.

"Nigh right up to top, ain't it?" Mam Rose demanded.

Persis had gone forward to look down into a dark pit the housekeeper had uncovered. The light did show the water swirling about. Mrs. Pryor studied the way that arose up a ladder leading to the kitchen.

"Not enough to worry about," she reported briskly.

Mam Rose's thin shoulders hunched. "I'm not stayin' here do the pen break and them big turtles git loose. Don't aim to have one of them climbing up."

Mrs. Pryor slammed the trapdoor back in place. "That's hardly likely to happen, Mam Rose, as you well know. And the sooner you get to mopping the better—all of you."

Seeing Persis' puzzlement she explained. "That is a fresh-water cistern down there. And part of it's a bathhouse. There's a stake side pen between it and the canal where we generally keep a supply of turtles. Turtle soup is excellent, if a little rich."

"You mean this house sits out over part of a pond?" Persis asked.

"Yes. It was channeled from the spring on purpose for protection against Indian raids. One could even escape that way into the canal by going through the turtle pond."

Persis could see the advantage of a supply of water, though she suspected it might be brackish and undrinkable if the overflow of the seaward canal rose in it. But swimming through a pond of turtles to escape a raid—it sounded like the wildest kind of fantasy. Yet Mrs. Pryor apparently accepted the idea as an added advantage of the house.

"The whole house is not over water," Mrs. Pryor must have caught some of her unease, "just the kitchen. Captain Leverett when he built used the Key method of mounting the house on heavy stakes driven well into the mound. The building, as I said, may shift a little—and it has—but it cannot be ripped loose. And hereabout it is only good reasoning to have another exit in case of trouble. There have been several massacres on Keys in the past and people have learned to

75

take precautions. The cistern is filled by the rain troughs—it may rise and then run off into the canal. We wedge the door here when that happens."

Persis tried to imagine a cellar, or what would have been a cellar in any proper house, filled with swirling water, including turtles. All she gained from that was a personal belief it was all a part of the barbaric wrecker life with which she need not concern herself. Turtles! She had seen some of the monsters turned over on their backs, their scaled limbs pawing futilely, and she had felt deeply sorry for the poor creatures, having thereafter no wish to taste the much vaunted soup.

As she backed a little away from the trapdoor she was startled by a crescendo of knocks from the outer door. Someone out there was beating almost frenziedly on the panel. Mrs. Pryor glanced around, and put down the lantern.

"Come!" she beckoned both Persis and Molly to join her. "It will like as not take the three of us—"

With one hand on the latch-bar, the housekeeper gestured for them to take position behind her, as if she feared she might be sent flying inward when she opened the door.

"Ready—" Mrs. Pryor warned during a short lull. Persis saw Molly brace herself and did likewise. Then the door, freed of its fastening, burst inward.

Persis, drenched by the incoming rain, cried out. From hair to shoes she was almost instantly as wet as if she had fallen into the cistern below. And so violent was the assault of water and wind she could hardly take a breath, gasping like a newly landed fish.

But the fury of the storm swept in someone else. Persis was only aware of a crouching figure who was

76

blown, or rushed near the hearth. Then she gave all the strength she could muster to aid Mrs. Pryor and Molly in, once more shutting and securing the door.

They forced it closed, leaving runnels of rain, even bits of torn leaves on the floor. When the bolts at top and bottom were again set Mrs. Pryor stood for a long moment breathing deeply, her round face red under the draggle of her soaked and wind-twisted cap and hair. Molly's hands were at her breast, which rose and fell with the deep gusts she drew into and expelled from her laboring lungs.

Only Persis turned to see who had come out of the storm. She shrank back, muffling a scream only in time. That—that *thing*—crouched by the hearth hardly looked human!

There were long dark sticks of legs, arms as thin, ending in hands like the claws of some huge predatory bird. And the rest of the body was covered with water-slimed leather, some of that in tatters, topped by a shirt so stained as to be nearly as dark as the leather. But it was the head—now swung around toward the girl—

In color it was as dark brown as the wretched rags of the shirt, and it bore no resemblance to any living creature. How could it? With those great upstanding ears like those of a bat, while the eyes were only deep holes not even showing a flicker of life within them. The nose was merely a raised lump in which Persis saw no nostrils, but the mouth was round, pursed, stuck outward from the surface as if this monster sought fiercely to suck at something.

Mrs. Pryor came away from the door. There was no dismay on the housekeeper's face as she stooped to pick up the lantern and set it once more on the table.

"Ill weather, Askra," she commented.

The tattered, mud-smeared creature out of the storm stood up stiffly, as if her joints were racked by rheumatism. Now Persis could see a tangle of coarse gray hair on her shoulders, rain-wet into loops which dripped on the floor.

She grunted and reached both bird-claw hands to the back of her head, fumbled there for a moment or two, and then that awful, unnatural face fell forward, lying, still held by a cord, to hang like a bib on her flat breast.

The newcomer was dark skinned, but her features were totally unlike those of the black servants. Instead she had a large, high-bridged nose jutting forward to overhang her mouth and chin, while her forehead slanted back in a way to accent the nose even more.

Persis had seen Indians in the North, the broken remnants of the once proud and feared Six Nations. But this very old woman was very different from those. For all her ragged and filthy clothing she carried herself as if she were mistress here. And she said nothing as she brushed back the matted elf locks of her hair. Her eyes slid past Mrs. Pryor and she did not answer the other's comment. Instead she looked directly at Persis.

Try as she might to break that steady locking of gaze the girl could not move her eyes, nor turn away her head. The other held her in a kind of trance by some force of personality, as if she could so reach directly into the captive's mind and read every thought lying there.

"Rockets!" That cry brought an abrupt end to their confrontation.

Lydia stood in the doorway from the hall. Her cloak was plastered to her body, streams of water ran from it.

"We saw rockets!" she repeated. "There's a wreck on the reef!"

6

Persis paced the hallway back and forth. She could not sit still, nor could she control the vivid pictures her imagination painted of what might be happening out there, beyond the walls of the house which shuddered under every lash of the wind. Lydia was strung up to a high rate of excitement, but even she did not again seek the dangerous walk on the roof, only chattered faster and faster about other storms and what had resulted from them. She had shed the dripping cloak and now sat on the bottom step of the stair talking, always talking. Until Persis wanted to cover her ears as Molly had done.

She grew so tired with her pacing that at last she was driven to a chair in the dining room where three candles made very small pools of light, and shadows hung over their shoulders like baneful beasts about to seize their prey. As Mrs. Pryor had warned, the food was cold— bread, jam, slices of cured ham, with not even a cup of comforting tea to wash it down.

Lydia still speculated on the prizes which such high seas offered—she seemed to have no thought in her head of lives which might be lost on those vessels caught in the full turbulence of the storm. But she was silenced completely when the crystals in the unlit chandelier over them gave a sudden sharp tinkle, clashing prism against prism, and the very floor under them appeared to shift.

Persis noted that Lydia's hand, resting on the table, closed in a tight grip on the edge of the board, her nails cutting into the heavy linen of the cloth which covered it.

But that lurch of the house was followed by a calm and Persis relaxed a little until Mrs. Pryor came in, herding Sukie before her, examining each windowsill for signs of a betraying trickle of water.

"Is—is it over?" Persis asked.

"Laws, no, Miss. This is the center—what they call 'the eye'—when that passes over we'll again have wind." There was something steadying about Mrs. Pryor, as if no torrent of rain, no fury of gale could beset her. As Persis had done she changed into dry clothing and reordered her old-fashioned coiffure, looking her usual self.

But the news she had brought was certainly not encouraging and Persis instinctively braced herself for a return of the fury. She had even lost all idea of time; it seemed to her that the fury had lasted forever. Was it night, morning—? However, tired as she was, she could not have crawled into bed with that rage of elements outside.

Then the blow did start again, even as the housekeeper had predicted, and went on for what seemed like hours and hours, never letting them go. Lydia stopped talking at last. Persis had barely listened to her chatter when the second hard assault began. Sometimes she could not hear anyway, only see the other's lips moving. They sat in the parlor, a single wavering candle flame between them. Once or twice there came such a crash that Persis was sure a part of the house had been beaten in. But she had regained enough of her own stubborn courage so that she refused to let Lydia see how stark her fear was.

What of the ships out there? The *Arrow* had been brought to the wharf so that its repairs could be more easily estimated. But with this second battering it might be left in a far worse state. Captain Leverett was on the open sea—daring his ship—and his life with those of his men. The rockets Lydia had sighted— would those who had fired them be as lucky as they of the *Arrow* had been?

Persis discovered Lydia was watching her closely, with some of the same searching which had been used by the tattered hag who had sought shelter in the kitchen hours earlier.

"Glad you aren't out there?" Lydia's lips shaped a hint of a smile. "The *Arrow* would never have lasted through this—and probably Crewe would not have dared to steer too close to the reef to help—not in *this* storm. And Crewe is the best wrecker on the Keys."

Persis did not want to think about the *Arrow*; she wished she could erase the sounds of the storm as well.

"How did he become a wrecker?" Persis asked.

Lydia pouted. "Because he is so stubborn. He has had his master's papers since he was eighteen; our father was an Indies merchant in the Canton Trade. He wanted Crewe to go in with him but Crewe had to have the sea. So he ran away on one of the China clippers. He was only twelve but he had the same stubborn temper even then!" She laughed. "He still does—hotter than hell, Ralph says—only he keeps it all inside. But when he lets go—" She made a gesture which suggested the scattering of bits of emotion. "Anyway, he is a natural-born seaman, and he worked hard. Then he got in with Palmer Briggs—"

Persis gave a start which she was sure that the sharp-eyed Lydia did not miss. Palmer Briggs was well known in New York—too well known and for the worst of reasons.

"Oh, Crewe never commanded a slaver." Lydia's chin lifted a fraction. "Only scum takes out one of those. But Palmer was interested in wrecking. He'd lost a couple of slave ships to the Navy and they were downright suspicious of anything he sent to sea. So he made a deal with Crewe—to try the Keys and see how it worked. Only right after that Palmer Briggs did fail, in fact he went bankrupt. And Crewe bought the ship somehow from the trustees who took over to settle affairs.

"Then he came down here and purchased this Key, from the widow of Sancho Mendoza who held it by Spanish law. He thought that the Key West men were working together to get rid of those they did not like. And they certainly had no time for Crewe. He's beat them to too many wrecks and made first deals with the captains. This house—he brought ships' carpenters in from the islands to build it." She looked around with pride.

"When my father died, Crewe had me go to school in Charleston in the Carolinas—" She made a face. "Don't do this, a lady never thinks of that, and all the

83

rest!" Her voice made clear her opinion of the school. "I kept begging him to bring me here. What a fool I was!"

Her expression was set now. "I didn't know, you see, just what it would mean being shut away on this—this desert! There was a girl from Key West at school—Sallie Mathews—and she had made life there sound so exciting. But there's nothing to do here. And I don't see how Crewe ever expects me to get married. Married to who— Dr. Veering? He's near old enough to be my father, and besides all he can think of are his plants. And the rescued people from the ships—they stay only long enough to get passage away. I might just as well be buried!"

Persis longed to ask how Ralph Grillon fitted into Lydia's dismal picture of life on Lost Lady, but she wanted no confidences.

"You're lucky." Lydia was watching her again with a slightly calculating look. "You have a good reason to go on to Key West, even to the Bahamas. Just don't let Crewe try to run things for you, too."

"There is no reason why he should take any responsibility for my affairs," Persis tried to make that sound emphatic.

Lydia laughed. "Crewe doesn't give reasons—he just goes ahead and does what *he* thinks is proper and suddenly you find yourself under his thumb. So watch out!" She lifted her hand to half-cover a yawn. "I'm sleepy. One gets used to this after a while, you know, and you *can* really sleep."

Persis took that for a hint. She did not in the least desire to climb the stairs to her own shuttered room. But Lydia had already blown out one candle and taken up the second. Very reluctantly Persis arose in turn, shielding the very small flame of the last candle with her cupped hand, and followed Lydia up the stairs. She wished now that she had suggested Molly would share her quarters but her pride kept her from carrying out that wish.

Once in her chamber she undressed only to the extent of shedding her dress and slippers, putting on her wrapper and lying on the wide bed ready for any alarm. However, perhaps Lydia was right, one did become accustomed to the continual sound of the storm. For, in spite of the fear she fought so hard to conceal, Persis did fall into a very disturbing sleep.

Disturbed by dreams— Once more she stood pressed against the wall of the upper hall listening to that whisper which might have come from invisible silken skirts brushing against the floor, seeing those slowly weaving glints of light. But this time as the presence passed her she was drawn after it in spite of every force of will she used to try and break free.

Then the walls of the corridor were gone, the house was gone. She was in the open, though around her, at a distance, was a barrier of stone. There was no sign of the storm. It was night and somehow very still, no insect call, not a stir of breeze, only the swish-swish which marked the unseen passing of the presence.

They came to the far side of the barrier. The glints now flickered with greater speed, but always in a constrained area. Then slowly, very slowly, those sank toward the earth, seemed to plunge into the dark surface she could not clearly see. And, at their disappearance, Persis was free.

She awoke. The room steamed with humidity and heat. Her clothing was plastered to her body and her head ached. But for a moment the dream lingered with her so that it seemed she would be not on this wide bed, in a room, but outside in the dark of a night where there was no moon, no star she could remember.

Persis sat up. There had been, she tried to tell herself sensibly, nothing really frightening about the dream. She had not herself been menaced in any way. Why did she then feel so weak, so shaken, as if she had to outrun pursuers bent on taking her life? She rubbed her hands across her sweat-dampened face. Only then she realized that there was no sound of wind or rain. And around the edges of the shutters where she could see was light.

Pulling herself off the bed she went to the near window, listened intently for any sound of the storm. It was as quiet as it had been in her first awakening here. Thankfully she jerked out the tags of rags that maids had tamped in to cover all possible cracks and looked out into a morning which was cloudy, yes, but still.

The vegetation had a ragged look. She saw several fallen palms, and the water in the canal lapped very high against the mound.

The *Arrow* appeared as if it had been hammed against the wharf, one side stove in. But there was no sign of the *Nonpareil* at anchorage.

Persis washed in water from the pitcher on the dressing stand, dressed in fresh underlinen and one of her own gowns which Molly had done her best to rehabilitate. It was a pink muslin patterned with small shiny dots, though it looked rather limp and ill used in spite of Molly's effort to refurbish it.

Now she was aware of being very hungry. Would the fires be lit again? She would like above all a cup of hot tea; her mouth actually felt dry when she thought of it. Tea and biscuits, and perhaps some of the fruit which seemed a usual part of any breakfast here.

There was no use in trying to make her hair curl

properly. The damp of the sea wind denied her that small vanity. So she combed and braided it up into a knot which was the best she could do. And then she went out into the hall. For a second the memory of her dream gripped her again—but it was only a dream Persis told herself firmly. She was *not* going to be continually set aflutter by her imagination.

The house was very quiet. Perhaps the rest of the household were still sleeping off the alarms of the storm. She hesitated for a moment at Lydia's door, half-inclined to knock; then felt no need. Rather she could find Molly, and the best place to hunt would be the kitchen.

As Persis went, the quiet of the house disturbed her more and more. She had an odd feeling that she was the only one now within its walls, deserted. An odd fancy and one she quickly quenched. Only, when she found the kitchen also empty, no fire set, nor any sign of Mam Rose and the others, she was again shaken.

The back door which they had bolted so firmly after the arrival of Askra now stood a little ajar. Instinctively, Persis headed for that. Mam Rose and the maids must have returned to their own cabins—that was it—and had overslept. It was not her place to awaken them, of course, but she could at least step outside and see what kind of a day it was.

A fresh sea wind pulled at her skirts and tugged vainly to loosen a lock or two from her tight top braids. Leaves and plants torn into fragments littered the ground. She could see no path through this mess, nor any sign of the cabins, though she continued toward the farther side of the mound, picking her way with care among the debris.

Then, there had been a slippage of the earth and shell of which the mound itself was made. Enough to uncover rough stones, set in a line which could only mean they had been placed there on purpose.

And two of those had been rammed askew by half a palm; its trunk now a splintered stump. Persis paused. Those stones—they should have stood higher—much higher! But how did she know that?

Wondering, she gathered up her skirts with both hands and edged past the wreckage of the palm to look at the remnants of what must be a very old wall. One of the long splinters torn from the palm had dug deeply into the surface of the mound at this point and there was something there—not stone—

Persis stooped, jerked a good-sized bit of palm frond loose, and dug into the loosened earth. A box! Of some dull metal which was the same color now as the ground which had held it.

It was narrow, about eighteen inches long. She wriggled it out of its niche and picked it up, to discover it was surprisingly heavy. Lead? A lead box. Something concealed here long ago by the Spaniards, or by a pirate?

She tried to force it open and finally had to admit that though she could see no lock, it was firmly closed. Carrying it carefully, she went back to the kitchen, in her mind a memory picture of the rack of knives on the wall there.

"Aaaaa—"

Persis jumped and dropped the knife, the blade of which she had been trying to force under the edge of the lid.

That witchlike creature who had been blown out of the storm was standing there staring at her with that same compelling, measuring look. Persis had never remembered feeling such a fear of any person before—

but Askra was far different from anyone she had ever met.

Now the Indian woman stretched forth a hand which was clawlike as to fingers, even the nails, dull and dirty, taking on the semblance of the talons of some unwholesome bird such as the vultures Persis had seen once or twice in the past.

"You find—ghost—thing—" The words were voiced protestingly, almost as if forced one by one with great effort from under the overhang of that beak of a nose.

Persis nearly snatched away her own hands to hide behind her back in denial. Then her stubbornness and independence strengthened her.

"I found this—out there under a stone." She pointed to the back door, tried to keep her voice as even and emphatic as always. There were no such things as witches—ghosts. She knew enough to be sure of that. And she was not going to let herself be stampeded into believing otherwise.

"Ghost thing—bad—"

Persis knew now what Molly had meant when she said that Askra's intent gaze did make one feel that the hag could summon powers beyond the comprehension of ordinary people. Only she was not going to give in to any such foolish idea!

The Indian woman stretched her hand out farther, extending her fingers as if to grasp the box. Now her eyes changed, were veiled as her wrinkled lids fell. She made, however, no move to pick up the box. It was just as if it radiated some form of heat which her hand could feel.

"Not of—" She no longer spoke English but rather a gabble of words totally unknown to the girl. "Bloody—it has been—it will be again. You take it."

Now using her fingertips, Askra pushed the box toward Persis.

"It is for you—a gift."

"A gift?" Persis echoed.

"A gift of blood. To your hand only will it go. And in your hand it will bring life—and death. *She* wishes it so."

"She—?"

Askra was already shuffling toward the outer door. She did not answer and in a moment was outside, the still unopened box left lying on the table. Persis was torn by two almost equal emotions. One demanded that she return the thing to where she had found it, scratch broken shells and earth over it. But she found that she could not do that. It had suddenly become so important that she *know*— She had to know!

The Indian woman had been obviously trying to frighten her; that was it. Molly said that most of the islanders held Askra in such awe that they gave her what she wanted and kept carefully out of her way thereafter.

Slowly the girl picked up a knife, inserted its point into the edge age had sealed shut, and began to pry. This had been a pirate stronghold once. The thought of some treasure crossed her mind but she forgot her uneasiness as she worked to loosen the leaden band around its side which apparently locked it closed. Loosening the end of one strip, she peeled that loose in a single piece. And once that band was gone, it was easy to raise the lid.

There was a mass of age-rotted fiber there. That she drew out carefully. Then a single object, well wrapped in what could only be a strip of oiled silk (gone crackly with age and giving forth a disagreeable smell) appeared.

Persis plucked gingerly at that, not liking the feel of it against her fingers. It unrolled slowly and she found she had uncovered a closed fan. But—

This was the one Lydia had shown her, with such a fantastic history! There was no mistaking the opal-eyed cats staring banefully up at her from the heavily carved end sticks. Except when she tried to open it, there was no spread. The thing was made to look like a fan, yes, but a second close observation showed no folds. It was a solid, heavy copy of the closed fan Lydia had displayed—even grooves along the top to suggest the edges of real folds.

And, she hated it!

Persis prided herself on her sensible approach to life. She certainly discounted Lydia's relished ghost story. This could not be Lydia's fan, of course, though it was so closely a duplicate, except that it must remain furled. Persis found that she shrank from touching it at all.

Instead, using the flaking, oiled silk to cover her fingers, she recovered it quickly, to fit it back into its coffin. Why did the word coffin seem to fit so well, asked one portion of her mind? But that was what it was—encoffined.

Hurriedly she piled the disintegrating fiber over it and slammed the lid back on the box. As best she could, she retwisted the lead strip, sealing it around the sides. Though, she was sure, not well enough to keep the sea damp from reaching the contents. But that did not matter. This was an instrument of evil!

Then she was astounded by her own thoughts. How could any object convey to her such a sense of heightened evil which this held? It was not natural in these enlightened days. She knew that witches and curses, and all the like, were only a part of such old romances silly schoolgirls traded and read in order to have the pleasure of shivering over impossible horrors.

Taking up the box once more she determinedly went out the rear door. This was going right back where she found it. And Askra's comments, or warnings, whichever those had been, were only the meandering of a half-crazed old woman who fed upon the awe and fear she aroused in the superstitious.

Persis found the hole from which she had freed the box and worked that back into its former resting place, pushing in shells and earth, tramping back and forth with stolid determination over the spot that it might stay safely hidden and buried.

It was not until she was back in the house again, washing her earth-stained hands that Persis felt comfortable. Nobody was going to find that again. Still, she had to fight down a small stir of curiosity. A fan which was not a fan—what had been its purpose? She was sure that the design on the end sticks had been exactly the same—the staring, enigmatic cats with their opal eyes giving them almost the look of life. She had just hung up the towel when she heard a stir in the silent house for the first time. Mrs. Pryor came in, her usual calm expression gone. Even several strands of hair had loosened at the back of her neck in a way which made her look more abandoned even than if she had allowed the whole mass (which Persis was sure was neatly pinned over a roll of padding) to stream free.

"The Captain—" She hesitated just within the door, her fingers twisting together over the sample spread of her apron, her face less pink than usual. "Signals from the ship—the Captain has been injured!"

"Captain Leverett? Are they bringing him ashore?"

"Yes, yes—we must be ready—"

Persis was already on her way. "Into his own room," she said firmly. "I will move my things. If you do not mind I can use Uncle Augustin's chamber."

"Of course," but Mrs. Pryor seemed hardly to hear her. She had unslung the ring of keys which she wore at her waist as her badge of office and was heading toward a tall cupboard on the left. "Hammond has gone for Dr. Veering—Hurt—never before—" But Persis judged that she was talking to herself now.

She herself sped down the hall and up the stairs. Once in the chamber she caught armloads of clothing Molly had labored to freshen and carried them across the hall, to dump them on the bed there. Her trunk—they would have to bring that later. She grabbed at brush, comb, mirror, and a bottle of toilet water which had miraculously ridden through the ordeal of the *Arrow* wrapped in three petticoats. Uncle Augustin's watch from the bedside table—

Just as she looked around to be sure she had forgotten nothing, Sukie came in, her arms laded with fresh bed linen and, behind her, Lydia. It was a much subdued Lydia, lacking that light malice which so often marked her face to give her such a discontented expression.

"I can't believe it—Crewe—!" she burst out. "If it's bad —" She bit her lip. "Crewe isn't one to take chances— ever—and— Not Crewe!" She gave a short wail, but as she did so Mrs. Pryor stalked in, behind her a second maid carried a pile of torn linen suitable for bandages, and small pots with oiled paper tied over their tops for lids.

"Don't you take on, Miss Lydia!" she said sharply. "Dr. Veering is on his way."

"Crewe—" Lydia was shaking throughout her body, and Persis, seeing how she might help, put her arm

93

around the girl's shoulder and drew her across the hall to that place of greater confusion where she had dumped all her possessions without thought.

"You have to have faith," Persis said. "And he's an excellent seaman, you know that." It was awkward for her to find words and she began embarrassedly to fold up underlinen.

Lydia's hand went out to smooth the full skirt of a tumbled dress. She did not look up.

"Crewe's always just—just been there," she said with a catch in her voice. "I could depend on Crewe."

"And you will continue to do so," returned Persis briskly, with a confidence she was not sure of.

7

But Crewe Leverett was not all right, nor was he a good patient. Where Uncle Augustin had withdrawn into a silent world of endurance without vocal complaint after his seizure, always polite, but remoter than ever to those who cared for his bodily needs (as if he himself had disowned that body at times), the Captain proved impatient and demanding. And his injuries were not light ones. He had a broken shoulder, two cracked ribs, and a slight case of concussion, gained during his efforts to save a Dutch brig piled up not far from where the *Arrow* had met its fate earlier.

Dr. Veering was able to keep him under the influence of opiates for the first hours after the shoulder was strapped and the ribs set. But even in his drugged sleep his voice would ring out suddenly in some sharp order. It was plain though he lay in his bed he was back in spirit on the brig. They had not been able to save the ship as they had the *Arrow*, though his men, under the mate, Lan Harvery, had managed to secure half the crew (those who had not been swept overboard at the first crash) and perhaps a third of the cargo, which was now piled below on the same wharf which had earlier held that taken from the *Arrow*.

Lydia provided no help in the sick room. Apparently the fact that Crewe was liable to the same dangers met by other wreckers came as a shock to his sister. And, Persis, remembering her own confusion and dismay when Uncle Augustin had suddenly changed from the dominate head of the household to an invalid, thought she knew how the other girl felt.

Save that he had not indulged Lydia's desire to travel it was plain that Crewe had done all he could to make his sister's life pleasant and without care. If she had learned any household duties in her Charleston school, such skills had long since vanished from her mind. So she proved awkwardly inept in the sick room. Somehow, without any discussion about the matter, it was Persis and Molly who backed Mrs. Pryor in the care of the Captain.

And, once he had regained consciousness, he was the most difficult of charges, demanding that, since Veering would not allow him out of bed, various of his crew and the islanders he employed be summoned to receive their orders. Until Dr. Veering rebelled and said that Crewe Leverett might command at sea, but the sick room was *his* quarterdeck and he would have no more of this going in and out.

That the Captain was running a fever Persis knew from her own observation whenever she came to bring
96

Mrs. Pryor, who seldom left his side, some draft or herbal medication she had asked for. His face was so flushed that the red showed even beneath the brown weathering the sea had given his skin, and his eyes were far too bright. He seemed to wear a perpetual scowl of outrage, as if he could not yet believe that this had happened to *him*. And he only was quiet when under drugs, which worried Dr. Veering.

"It is the head wound," Persis heard him tell Mrs. Pryor. "This continued excitability may have been caused by that. I have never known Crewe to be so unreasonable before. There may have been a slight fracture of the skull. But we must keep him quiet—that above all. Nothing to arouse him further."

They divided their time so there was always one at watch in the room. Molly reported twice he had aroused and demanded to know—with words she would not repeat—what a strange female was doing by his bedside. And before she could answer he slipped away from consciousness again.

It was the early morning of the second day that Persis took her place in the chair which faced the bed, dismissing Molly and Mrs. Pryor to get the rest they needed. A single candle burned as the day without was still only the faintest gray streak across the sky. And, though the netting veiled him somewhat, she found herself studying his face, hoping that she was right in her guess that he was sleeping more naturally and that the fever was going down.

He was wedged in with pillows so that he could not inadvertently roll onto his injured side. But now and then his head turned on the higher pillow behind him as if he could so shake off some fragment of an unpleasant dream, and that scowl seemed to have permanently creased his forehead.

There was a bristle of pale stubble across his chin, cheeks, and upper lip, but he slept with his mouth closed. And, in spite of his scowl, Persis began to realize that Crewe Leverett might be termed a fine figure of a man. The stiffness of their last interview had left him; he looked younger, less foreboding.

His head turned again and she saw his tongue tip travel over his lips. Quietly she arose and went to the bed table. As she had seen Mrs. Pryor do many times the last two days, she dipped the edge of a small linen towel into a basin of water and, parting the netting, she stooped to wipe his face with the damp cloth. Not once but several times. He sighed and half-opened his eyes.

There was a feeding cup with a spout, another of Mrs. Pryor's sick-room aids. Persis used that to give him a drink, and he swallowed thirstily. She dared to touch the skin on his forehead—it was damp and not, she thought, entirely from the toweling. Perhaps the fever was breaking! Then she discovered that his eyes were fully open and he was gazing up at her, the scowl gone, just puzzlement mirrored in them now.

"You are not—Lydia—" His voice was a harsh whisper.

"I am Persis Rooke," she returned and allowed her fingers to slide down to cover his mouth. "I was on the *Arrow*. Now rest, Captain Leverett, you have been hurt and have a fever."

But he did not close his eyes she noticed as she turned away from setting the feeder back on the table, and drew again the bed net. His eyes, dark as they had seemed earlier, were really blue, not the light, more shallow blue of Lydia's—rather like the blue of the deep ocean he had set himself to master.

A thought struck her. "Do you want Lydia?"

98

For the first time his lips shaped a shadow of a smile. And even as faint as that was, the change in his face startled Persis. She had seen him angry as he had been on board the *Arrow*, she had seen him handle what must have been a daunting duty when he officiated at the burial of Uncle Augustin, but she had never seen the least hint of lightness or youthfulness in his expression before.

"Lydia," his voice still was hardly above that whisper, "is not well versed in sick-room attendance."

"She probably has never had to face it before," Persis returned tactfully.

"And you have?"

"My uncle was ill for many weeks before we left New York," she answered composedly. "Molly, Shubal, and I were all he had to depend upon."

"Molly—" Once more he looked puzzled. "Oh, the one who pours a draft down you whether or no. She reminds—me—of—my old nurse—"

His eyelids were drooping, his voice slurred away into the even breathing of a sleeper. Just then Mrs. Pryor came in, carrying a tray piled with various bowls, napkins, and armed with such an air of purpose that Persis did not go back to her chair.

"I think his fever has broken," she reported.

Mrs. Pryor made her own examination. "Praise the Lord, and it has! Did he wake?"

"Only for a moment or two. I gave him a drink of water."

"Good enough. We shall get some broth into him today." The housekeeper bustled about, changing the things on the night table for those she had brought with her. Persis offered to take the discarded bowls and cloths away.

"Kind of you, Miss Rooke. Then I suggest you lie down. You look a little peaked." It was plain that Mrs. Pryor had already dismissed her.

Persis put the tray on a table in the upper hall, to be picked up by Sukie later, and went to what was now her chamber. She found Molly there and also two cans of water, one hot, one cool, waiting.

"He's better. The fever broke—"

Molly nodded. "He's a fighter that one, just like Mr. Augustin. Only he doesn't have the weight of years on him to hold him down. Miss Persis, you look worn out. Take a nice sponge bath now and get to bed. I'll bring you up some toast and tea and then you just sleep and—"

She had been folding aside garments in the lower drawer of the chest apparently hunting a fresh night rail. Now she straightened up, something else in her hands.

"Miss Persis, whatever in the world is this? I've never seen it before!"

Persis took one long look and could not believe her own eyes. The fan—the opal-eyed fan!

"Open it," she demanded.

Molly shook her head. "It doesn't open. The sticks seem all stuck together like—"

Then it *was* the fan she had found—the one she re-buried! There could not be two such around. Was she haunted by the thing?

"It isn't mine, Molly," she forced calm into her voice. "Put it back in the bottom drawer. Someone must have forgotten and left it there. I'll ask Miss Lydia about it."

But all the time she sponged her tired, hot body, put on the night rail Molly had laid out for her, and then crawled into bed, she was seeing that fan as Molly had held it. Who had known that she found it—only that Indian Askra. And why would *she* dig it up again and hide it in Persis' room? The girl was afraid, afraid enough to wish that Molly would hurry back with the tea and toast she had promised. She wanted to ask Molly to stay with her. But what reason could she give? She had no proof except her own word that she had indeed found the fan in the sealed box (she wondered what had become of that) and reburied it again, because just to hold it made her frightened of it.

Settled back against her pillows she kept her eyes on the drawer into which Molly had dropped the fan—if it were a fan at all. She almost expected to see that drawer inch open, the black carving with the staring eyes of the opal rise into her sight again.

She would take it out the first chance she got and throw it straight into the canal, making very sure that no one, especially Askra, saw her do it. That was the answer and, having made that decision, Persis' mind was a little more easy.

She found when Molly did arrive with the tray that she was not very hungry after all. But there were some slices of fresh melon, thinly slivered and made tasty by a sharp new vinegary sauce which pleased her better than the conventional toast and tea. Then Molly drew the shutters a little to keep out the sun and Persis settled back, sure that she could not sleep, only to do so.

It was perhaps the afternoon heat which aroused her, for she turned uncomfortably in bed, realizing that her night rail was damp on her body and her hair plastered dankly to her forehead. If there was any sea wind now—and certainly the gale had left them long since—the shutters kept that out along with the punishing sun.

There was no going back to sleep again. Persis sat up in the huge bed and rubbed her forehead, brushing away her hair. She licked her lips experimentally and tasted the salt of her own perspiration. The memory of Mrs. Pryor's explanation of the dark and rising water under the kitchen, that it was at times used as a bathhouse, somehow crept into her mind. But a second memory of the turtles quickly banished it. She had made do with a sponge bath before, she could certainly do so again.

As she slipped over the edge of the wide bed she looked toward that drawer in the chest. Was it or was it not open a fraction? She did not in the least want to go and make sure. But there was still, she discovered, a half-filled jug of water on the commode and that she used with vigor, sprinkling her body thereafter with the lavender water which might not be cooling the least but which made her feel fresher.

Molly had laid out clean clothing. There must be a great deal of washing necessary on Lost Lady. Certainly no lady in this heat could use the same body linen a second day. And now she was hungrier than she had been earlier. Thoughts of ham and biscuits, of some of the baked fish and fruit Mam Rose seemed to have a fine hand at serving filled her mind.

Her dress was her own—a cream muslin with small, meticulously printed moss roses scattered across it. And the style of it was far more staid than the lace and ruffles which Lydia affected and which did become her golden prettiness.

Lydia—she had not come but once to see her brother and then, viewing him flushed with fever, deliriously calling to his men, she had beat such a hasty retreat that she might never have entered the door of his chamber at all. She had looked both sick and scared.

There were people like that, Persis thought, as she brushed her hair carefully. They could not face up to any illness or hurt. But though she knew they existed, Persis had never been able to understand them. What had Lydia been doing all these days? Certainly not running the house, for she had early given evidence that she left that strictly to Mrs. Pryor.

The door behind her opened softly and slowly. Persis seeing that movement in the mirror felt a small lurch of fear. She had not forgotten the strange fan, no matter how hard she had tried to put that firmly out of her mind until the time came to deal with it.

"Molly!" Her recognition was in small part real relief.

"Miss Persis, you should have called me."

"Why? I'm past the age when I have to be buttoned and tab-tied into my clothes—well past. Do you realize, Molly, that in a couple more years or so I'll be what you New Englanders term a 'thorn-back'—a real old maid." She laughed at the outraged expression on Molly's face. "Come, admit it now. Here I am near past twenty and no men ever thought to offer for me. Nor has anyone had the good taste to seek out my company beyond the merely civil."

"And why?" Molly exploded angrily. "You never saw nobody but them who was old enough to be your grandpa! It was a crying shame that Master Rooke was so set on his own affairs that he never noticed you was growing up and needed company like all young maids!"

Persis was a little surprised at Molly's heat. The maid had always appeared to accept Uncle Augustin's way of life as a proper one and Persis' place in it as suitable for the lady she labored to make of her.

"Yes, I don't think Judge Sims would ever have

made me an offer, though he was polite enough. And Mr. Hugues only looked at me as if I were a chess piece." The girl laughed. "Uncle Augustin had his own ways, Molly, and after all he gave me a good home, schooling, and a lot more to be thankful about. He was so old I suppose I was always just a child as far as he was concerned, and he can't be blamed for that."

She leaned forward a little to look at herself in the too-ornate mirror. With her hair all down about her shoulders she did look younger of course. But since she had left school and taken on such responsibility as Uncle Augustin seemed to require of a female, she had somehow never thought of herself as a girl again. Never had she had Lydia's quick changes of mood, her outspoken criticism of her elders, and her self-centeredness.

And certainly she had none of Lydia's prettiness. She did not quite understand now why she picked her hostess as a measure to judge her own self-lacks, save for the past two years her only contacts with former schoolmates had been a couple of decorous tea drinkings a month and the attendance at three of their weddings. Though Uncle Augustin had never forbidden her to invite friends to his house, she had somehow innately known that to do so would be taking a liberty on her part which she had not been prepared to do.

Did she *look* old? Compared to Lydia, she probably did. No wonder Mrs. Pryor had considered her staid and sober enough to act as a relief nurse for the Captain. Perhaps the housekeeper credited her with even more years than she could count.

"Look at yourself, Miss Persis." Molly had already taken brush and comb away from her mistress and was starting to pin and braid, reducing her too-fine and flyaway hair to decent order. "There's girls much

104

less favored as has been wearing a wedding band for some years. You —" she stepped back a little to survey Persis, "you make too little of yourself, Miss Persis."

"You're very comforting, Molly, to an old maid—"

Molly's face flushed. "Now don't you never say that 'bout yourself, Miss Persis. We think ourselves into things. I've seen that happen a mite of times. I've watched you, Miss Persis," she continued. "You owed a duty to the master right enough—him taking you in and all. But you gave him back all that you could. And it wasn't fair that you never had a chance to be yourself."

Then Persis said a thing which surprised her as much as it must have Molly.

"Myself? I don't know what self I really am, Molly."

"Then," said the maid firmly, anchoring the last loop of braid firmly into place with a bow of rose velvet ribbon at its base, which she pinned on with a defiant air as if she expected Persis to protest such frivolity, "it's time you're findin' out! An' don't talk to me about 'thorn-back' and old maids—I won't hear it. There you are—as elegant a young lady as ever came out of New York. Miss Lydia may have all the curls and the laces, but you've got something else. And—" she reached in her apron pocket and pulled out a small piece of paper which had been overfolded twice and then stuck together with a blob of red wax. "I was asked to give you this here—by a young gentleman, no less. You remember who you are and make the most of it, Miss Persis."

She went to lay away comb and brush and tidy up the room. Persis fingered the note in sheer surprise, before she pried loose the wax with a fingernail and read the few lines of bold script black and heavy across the page.

105

Miss Rooke:

I hesitate to ask such a favor of you but the situation is such that I cannot go openly to the house and I have information of great value for you. Upon my last meeting with Captain Leverett he forbid my visiting his house, or indeed his island. But this knowledge is of such importance that I have taken the risk of both offending your sense of propriety and encroaching upon forbidden waters to bring it.

You have, Miss Lydia informed me, inherited certain properties in the Bahamas. I have a recent report which may well affect your claim in this direction. If you will allow me to explain it to you, come to the point of the Key, beyond the ruined mound, as near to sunset as you can manage and I shall meet you there.

Ralph Grillon

Persis read it through twice. Wisdom, she thought, suggested most firmly that she ignore such a missive. On the other hand Ralph Grillon *was* from the Bahamas; he might even have known of the Rooke family there. If he did have such information as he said, it could influence her own future plans one way or the other. She did not in the least care for such a semisecret meeting as he suggested, but she was well aware now that there had been a fierce altercation between Captain Leverett and the Bahamian on the day Uncle Augustin had died. At the time she had only half-heard, and hardly attended to the story, but it seemed that the two captains had met outside the house and Crewe Leverett had warned off Ralph Grillon in a no uncertain way—saying if he caught him again on Lost

Lady he would take steps which would effectively insure that the *Stormy Luck* would never harbor here again.

Since Persis had guessed that Ralph Grillon was more one to take such a prohibition as dare, she was not surprised he had returned. But she did not want to be drawn into any difficulty which might lie between her host and the captain from the Bahamas. On the other hand she must learn to stand on her own two feet.

Persis knew how easy it was to drift into dependency on someone, as she had on Uncle Augustin. Even now she worried when she thought of what might lie ahead. And if Ralph Grillon—Why, he might even know of a lawyer in the Bahamas who could act for her, since the wreckers dealt much with courts and legal matters. Yes, she would see him.

The note she folded and put away in her small purse. Then she wondered if she should not consult with Lydia. To go with the other girl might be well. Only she had some of Uncle Augustin's need for family privacy. The story of her Bahamian inheritance was not altogether such a savory one. Even in discussing the broad outline of her inheritance with Captain Leverett she had not mentioned what lay behind the very generous gesture of the widowed Madam Rooke. Molly now, and perhaps Shubal—but they were family. No, she would not speak to Lydia.

Once more she found that the veranda was the center for dining and lounging. Lydia sat in a cane chair, yawning over a book which she declared was too tedious for words after she made a perfunctory inquiry concerning Crewe. Sukie brought a tray of food and Persis ate with a good appetite. As she had slept late, the hour Grillon had appointed could not be too far off. Now she must devise a way for reaching that part of the island he had indicated.

She thought she knew her way, for the burial ground which lay on the highest point of the Key looked down toward the point. And, though she hated to use family sorrow as an excuse, she announced that she would like to take some fresh flowers for Uncle Augustin's grave. Lydia yawned, advised her to wait until it was cooler, and then went reluctantly to interview Mam Rose, since apparently she had been forced by Mrs. Pryor's stay in the sick room to assume some small duties in the house.

Persis arose and took the path which led first over the shell-strewn mound and then down into the low, strange, vegetation. She culled as she went two handsful of brilliant red flowers, the first she could sight, thinking at the time that such a tribute might amuse Uncle Augustin but would hardly be his choice. Their colors were too bright, their appearance of vitality too strong.

Leaving them by the wooden cross on her uncle's grave Persis deliberately turned in the other direction along a path even more nearly overgrown. Here she had to hold her skirts firmly close to her lest they catch again and again on the spikey arms of low bushes, as she headed for the rendezvous Ralph Grillon had appointed.

8

"Greetings, Miss Rooke."

Persis started; Ralph Grillon had appeared so suddenly he might have risen out of the ground. She had rounded a large rock and was looking across the shell-strewn sand to the now-tamed wash of the waves, still holding her full skirts about her. Whether he had meant to startle her she did not know, but she eyed him with very little welcome.

"I had your note," she returned abruptly, attempting to summon to her own voice some of the brusqueness Crewe Leverett used. Persis found Ralph's good looks, his air of recklessness, both drew and repelled her. Perhaps more the latter because she associated trust always with Uncle Augustin's air of quiet reserve.

"Come." He held out his hand. "If we sit here we cannot be overlooked from the house." He pointed to a log of drift half-buried in the sand, perhaps so deeply anchored that not even a storm, unless one strong enough to wash away the whole of the island, could shift it.

Persis folded her hands before her. "You said you had a message of value for me." She refused to soften her voice. "I shall be missed since I have been helping Mrs. Pryor care for Captain Leverett."

He smiled, in no way abashed by her refusal to be ushered to the seat he had chosen.

"Yes, Leverett met bad luck at last, didn't he?" Grillon sounded cheerful about that. "Or maybe it was good luck—a soft bed ashore and near all the females in the Key fussing over him. But it will be some time before he takes out the *Nonpareil*."

"I did not come here to discuss Captain Leverett," Persis reminded him sharply. For all his charm, and she did not deny that he had it, she decided she did not in the least envy Lydia her beau.

"No, you came here for the news I promised you, but I can't say that is good, Miss Rooke. By all accounts, your uncle—since you seem to want to speak frankly—was hard set financially when he started down here. Well, that will on which he pinned so much hope may not be worth the paper and wax of its making."

"What do you know about my uncle's affairs?" Persis withdrew a step or so, again surprised. She had not even discussed the full of the tangle with Crewe Leverett in their one meeting before Uncle Augustin's burial.

"You'd be surprised how quickly rumor spreads hereabouts when there is something new to talk
110

about," he countered. "And Mr. Rooke had some interesting conversations with Captain Pettigrew before the *Arrow* came to its dismal end. He asked a lot about the islands, enough to make the Captain interested. And since Rooke is not a common name, it is well remembered in the Bahamas. Old Madam's will was the talk of the town when it was proven. Only she didn't have the right to be so free with Rooke property, you see. James Rooke had a child—legal born—all proper. And that child has a good claim, a better claim on old Madam's leavings than Augustin Rooke or you." Ralph was watching her, still smiling, and she could not read any maliciousness into that smile. Also, that he was speaking the truth she did not doubt, or at least what he believed to be the truth.

"But there are documents proving that James Rooke died—at sea," Persis protested.

"Which is no reason to say that he did not sire any offspring before he took off on that privateer, is it? Even Madam had her troubles with the court clearing her title to what there was in spite of proof of James' death. I am afraid James was not a very good boy." Ralph Grillon leaned his back against the rock which screened them from view. He had thrust his thumbs into the front of his belt and now his fingers beat a soft tattoo on the salt-stained leather of that.

"No, James was never the pattern of a good and dutiful son. After old Rooke finally paid up a last round of debts and said his son could well live at the expense of the devil, since he had already chosen to ape his satanic majesty, they did not keep in touch.

"Though I did hear that the old man had second thoughts before he died, and tried to find James—even left a letter for Madam which kept her hunting, too. Until your uncle obligingly sent her the proof that

111

James was safely dead. But James had left a child, all right—"

"What proof of that have you?" Persis demanded.

"Oh, there'll be proof when the proper time comes. If you go on to the islands, Miss Persis Rooke, you'll find more trouble than any female can rightly face. But there's a way out—a very good way. You help me— I'll help you."

"In what way?"

"I know the lawyer who is ready to slap down old Madam's will if you try to prove it. But he and his client are not unreasonable. Seeing as how you are, in a manner of speaking, an innocent party in all this and a lone female. They'll make a settlement which will give you enough to get back north again. Up there you can manage—"

Persis studied him. His confidence was complete. She must accept that he knew exactly what he was talking about. And there were perhaps remnants of Uncle Augustin's estate left in New York. They would—she, Shubal, and Molly (because they were family and she must consider their future as well as her own)—have to live very frugally. The house could be sold; it was a good one in a district considered the height of respectability. And there might be other small sums she could count on. And, she could teach. Though she did not look forward to that. But Miss Pickett would give her a letter of recommendation.

Only, before she gave in, she must know more and not just accept Ralph Grillon's word. In her mind Persis tried to marshal all her confidence in herself, her belief in Uncle Augustin. He was not, in spite of his severe reverses, a man to travel to this wild place in spite of his illness, unprepared. He must have made inquiries of his own. Did Ralph Grillon imagine that she would meekly accept his word and take the first possible ship back to New York?

"I must take my uncle's papers to a lawyer in Key West," she said slowly. "Then I can make up my mind on his advice. But you spoke of a bargain—if you help me, how do I help you?"

Captain Grillon lost none of his good humor. "Fair enough—but remember these lawyers know all the tricks, and when it comes to arranging an inheritance some of it sticks tightly to their own fingers when they handle it for you. So no matter what one advises, the settlement of which I speak would be more to your advantage—yours without the gamble of a court case and the expense of a greedy lawyer.

"Now with what I can do for you being settled, we come to the other part of the bargain, even as you suggest. Crewe Leverett has warned me off this Key in no uncertain terms. I don't want to challenge him openly. It would not look well to fight a man over the right to come courting his sister. Yes, it's Lydia I want to deal with. You do what you can to help me there and I'll find out what I can in the islands which may be to your advantage.

"Leverett has no right to warn me off, you know. He hates Bahamians because he had a run in with one the first year he set up here. And he came out of it with a ship that needed some repairs as well as a couple of men to bury. So to him all from the islands are like scum. I'm not saying that we're saints. But we hunted these reefs before your United States made such a parade of declaring them off limits. And a lot of us don't take kindly in the least to that. Why should we have to risk our ships and our necks getting in a wreck and then have a court of another country decide proper fees—as well as collect taxes?"

Persis stood very straight and chose her words carefully.

"I know very little about your personal problems, Captain Grillon," she said quietly. "But as for your proposed bargain, that I find highly distasteful. Captain Leverett is now my host, in addition he saved my life and that of my uncle. At present he is bedfast because he suffered injuries attempting to do the same service for others. I think you must have a low opinion of either my intelligence or my honesty when you suggest that I aid his sister in actions he completely forbidden. No, I shall not accept such a bargain. I bid you good day, sir."

For the first time that half smile was gone from his lips. And something looked out of his eyes for a second or two which Persis believed she had not seen in Crewe Leverett's even when irritation had reached a peak of his emotions. But she held her ground valiantly, meeting that gaze as bravely as she could.

Then, he laughed. "You are a proper miss, aren't you? Do you tattle too, I wonder!"

Persis threw the note he had sent her at his feet. "I shall not dignify *that* with any answer, sir. But I intend to do as I have planned, go to Key West and consult with a lawyer. After that will be the time to make my own plans. But they *will* be my own plans."

Ralph Grillon flung up both hands with a small gesture. "So be it, Miss Rooke. But Lydia cannot say now that I did not try. She worries about you, knowing your situation."

"Which is no concern of anyone save myself." Turning her back upon him, Persis marched up along the faint path. So he had discussed her with Lydia, and probably half the island knew by now that she was near penniless and had a dark future into the bargain.

114

But that he would have dared suggest she play his game—she sucked in her breath sharply. Some men did hold a very low opinion of females, judging them incompetent to manage any affairs. Yet what man had ever tried to run a household smoothly, keep the peace between quarreling servants, make sure that the master under that roof had instant and excellent service? Perhaps were they to attempt all that for even a day or so, they would not be so quick to believe that females could be talked—or "sweet-talked" as Molly would put it—into some action which utterly lacked all principle.

She was flushed, not only with the heat of her walk, but also by her indignation that Ralph Grillon, and perhaps Lydia, would believe she would be party to arranging in some manner secret meetings between her host's sister and a man he particularly disliked! Had Ralph Grillon thought his threat of impending ruin of her hopes would be enough to coerce her into such action?

More than ever she wanted to get to Key West, to find a reputable lawyer there, and learn just where she did stand and how much of Madam Rooke's now seemingly illusive fortune she might be able to claim. She could make no real plans until she did learn that, and not as a second- or third-hand rumor from a man who wanted to use her for his own purposes.

Persis was so intent upon her own thoughts that she gave a start as she came up to the graveyard of the Key. Where she had left the already wilted bouquet earlier, a figure in a black coat knelt, both vein-ridged hands covering his face. But there was no mistaking Shubal.

The girl crossed quickly to touch the old man gently

on the shoulder. "Shubal—should you be here? The sun is very fierce."

He looked around and up at her, his face a worn mask of the man she had known for most of her life.

"Killed himself, he did," the servant burst out. "The doctor told him it would be the death of him—I heard it with my own ears. I may be nigh as old as Master was, but I ain't deaf! He went ahead, just like he always did, no matter the cost, when he thought he was doing right. But it ain't right, Miss Persis, it ain't right for him to be lying here, not able to do what he set himself out to do. He won't rest easy—"

"Yes, I think he will," Persis said slowly and distinctly, trying to break through the other's wall of misery. "Because we are going to do it for him, Shubal. He knew that—when he talked to me he told me what was to be done."

"Miss Persis, how are you going to do anything—?" It was plain, almost irritatingly plain, that Shubal considered her abilities scarcely higher than Grillon had done.

"We're going on to Key West, Shubal, and see a lawyer. I have all of Uncle Augustin's papers. He gave them to me. We'll find out there just what our next move must be."

Shubal shook his gray head. "The master—he had a way with him, Miss Persis. You never saw him face down angry men and him with nothing in his hands but his cane. He should never have come here." Shubal pounded his fists together and his voice rose. "Never have come!"

"Could anyone have stopped him, Shubal?"

The old man sniffed and wiped the back of his hand across his nose. "I guess not, Miss Persis. He was never one to be reined in. His father was killed so young, you

116

see, and the master had to grow up quick. Then he was an agent for the General—General Washington—rounding up supplies, trying to get support— He was just as much a soldier as his father, though he didn't wear the coat, nor the name.

"There's no one like the master, Miss Persis—" His voice trailed away and there was such a lost look on his old face as to hurt Persis more than the death of the man she had respected and felt a duty to, but whom she had never loved. Shubal had loved, and lost, and now his world was in pieces around him.

"I know. But, Shubal, he has left you something to do." She added her own interpretation of what was needed to bring Shubal back to his old self again. "He wanted you to help me finish what he had begun. And you can, Shubal. You know more about Uncle Augustin's affairs than I ever did and you must advise me."

For the first time he looked directly at her as if he saw her clearly.

"Yes, many's the time he said to me, 'Shubal, you're my left hand, the one which is needed to help along with the right.' I was with him overseas, in some mighty queer and dangerous places—" Shubal's head came up proudly. "Depended on me a lot of times, he did. Why, I've carried a pistol in my pocket with my hand near to it, 'cause he would never take anything but that cane of his. Yes, he depended on me then—"

"And even more now." Persis pulled a little at his arm, drawing him to his feet. He stood straighter, a faint flush high on the cheekbones of his worn, gaunt face. "I'll need you, Shubal, so we can do just as Uncle Augustin wanted."

"And we will, Miss Persis, that we will!" There was more force in his tone than she had heard for days. "First thing is we must get to this Key West—"

"Suppose you find Captain Pettigrew," she suggested action which would keep this alert interest alive in him. "See what you can discover about how he is going to get transportation there himself."

"That I will!" And he turned away from the small graveyard with a firm step.

Persis watched him for a moment and then continued back to the house. The long evening was closing in. She wanted to go through the papers in the portfolio more closely. Perhaps there was some name therein to suggest who in the Bahamas might be considered trustworthy. Though after Grillon's revelation she must be very wary of the lawyer of the Rooke estate. It could well be that he would be bound by family ties to serve this mysterious new claimant.

Also, there was Captain Leverett. She had been taking a night watch between Molly's and Mrs. Pryor's turns and she had no intention of shirking that. In fact, it was odd, but she found herself looking forward to those very quiet hours sitting by a shaded candle, listening for any sound from the big bed, but also able to think her own thoughts.

Her own thoughts—they were now in a queer muddle. Life had always been well ordered. There had been school. And, after she had been deemed of an age to quit Miss Pickett's supervision, there had been the household to manage. A little shopping, sewing, reading—looking back now, those days which had seemed so well filled appeared empty. Oh, she had made herself useful; there were also the household tasks which were the mistress' alone. But they had been very dull!

For the first time Persis allowed herself to admit that. Dull, dull, dull! The word repeated itself in her mind as she went up the inner stairs of the house. She had accepted that dullness because then she had nothing to compare with it. Now—

"So there you are!"

Startled so quickly out of her own thoughts, Persis saw Lydia waiting at the top of the stairs. The other girl was not wearing her usual finery. Rather she had pulled about her a wrapper of heavy Indian muslin, while behind her was Sukie, laden down with a big sponge, several towels, and a small basket in which there was both soap and a bottle of toilet water.

"The storm filled the bathing pool well." Lydia pulled her wrapper tighter about her. "We can have the use of it to cool ourselves."

That darksome hole below the kitchen floor! Persis looked at her in startled amazement. Did Lydia mean go down *there*!

"Didn't Mrs. Pryor tell you? It's just right now."

"The turtles—" Persis said the first thing at the fore of her mind.

Lydia laughed. "Lord, they're penned up near the canal; we don't go near that part. But it's good to splash about in all this heat."

Persis considered the suggestion carefully. She had a good idea that Lydia was not speaking of something which she herself did not consider perfectly ordinary. And since the sea wind had died, Persis' walk to the shore had left her feeling unpleasantly hot. The sponge baths which suited a lady might perhaps not be all one needed in such a climate as this.

"Wear an old shift," Lydia advised her. "And don't worry about towels and such; Sukie has plenty."

There was a note of challenge in Lydia's words. And Persis decided that she was going to accept the invitation. If there was any danger, she was sure that it would never have been issued.

"I'll hurry." She passed Lydia and began to unbutton and untie almost before she closed the door of her room. This was a new form of excitement, a new part of this life which was not dull.

She dropped the petticoats which were so hot and dragged so, at once; unlaced the stays which chafed her. She had an old shift, and there was her wrapper, her slippers. She stopped only to snatch that ridiculous bow out of her hair, Molly's attempt to enliven her appearance, and then she did join Lydia who was waiting, openly impatient.

The trapdoor in the kitchen had been flung open and the light of a lantern gleamed up from below. Persis could not hesitate with Lydia already setting foot on the ladder to descend matter-of-factly.

So she followed her hostess down rungs which were damp with memory of the storm, to step out on a platform of wet stone where two lanterns gave a measure of light.

Lydia gestured to the right. "That's the cistern. It's both rain and spring fed. We dip in over here—"

"Over here" was to the left where there were water-washed steps leading down into the flood. Lydia handed Sukie her wrapper and kicked off her slippers. But, Persis noticed, she used caution as she went down the steps where the water washed first her ankles and then her knees, and then to her waist. She took those steps one at a time and held on to a soaked rope which served here as a banister.

When she halted, she was breast high. Then she looked up to Persis.

"It is no deeper in this part—unless the storm has raised the water level. Sukie, give me the soap." She deftly caught that as the maid tossed it down to her and fell to lathering her hands and arms. Gingerly,
120

Persis began the same descent. The water was chill, or seemed so at first, in here shut away from the sun and the air. And the smell was strongly that of the sea. But it was good to feel it against her skin, cooling as it rose up about her body.

Reassured by Lydia's unconcern, she joined the other girl.

"One can swim out to the canal—even out to sea that way." Lydia held out the cake of scented soap and pointed with her chin toward the left where the lantern light failed to show any sign of wall. "Crewe opened it up in case of Indian attack. Other houses have cisterns and pools, but this is the only one with an escape way."

She scooped up handsful of the water and splashed her face.

"Cool—it is so good to be cool!" Then she ducked down until the water ringed her neck. "Crewe swims, but he won't teach me—or at least he's never home long enough to take the trouble. There's another rope under the water—you hold that and pull yourself out if you have to. Ahhh—" She closed her eyes blissfully.

Persis used the soap. It had the clean tang of herbs against the stronger scent of the sea, and the water was like the softest of linen enfolding her body.

"Miss Persis!"

She edged around to face the water-covered steps down which she had come so cautiously. Molly had elbowed aside the island maid and stood with a distinct frown of disapproval on her face.

"Miss Persis," now she spoke as she had when she had taken over Persis' childhood welfare and entertainment, "you come straight out of there—no tellin' what kind of nasty fish or thing can be swimming around waiting to get at you!"

"There's a net across the sea entrance," Lydia said, glancing from Persis to Molly and then back again with a rather sly set of eyes, as if she wanted to see just how much Persis was ruled by Molly's disapproval.

"I am perfectly all right," Persis summoned up confidence. "You need not worry, Molly."

At least the maid did not voice the rest of the arguments Persis had no doubt were burning on her tongue. But she became an embodiment of complete disapproval until Persis, having asserted her independence and knowing that she still had her duty of watching Captain Leverett, haltingly climbed the steps once again.

With a distinct sniff, Molly flung around the girl the large towel she had taken from Sukie.

9

Persis had asserted her independence but, she discovered, she had not won Molly to acknowledge that in turn. The maid was ominously silent as she escorted her mistress back upstairs to her own chamber. So much so, Persis was piqued into speech.

"You should try bathing so, Molly. It's wonderful to be so cool in this weather!"

The maid sniffed.

"There's worse things than bein' hot, Miss Persis. If Miss Lydia wants to go rampagin' around so, you need have no reason to join her. A sorry sight you make now, both of you!" Her tongue held a sharp edge Persis knew of old. Molly was really upset.

"But—they all do it," the girl pointed out. "And

when the weather is so hot it is wonderful to find a cool spot—"

"Miss Persis, you was raised a lady. And a lady don't go around bathin' out in the open like that. I think you'd be ashamed."

Molly set her lips tight together, as she could on occasion, and Persis sighed inwardly. There was nothing one could do when the maid was in this mood of righteous indignation.

Under Molly's eye she dressed, submitted to a none-too-gentle repiling of her hair. And she noticed in the mirror, as she watched Molly work at the edifice the maid thought due a lady for a public appearance, that the other's pursed mouth did not relax. Persis began to guess that perhaps more than her indulgence in the swimming pool irked Molly, and that feeling grew on her until she at last asked:

"Molly—what is the matter with you? There is something behind all this—"

"Miss Persis, I was brought up to speak my mind when it was necessary, and right now—" For the first time her air of indignation was disturbed and she hesitated as if lost for words, before she continued briskly:

"Miss Persis, you went down to the beach to meet that Captain Grillon. Don't you know that the Captain who's lying right across there on his bed, a sick man, has said that that Grillon is no better than a pirate and has ordered him off the island? Now that Captain Leverett isn't able to take care of him, the fellow comes sneakin' back and you meet with him as bold as—as—"

"Brass?" Persis suppled the last word of one of Molly's favorite expressions. "All right." She swung around sideways on the stool before the mirror, hardly giving the maid the chance to anchor the last hairpin
124

securely. "Yes, I met with Ralph Grillon. He sent me that note *you* brought me saying he had news—important news—for me. And it was important, Molly. Captain Grillon sails out of the Bahamas, and he knows what is going on there. I may have no right to anything Madam Rooke left Uncle Augustin in her will. It seems that her husband's son left a child—and, if so, the will can be challenged."

"Miss Persis, you ain't just goin' take *his* word for that?"

"Not altogether, but he was very sure in what he had to tell me—so sure he offered a bargain."

"What kind of a bargain?" Molly's disapproval had vanished. She watched the girl now with complete attention.

"He wanted to keep in touch with Miss Lydia with my help. In return he would help settle matters in the Bahamas through a lawyer he knew. Of course, I told him that that was impossible. If he wanted to court Lydia he must do it openly and face up to Captain Leverett."

"Miss Persis, I wouldn't take that one's word that the sun was shinin' if it were out in the sky right over my head! I've seen his like before—swaggerin' around an' talkin' big. He got his comeuppance from the Captain the day the master died. An' all Miss Lydia's carryin' on didn't make a mite of difference either. They had a fight one other time over a wreck, and the Captain got the better of him. I wouldn't listen to no story he had the tellin' of! You get the Captain, when he feels better, to listen to it all. He'll put it straight for you."

"No, Molly. I can handle my own affairs. And I won't depend on Ralph Grillon for any help—that I promise you. What we want is to get to Key West and

125

find a lawyer there. I have all of Uncle Augustin's papers. He can use them to make inquiries for me. It may be, Molly," she said soberly, "that Captain Grillon was not exaggerating. If this other heir does exist, then I will have lost all Uncle Augustin hoped to gain by coming south."

"*If* he's right!" Molly sniffed again. But a moment later she added, as if the dire meaning of Persis' words had come to her, "But—Miss Persis, what will you do then?"

"We have the house in New York." Persis thought of the first asset. "That can be sold. It is a good house, Molly, and should fetch a good price. Then I can teach. Maybe Miss Pickett would find a place for me. Also, though Uncle Augustin was poor compared to what he had been, there is still some money. And you and Shubal have your pensions—those will come first."

"Not if you need the money, Miss Persis!" Molly shook her head decisively. "And you have only this Grillon's word that it is so—"

Persis wanted to cling to that hope also, but she disciplined herself quickly. Perhaps a female was not credited with a practical mind but she thought it best now to plan on receiving the minimum and not the maximum of an estate her uncle had left her.

"Molly, bring me the portfolio. I think there is some time before dinner for me to look through it again. Certainly if this heir exists, the lawyer in the islands must have warned Uncle Augustin of it. Unless he or she has been very recently found."

The maid went to the trunk and started to lay aside the contents which had not been placed in the chest drawers in the new chamber.

"Now that's a funny thing," she said. "I remember

as well as if I saw it now, that it was under three night rails. But here it is on top."

She came back to Persis with it in one hand. "And nobody's been in that trunk but me and you. Did you have it out, Miss Persis?"

"No—" As Persis took it into her hands the cover moved. She held it closer to the light. Just as Molly had been so distinctly sure where she had put the folder, so had Persis been sure that it had been locked. But plainly the cover was now ready to open at a touch.

"Molly, my jewel box—Uncle Augustin's watch—is the fob still there, the one with the small key on it?"

The maid made a quick search. Persis' jewels were certainly very modest: a necklace of coral with matching hair ornament, bracelet, and earrings—carved into roses, two gold chains, one with a locket, and an ivory pin, and a set of jet which had been mourning jewelry for the mother she could hardly remember. Uncle Augustin's watch was there, with the key still fastened above the carved seal which formed the carnelian fob he had brought from London.

Persis examined the lock of the portfolio closely, holding it near the candles which Molly had set on the dressing table. Tiny scratches. She was sure those had not been there before! But she could not swear to that. If someone had forced the lock—but who—and why?

She moved quickly to pull out the papers, checking through them hastily. As far as she could see everything was there—the old letters, Uncle Augustin's will, the depositions of the privateer's men. Everything—but she was very certain someone had rummaged through them. Though she could not prove that either. Ralph Grillon? No, he would not have dared enter this house, for all his reckless self-confidence. But he might have bribed one of the islanders.

Only she doubted if any of the housemaids would be able to read. Sukie certainly could not. And Molly would not have done this. Persis shuffled the papers back into the portfolio. She was right, she discovered when she tried to close it—the lock had been broken.

"Someone has been looking through this," she kept her voice as calm as she could. "Molly, could you hide it among your things?"

"Miss Persis, who in this house—and why?"

"I don't know any answers, Molly. But the lock has been broken, only nothing was taken. And these may be highly important."

"You just give them to me. Nobody is going to get at them again, Miss Persis. What a thing to have happen in a respectable house!" The maid flushed nearly as red with indignation as she had been when she had discovered Persis enjoying the pool.

The thought that her belongings had been searched was a blow—a threat. It couldn't have been Ralph, and she did not see how any of the servants might have done it by his bribes or orders. Then—Lydia? But she had no right to imagine that the other girl would do such a thing. Save that she was plainly fascinated by Grillon and, in defiance of her brother, might be moved to some reckless act to prove her partisanship with a man she plainly greatly admired.

"Don't you worry none, Miss Persis," Molly held the portfolio against her heavy breasts as if she would defy anyone under this roof to wrest it from her. "I'll see as how no one gets to this again!"

They dined by candlelight for the first time, the three of them together, Mrs. Pryor (who declared herself well satisfied with Captain Leverett's turn for the better), Lydia, and herself. And Lydia talked vivaciously as she always did, flitting from subject to
128

subject. Only Persis found it hard to maintain polite interest in her hostess' chatter. She kept wondering if Lydia had been the one to invade her chamber, search it—perhaps the note from Grillon had been partially to get her out of the way before such action could be carried out. Grillon had offered her help, but could it just be the other way around—that he wanted to assist the mysterious heir and had come to get knowledge, one way or another, of what authority Uncle Augustin had brought south with him? She had made no great secret of the portfolio earlier. All knew it was her uncle's and contained papers of importance, though she had not gone into details over its contents with even Captain Leverett.

For the first time she considered a new and startling thought. Captain Leverett—he had offered her assistance in Key West. Yet Grillon had said he could not venture there—that there was a writ out against him. Her uncle, Shubal, either one of them without telling her, might have appealed to him. Also, there was Captain Pettigrew of the *Arrow*, still bound here on the Key with his crew. How much had her uncle talked with him during those hours when she had been so miserably sick in her cramped stateroom? It would be easy for Captain Leverett to get one of the servants to secure the portfolio, go through the papers. He had slept most of the afternoon Mrs. Pryor announced with quiet satisfaction, but she had left Sukie with him on watch since his turn for the better was so pronounced.

Only—while she could picture Ralph Grillon rifling, or causing to be examined her belongings—Persis could not visualize similar action on Crewe Leverett's part. There was something petty—and—and perhaps dangerous enough to make her uneasy, in that action.

129

While the Captain accepted danger as part of his daily life—it was a different kind of danger altogether.

"Miss Rooke—" Persis looked up quickly, hoping that her preoccupation had not been apparent to them all. She was not even sure her murmurs had satisfied Lydia who was now consuming a coconut custard spoonful by spoonful with the air of one who had not been enough appreciated for her social expertise.

"Captain Leverett has expressed a desire to see you, if it would be convenient," Mrs. Pryor continued, again with that air of vague disapproval which Miss Pickett in her day had used to such advantage.

Persis guessed that while the Captain was fevered and practically unaware of his surroundings, the housekeeper had welcomed her aid in nursing. But now that he was in his right mind, if not mended of body, visits to the sick room certainly did not meet with her approval. In her present mood Persis was perfectly willing to agree with the housekeeper.

"Whenever it is convenient I shall be very glad to accede to Captain Leverett's wishes," she answered with all the primness of her school days.

Lydia suddenly laughed. "You sound as if the last thing you want to do is to see Crewe. Is he so trying as a patient then? He has the temper of a devil, you know—a cold, sarcastic devil!" Her tone had been light but she ended with such vehemence and a look in her eyes which matched that of her brother's at his most exasperated.

"Very few men," Persis remarked, "take kindly to being ill. Uncle Augustin at times would have no one near him save Shubal. But your brother was unconscious, I think, most of the time, of who cared for him." She remembered her own short conversation with a

130

rational Crewe Leverett, but saw no reason to enlarge upon that.

She mounted the stairs in Mrs. Pryor's wake, breathing a little fast. It was so like, somehow, being summoned into the presence of Miss Pickett to have one's sins of admission and omission reckoned up judiciously against one. And—but what had Crewe Leverett to do with her? She had helped to tend him during his illness, mainly because she still owed him the debt of being alive. Of course, her meeting with Ralph Grillon could well have been witnessed by some islander (she would be the first to admit she was not skilled in the processes of intrigue), and if that were so— then, she decided swiftly, as Mrs. Pryor lifted her hand to rap on the Captain's door, she would admit freely all that had passed between them. She certainly owed no loyalty nor duty to the Bahamian.

There were a number of candles alight in the room and a kind of curtain netting pulled over each of the open windows, while that veiling about the bed had been drawn back to fully reveal the man resting there.

He had been shaven of his stubble of beard, and, though his face looked a little sunken, his eyes overlarge, he had certainly taken a great stride back toward becoming the self he had shown when she had last seen him.

"Miss Rooke—"

She found herself, without knowing just why, falling into the pattern Miss Pickett had so drilled into her pupils, and making a curtsy. As if, she thought, with a kind of nervous laughter rising from within her which she struggled hard to curb, they were somehow being introduced for the first time.

"I see you find yourself better, sir," she schooled her voice to its most formal tone.

For the first time she saw him smile fully. And even on that worn face that change of expression made him shed both years and authority.

"I understand that I owe that somewhat to your efforts, Miss Rooke."

"I am well acquainted with nursing, Captain Leverett. My uncle was long in his bed after his seizure. But here I did little enough—only aided Mrs. Pryor when there was need."

"Come here!" With his good hand he beckoned sharply, his smile gone now, that familiar faint frown of displeasure easy to see.

Persis' chin lifted a fraction. He need not believe that he could carry his shipboard commanding ways here and against her. If that was the tone he habitually used with Lydia, she did not wonder that his sister made her own schemes for the future. But Persis did move a step or two forward into the direct light of the candles, to discover that he was surveying her with a steadiness which made her uncomfortable.

There was no subtlety about Crewe Leverett she learned a moment later for he said, without any dressing of polite usage:

"I understand you met with Grillon—down on the point."

There must be plenty of eyes on Lost Lady Key to watch and report, Persis thought. But his own brusqueness aroused answering resistance in her. She was *not* his sister! At that moment she thought she could forgive Lydia any wiles she thought to use against this man.

Only long ago Persis had learned that truth in itself could be a potent weapon, sometimes disarming an attacker who did not expect it.

"I did," she returned quietly.

Crewe Leverett's frown deepened. "He dares—because he thinks I am helpless!" There was anger in that small explosion. "What did he want?"

"To strike a bargain."

"A bargain?" Now she had succeeded in surprising him and for that she felt an odd little twist of pleasure. "What kind of a bargain?"

"News for news—of a sort. He had a tale of the Bahamas he thought of interest to my future—"

"And," Captain Leverett interrupted, "he wanted information concerning this household in return? Was that it?"

Persis shrugged. "If you know all—why ask me, sir? I will tell you this much, I am your guest, uninvited and unwilling, but nevertheless, your guest. There was no reason he should expect me to fulfill the conditions he desired."

"Sit down!" Again that abrupt command. Mrs. Pryor moved from the doorway to draw forward the same chair Persis had known during her night watches. The last thing the girl wanted was to prolong this interview, but for the moment she saw no way of escape. "And you, Mrs. Pryor," he turned his head a fraction on the pillow, "leave us, if you please. But keep an eye on Lydia."

Such sharp orders. Persis glanced at the dignified housekeeper, more than half-expecting to see some sign of resentment at being dismissed so summarily. But if that lay in the old woman's thoughts no such emotion showed about mouth or eye. She gathered up a small tray on which was cup, spoon, and covered bowl.

"A quarter hour, Crewe," she said, "and that is all. It is more than the doctor would allow if he were here."

133

The Captain waited, but he gave an impatient grunt before the door had quite closed behind her.

"So you turned him down, did you?" Crewe Leverett raised his good arm, scratched his chin. "I take it that annoyed him a little. Grillon is not used to anything in petticoats being indifferent to his wishes."

The Captain, catching Persis' outraged expression, laughed. "Ah, that fetched you, didn't it? But you're going to tell me more—what did Grillon have to offer on his side of the bargain?"

"Nothing," Persis fought to keep her voice neutral. The man was insufferable! As if she could ever appeal to *him*! All she wanted now was to escape to Key West. She was not a ninny and in spite of Uncle Augustin's put-downs in the past she thought she had intelligence enough to seek the proper help in the proper places. "Nothing," she repeated, "except that which is a private affair of my own, concerning my uncle's visit to the islands."

"So? Well, I have a warning for you, Miss Persis Rooke, in the places where Ralph Grillon foregathers with his kind you would be a nice tempting pigeon meeting hawks. His hands are not clean, and a good many of us know it. We have our turncoats just as any profession may, Miss Rooke. There are captains who will make bargains and run their ships on some convenient reef, then share secretly with the prize money."

"Pirates," she could not resist that one word which had lain at the back of her mind ever since she had come into this house.

He gave a half shrug and then winced at the pain from his shoulder.

"If you wish—pirates. These waters have long attracted the lawless. There has been blood spilled up and down the Keys and not all that of enemies either.
134

In fact," he hesitated as if there was something more to be said and then, seeming to have come to an inner decision, he added—"we go in peril right now."

"From Ralph Grillon?" She could not believe that.

"Hardly. Grillon may be a mosquito, annoying enough but easy to be handled in time. No, I am thinking of Indians."

Persis was diverted from her own wary thoughts enough to echo that last word—"Indians!"

"The ship we went to help," he appeared frank now, "had bespoken earlier a gunboat out of Key West. That had sailed to carry the news of a massacre at Crow Key and so to warn us all. So far Lost Lady has never been threatened. Those who built here, the Old Ones, are dead. But the Seminoles the Spanish brought in to wreck their mound cities believe that certain places are still under unseen guards. I have tried to foster that—there's a strange old woman—she's a kind of witch as far as they are concerned—"

"Askra—she came here during the storm," Persis said as he paused.

"Yes, Askra. She has the face of the Old Ones—knows a lot of their 'magic' if you want to call it that. The Seminoles are afraid of her powers. She comes here because the mounds are or were sacred to her people and I have allowed no interference with her. So far we have escaped any raids. But that does not mean we shall continue to do so. And the report I was given was a serious one.

"Unfortunately the *Nonpareil* as well as her master took a crippling beating in that storm." His legs moved under the covers on the bed as if he were uncomfortable. "I've told Veering to keep off Verde, and I've sent Macmasters to do some recruiting in Key West—"

"You sent a ship to Key West! But I could have gone—"

"In a fishing smack, hardly better than a native dugout?" he asked. "I don't think you would have chosen that form of transportation."

He was probably very right, Persis thought gloomily. She had no relish to continue her trip by sea, and thought she could only bring herself to it on a larger ship.

"Yes, we have arms, powder, shot, and this house and the hotel have both been designed as forts. But it means that we must take every precaution, Miss Rooke. No more wandering along the shore alone—nor meeting with Grillon."

"I did not and do not intend either of those," she told him coldly. "But neither do I wish to remain here. If I carry out Uncle Augustin's declared wishes I must have legal help—at Key West."

"As soon as it can be arranged," for the first time Crewe Leverett sounded tired, "you will be accommodated, Miss Rooke."

Persis arose quickly from her chair. "I fear you are overtired, sir. Please let me summon Mrs. Pryor—"

His scowl became pronounced. "Summon the devil if you wish!" he snapped and turned his head from her.

The girl was only too glad to leave the room, meeting Mrs. Pryor and Dr. Veering coming up the front stairs.

She nodded to both, but they seemed so intent on a low murmur of conversation that she hardly believed they saw her. And inside her own chamber Molly was waiting, plainly excited about something.

"Miss Persis, that old Indian witch—she's come back—and she talked to Mrs. Pryor—out in the yard where they couldn't be overheard. She kept looking at the sea as if she expected another storm. Do you suppose she knows about something like that? They say they do—like animals—they can smell out a storm."

"I don't know." Persis thought of her last ordeal by wind and wave and wondered how any rational being could abide living under such a threat. In spite of her long time abed this morning, she now felt sleep creeping up on her and was only too willing to yield to that now.

10

Persis awoke quickly, as if someone had called her name. There was the very fleeting memory of a dream and she was breathing hard, her body sweating so to dampen patches of her night rail. Pushing aside the light sheet she had pulled over her, she sat up to listen.

There was no sloughing of wind. But there was something else. A rise and fall of a voice chanting words she could not understand.

Moonlight lay in patches on the floor, bright enough to rival candle flame. Persis slid to the side of the wide bed. The sound—the threat from the dream she could not remember. She was fully awake now—not only awake but apprehensive. She felt out with one foot and her toes touched her slipper. Yet she did not bend forward to secure it on her foot. It was as if she must not move, must not allow herself to be noticed—

Noticed? By what—or who?

That same strange, awesome feeling which had come upon her on the night she had gone to retrieve the portfolio, hung in this chamber. There was moonlight enough, when her eyes adjusted to the half dark, to make sure that she was alone. But—

Fear choked her, such fear as she had never known. It was as if she drew this terror to her whether she would or not, and was a magnet for it. Her hands crumpled the edge of the sheet, pulled it up to her mouth and she bit down hard on the folds of herb-scented cloth, seeking so to stifle her terrible inclination to scream, to—to—move into what might be greater terror.

Persis tried to interpret those whispering sounds. Though she could not understand them, they played upon her so that she knew she was swaying back and forth in a grotesque answer to their broken rhythm.

She wanted desperately to close her ears with her hands, but she found she could not. It was as if she were frozen, one foot off the bed, the other half-curled under her—searching the room—or what she could see of it—wildly—for what her inner sense told her was there and what her eyes and the remnants of her sensible confidence denied could be.

There was a dark shadow along the front of the bureau. One of the drawers had not been firmly closed, and now showed a noticeable gap. The portfolio? Had someone crept in during her period of sleep and searched for it again?

But—what she felt here—Persis slowly moved her head, it required a vast amount of energy and determination to break that strange apathy which held her to do that. There was no one in the room.

She forced herself to drag the wet linen self-applied gag out of her mouth. This was just the remnants of a bad dream—it had to be!

Only all her arguments could not expel the fear which still imprisoned her like an evil cage. And she stiffened, her hands clawing at the sheet.

The glimmer of light, flickering of sparks of light! That she had seen before! In the hallway. It was cold—cold. Something old, something which she could never understand and did not want to, was here, growing stronger and stronger—stronger—

With a little cry she could not stifle, for the first time in her life, Persis fainted. Or was she purposefully overcome by that thing which had nothing about it except dark purpose and overwhelming fear?

Dream—was it a dream which awaited her like a great beast in hiding? She could not have told. Save she was swept up into another time and place.

It was as if her body (though she was no longer aware of even having a body) floated in the sky. Though she had never remembered seeing colors in any dream before, such were all about her now, strident, cruel, threatening.

She was a prisoner of some force which willed her to look—to watch—

While what lay beneath her was so alien to all she knew that she felt totally lost.

This was not day, but night, and fires leaped high. Still the colors were there—the red of blood, the green of a poisonous vine, the yellow of a snake—all comparisons which flitted through her mind were those of wrongness, of evil. There seemed to be a stench composed of vile deeds and imaginings arising like the

140

smoke from the torches, to taint her spirit as the smoke tainted the air.

And there were many of those torches, some borne by those in canoes who paddled purposefully toward what lay directly below Persis—or below that part of her which was caught in this dream. For what did stand there, the water of a small lake washing at its shell-armored sides, was a tall hillock of which the top was squared off after a fashion, though it angled inward toward the crest. While the crest itself was a platform with stone planted in its middle.

Up the side of the hillock were steps cut away and shell-paved, while on either side of those were planted more torches, even as there was also a veritable wall of them set around the outer edge of that top square.

Those in canoes did not move toward the stairs, rather their craft gathered in ranks around the outward skirts of the mound. But near the stone at the crest were others who waited. And, though their bodies were human, broad necklets upon their chests, their heads were encased in masks—with huge plumed crowns all in the forms of snarling visages of animals. One looked out from between the threatening teeth of a huge spotted cat. Another was snouted and fanged like an alligator.

And, very dim and far away, a thin chanting reached Persis. She felt that she was on the very edge of learning some mystery. But it was not a mystery of her kind and she had no desire—no right—to understand.

There came a last canoe, bearing at the bow a man who was not masked, but rather plumed and crowned, and about him there was the air of one who gave orders and was speedily thereafter obeyed. While behind him, between the two paddlers who maneuvered skill-

141

fully to bring their light craft to the beginning of that stairway of light, was another figure, but so draped in white that Persis could see neither face, nor hands.

The crowned chieftain stepped easily to the small landing which lay at the foot of that stairway. Then he turned and held out his hand while the paddlers brought the canoe around a little so that the figure in white could also disembark.

Persis, though she could not tell why she knew, believed that this was a woman, a young woman. And from that swarthed figure there came a breath of fear as strong as if the sea wind buffeted Persis.

Up they went, step by step. The chieftain first, proud, his face one which teased Persis' memory for it seemed she had seen its like before—with the jutting beak of nose, plugged on one side in the nostril with a disk of green stone. He made no move to urge on or aid his companion.

Yet that other climbed, step by step. And her fear arose with her like a sour breath of corruption. So they reached the top. Then two of the animal-masked men moved quickly to the side of the white-shrouded one. They wore gloves as Persis could see when they raised their hands, but the gloves were skillfully fashioned of skin, while talons set in them glistened in the light.

These ripped and tore. Rags of white fluttered to the pavement of shells. A girl stood there, her young brown body brought into life by the torches. She made no attempt to raise her limp arms. Her face was passive, her eyes staring straight ahead. They had drugged her, these priests. Persis did not know how she was certain of that. But the drug controlled only her body. Trapped inside the victim's mind was alive, and fear was eating at her.

With the ease of long practice the cat-headed priest

stooped to catch her ankles, the alligator already gripped her shoulders. Unresisting she was limp in their hands as they swung her up and across the stone.

No—she would not watch! Persis had no eyes to close—not in this dream. But her will arose with such a fury of revulsion that she struggled as the poor victim could not. There was a vast silence. The chant which had reached her faintly had stopped abruptly.

Away—Persis summoned all of her will. She *would* wake! She would!

It was like suddenly finding a way out of a prison, the falling to the floor of a bar across a door. She was—out!

Once more she opened her eyes, saw that she lay so close to the edge of the bed (her hands tightly gripping the rumpled sheet until her fingers ached) that she might have rolled to the floor. Still the nightmare held her for several breaths and she looked about her, eager to make sure of where she was—and when.

That had been unlike any dream she had ever had in her life. It was—real—even if she had had no part in it but was only an onlooker. She raised her head and was aware that that distant sound of chant was gone. *It* had not been of the dream. She had heard it before she had been caught in that nightmare.

Askra! The woman who might be the last of her tribe, who was credited with strange powers, and who was allowed to return to the Key to carry out communication with her dead (or so they said) because she could overawe in turn even the fierce Seminoles who had invaded and taken the lands of her people.

Had Persis this night somehow looked into Askra's memories? Yet the girl had the feeling what she had witnessed had happened very long ago. The mound, the lake around it—those had stood clear, well tended.

143

And there had been no house. Still she was certain that it had been the same mound as that on which the house now rested. What had Lydia said on that first day here—that this was blood-soaked ground with its own ghosts—the Old Ones Askra believed in—the Spanish—the pirates—the Spanish again—and now people of her own race. She sat up in bed and looked at the room with its bars of moon and its shadows. If evil was done—murder—over and over again in a place—then did that evil still hang like a dark cloud above it—perhaps forever?

There was, she drew a tentative breath, an odor in the room—some night-blooming flower? Perhaps—but she did not fancy it. And she felt queer and giddy. If only there was someone within reach she could go to now. Molly? No, it would be foolish to seek out the maid for no other reason than a bad dream.

However, she sought for her second slipper and firmly pushed her feet into them. She had to go to the window, to look out and reassure herself that the here and now was back. Without waiting to pick up her wrapper from the foot of the bed she did just that.

The moon shone on the causeway now uniting the mound and Key. There were no canoes, no torches. She wanted light within her room as well, though she knew the folly of sleeping with a candle aflame. Yet at the moment she did not feel as if she would ever truly sleep again.

Moving to the small side table she struck a spark from the tinderbox, and watched the welcome cone of fire answer on the wick. Then, she did not know why, she took up the candle, shielding the flame with her other hand, and moved to stand at the door—though she did not open that.

Instead, she listened. There were sounds out of the

night—rustle of leaves, others made by insects. But nothing she could connect to either the chant or the uneasy feeling of the presence which had haunted her first awakening.

It was when she turned reluctantly once more to her bed, determined that she must fight sleep lest she somehow return into the world of nightmare, that Persis saw it.

A dark rod was lying at the foot of the bed, as if someone had twitched loose the netting there and laid it for her to see. She held the candle closer, until it nearly set aflame the netting before she jerked it back again.

The fan!

A glance toward the chest told her that the bottom drawer gaped open far enough. Someone had deliberately taken it from where Molly had put it and laid it here for her to find.

It cost her high resolution to touch it, draw it out into the full light of the candle. In her hold it was heavy, seemingly oddly balanced. And this *was* the one she had found buried! It could not be opened—as if it were a box made to resemble the fan Lydia had taken such malicious amusement in showing her. The opal eyes of the cats watched her, not with menace, but with the detachment of the furred kind. As if they were waiting for something—or for some action on her part. But how had it come here?

She had buried it, Persis knew that, she could even sense this moment the very feel of the earth and stones she had pressed with all her might down around the lead box which had held it. And then Molly had found it among her things. Yes, that *was* the drawer she had hidden it in for a space. And it would seem that it had been deliberately left in the open this time in mockery—to prove to her that she could not rid herself of her find.

Shivering, the girl collapsed on the edge of the bed. She would have given all she possessed, all Uncle Augustin had hoped to obtain to insure her future, to be safely back in New York. There was an uncanny shadow over this house—though she had never believed truly such things could honestly be. Now it would seem she was partially its victim.

She set down the candle carefully on the bedside table, wishing at that moment she possessed a dozen more to make a barrier of light around the bed. No—that made her think of those torches and the wall of light they had furnished for that very sinister crest of the mound!

If she could only hurl the fan away from her—out the window—into the vegetation where it might be lost forever. But though she willed fiercely to do just that, she could not move. This was like being caught in another dream. Was she? Could dreams be layered one upon the other so she might now think herself awake and yet not be?

But if anything was real in this suddenly frightening world it was this room, the bed—and what she held in her hand. Persis concentrated on the fingers which held the fan so tightly, loose—throw—

She brought up her other hand and began to straighten them one after another. Then she paused. There was something new stirring beneath the fear which was like a cloud of poison in this room. She—she had sat so before, and there had been—

For a moment the room beyond the reach of that single candle wavered, showed a ghostly otherwhere. Not the mound and the masked priests. No, rather rough walls. And she was a captive there—waiting—

146

Ah, but she had the answer—it lay right in her hands. Persis no longer tried to throw aside the fan. Instead she gave a turn to the narrow end. What it contained slid out smoothly, a delicate and deadly length of steel. Though she could not know it, a small, crooked smile shaped upon her lips, and there was a new depth of light in her eyes.

She held a dagger, nonetheless deadly for being so short. It would be long enough to cut a man's throat—or even find his heart. The opal eyes of the cats flamed in the half light, promising. Persis dropped the fan-shaped sheath, put the forefinger of her other hand to the needle-tip of the hidden blade.

This was a key to unlock the door of desperation. As she held it so, once more shadows moved in her mind. Not memories of hers, rather a faded picture which might have come from a long distance, or far away in time. The girl she had seen brought to the mound in her dream—*she* had had no such weapon—it had not existed then.

But there had been a later captive, as helplessly entrapped here. And this had been her way to safety. Persis' hand no longer tried to reject the touch of that blade. Why should she throw from her the one defense left.

Soon *he* would come; she knew it as well as if she already saw him walk through the shadowy doorway. Then she must play her little game, be one who cowered and feared—bring him close—even endure his touch until—until she could use the steel she held!

She was breathing fast, the tip of her tongue passing quickly back and forth across her lips.

Slowly she turned the blade in the candlelight. From it shimmered kind of radiance, cold and deadly. The girl watched that half-bemused—but at the same time she was listening. When would *he* come? Perhaps

147

it was part of his cruelty to keep her waiting this way. But he would discover—she moved the blade lightly through the air. The point caught on one of the folds of the net around the bed, and slit it easily apart.

So small a thing, but the action jerked Persis from her bemusement. What—who—? She dropped the blade, her hands going to press against her cheeks. Her skin felt hot, fevered. Was she ill and those dreams part of delirium? She was—she took firm hold on her thought—Persis Rooke! This was a room which had no confusing shadows to cloak it. And what lay before her—

With a shudder she thrust the thin blade back into the concealment of the mock fan. Though she had been only a spectator at the grisly torch-lit scene of her too-vivid dream, this time she had been near enough awake to at least confusedly realize she was in a house. Who had been there to open the drawer where she had hidden the fan earlier, who had brought it back? And why—?

The lost lady—?

Persis made herself give searching survey to the room. A woman had vanished years ago, many years ago, leaving a dead man behind her. Where had she gone? There must have been no escape from the Key for her. If she had killed the man, who would have forced her—had she just walked into the sea?

It was the hidden fan which had so strangely reappeared which troubled her. She forced herself to pick up the blade, slip it once more into the case which had held it. That quick twist of the fingers which anchored it within—how had she known that must be done?

Throw it into the sea? But even as she picked up the fan-shaped case she knew—against all reason—that she could not do so. Now as she held it once more her
148

fingers tightened around it protectingly—Protectingly? Yes, she had to keep this—there was a reason. It was as if a thin voice, very far away, was raised in warning.

Persis got to her feet. Her body was clammy with sweat, her night rail clung to shoulders and thighs, as she moved, with the wavering steps of someone who has been a long time ill and was trying to walk again for the first time, to the chest of drawers.

Into that she pushed the mock fan, pulled the clothing over it. Her mouth was dry; she longed for a glass of water. And when she went back toward the window her hands were shaking so that not all her power of will could still them. Once more she looked out into the night.

There was a torch below now. Against the dazzlement of that light she saw a hunched shape. And there was something wrong with the outline of the head.

That turned, so it was plain in profile against the torchlight. It—it was one of the priests! One of the animal-headed ones who had awaited the sacrifice. Persis blinked and blinked again.

No, there was no canoe. Just a single torch. And she was not on the mound of her dreams, rather in a house which used its remains for a base. The torch disappeared. But surely that had been no human face she had caught a glimpse of—

There was no sound now but a distant wash of waves, the sigh of wind outside. She was oddly free. All she had sensed—in her dream—and in her awakening to find the treacherous fan close at hand—was gone. Also—she felt suddenly sleepy as one does who is drained of all strength or who has been drugged.

She stumbled back to the bed, one small fear still stirring in her. To sleep might mean to dream again.

She must not let that happen—she must not! But her weighted eyelids closed against all her determination.

If she dreamed again it was not so vividly, nor could she remember any of it, when she struggled out of that pit of unconsciousness the next morning. However, the face she looked up into was not Molly's usual round features with their ever-slight flush, but rather Sukie's browned features.

The island maid set down a covered cup on the small bedside table, her eyes more for that duty than for Persis who hunched forward on her pillows, coming fully awake at this surprise at the change in routine she had known for so many years.

"Where's Molly?" she demanded almost too sharply. Sukie glanced at her sideways as if she did not quite like to be where she was. Persis had never noticed her much before, now she was a little repelled by the girl's harsh features. She must be of mixed blood as many of the islanders were. But the jut of her nose which looked out of proportion with the rest of her face was reminiscent of Askra's. Perhaps she did have some remote strain of the archaic blood of the people who had built the mound. The mound—Persis battled down her vivid memory of that dream.

"She's ailin'. Stayed in bed." Sukie sounded sullen. Perhaps she resented having to take over new duties.

"Ailing!" But Molly was *never* sick. In all the years the maid had seen Persis herself through the ordeals of measles, colds, and a lengthy bout of fever (which did not, thank God, turn out to be smallpox as had first been feared) Molly herself had been a tower of strength.

Persis scrambled out of bed, thrust her feet into her slippers, and grabbed the wrapper from where it lay across a chair. With her hair still in the braids Molly herself had made last night, she was already on her way to the door.

She heard Sukie say something she did not wait to catch, instead she headed for that second flight of stairs, hurrying to them with only the care of catching up the front of her wrapper so it would not trip her.

A few moments later she was in Molly's room, just in time to support her head as the maid retched miserably into the slop pail, runnels of sweat on her cheeks from the thick beads gathering on her forehead.

The attack over, Persis eased her back on her pillows.

"Somethin' I ate," Molly got out between gasps of breath. Under Persis' fingers on her wrists her pulse was laboring. "Please, Miss Persis—I—hurt—"

Her big hands pressed against her thick body just under her breasts and the eyes she turned on Persis begged for reassurance and comfort.

11

"A severe bout of indigestion," Dr. Veering gave his verdict in a precise voice. "The eating of our raw fruit by those not accustomed to such fare has been known to produce just such symptoms. Your man has something of a like nature—"

"Shubal!" Persis broke in. "But how—"

"Mrs. Pryor heard him being ill in the night. I would advise a very light diet—say broth—perhaps a custard," the doctor continued. "But I have given them both a draft, and do not offer them food until they ask for it. And how have you been feeling?" He peered at her with the intent he might have given to some plant he wished to classify—the closest and most measuring look Persis remembered ever having from him. "You do not look quite the thing yourself, Miss Rooke."

"I had a nightmare," Persis replied. "But you are sure—about Molly and Shubal? Molly has never been ill that I can remember."

Dr. Veering shrugged. "Such a history does not guarantee she never will, you know. But I would say that the worst is over. She and your manservant need the rest—and then judicious feeding up. Leave it to Mrs. Pryor, she has had much experience with such indispositions."

But when the doctor had left the room, Molly's head moved on the pillow, her eyes looked wide and frightened.

"It ain't like he said, Miss Persis," her voice was weak but urgent. "We didn't eat any food that wasn't served to the family. We—we was overlooked!"

"Overlooked?" Persis could not understand.

"It was done a-purpose, Miss Persis. Me, I'd swear m'dyin' oath to that."

"Poison!" Persis stared back at the maid, completely confounded.

"Not bad enough to kill us maybe." Molly's face looked very wan, even her full cheeks seemed to have collapsed into wrinkled folds. "To keep us abed—maybe away from you."

"That is silly!" Persis retorted more sharply than she meant to. "We're not in any danger. Molly, it is impossible and don't you dare say anything to Mrs. Pryor like that! We're guests here and not prisoners."

The maid reached out her hand and caught at a fold of Persis' skirt as the girl got to her feet.

"There ain't no way of us gettin' off this island, less they help us. And there's that witch woman hangin' around. Mam Rose said as how in the old days they killed people—sent 'em out, as they said, as messengers to their old heathen gods. The Captain, he's let that

153

Askra come here and call upon those gods. She was a-doin' that last night. I heard her, Miss Persis. How do we know that she didn't want to send us somewheres—we being strangers an' no one carin' 'bout us here? She knows herbs—she could—"

"Was she in the kitchen when the cooking was going on?" Persis demanded. Molly's wild idea had a kind of crazy logic. She remembered, in spite of all her efforts, her own terrible night—the dreams—and finally watching the torch held by the masked figure disappear into the thick vegetation below.

"I wasn't in the kitchen all the time, Miss Persis. How would I know? Only all them others—Mam Rose, Sukie, the rest, they steer a wide path around her and they're afraid of her. They say she has powers—"

Molly grew more animated as she talked, as if the need for making an impression on Persis gave her the strength she had lost during her bouts of nausea.

"Was you sick last night, Miss Persis?"

Could one call those vivid dreams a kind of sickness, Persis wondered. But she refused to allow fancy to stray so far.

"No. I just had a couple of bad dreams," she returned shortly and positively. "Now, Molly, you heard what the doctor said—eating unusual food can bring about the reaction you, and apparently Shubal, have had. We are strangers here and are unaccustomed to some of the fruit."

"It was done—a-purpose, Miss Persis, you'll see—it was done with a purpose." Molly settled her head back on her pillow. "Jus' you watch out good. There's somethin' mighty queer happenin' here. I ain't one to go seein' what ain't solid an' what I can't touch, but now I have a bad feelin' 'bout this place, Miss Persis. Seems like we'd better get away as soon as we can."

154

"Yes," to that Persis could agree. She smoothed the bed cover and moved the shutter of the near window so the hot beam of the sun would not touch Molly's wan face. "I promise you, Molly, that's just what we're going to do."

But that the illness of the only two she could completely trust under this roof had been planned—that was too wild to even consider. She paid a visit to Shubal and found him asleep, his face against the pillow carrying a greater appearance of age than she had ever seen. But Shubal *was* old—nearly able to match Uncle Augustin in years. As long as his master had been alive one had not been so aware of that. It was as if his constant preoccupation with Uncle Augustin's needs and desires had so filled his life that even age could not threaten him. Only now that that occupation was gone he had nothing to fill the void and was so empty he was only a fading shell of a man. She must keep appealing for his help, let him see that he would be, was, of use still—that she must have his aid. That, Persis thought, might give him a new lease on life—or at least she could hope so.

She met Mrs. Pryor as she came down into the second hallway. The housekeeper had just come out of Captain Leverett's chamber and there was a kind of quiet triumph on her face as she exhibited a tray on which only used dishes remained—no sign of food.

"He made a good breakfast," she greeted Persis. "And he threw a saucer at the houseboy when he would not help him to do more than sit up with a second pillow." She appeared to believe that a most encouraging sign. "He might be glad of a little company, Miss Rooke, if you are wishful to offer it."

"Perhaps after a while." Captain Leverett was no
155

longer her problem, Molly and Shubal were. "My servants—"

"Ah, yes, Dr. Veering told me. It is not unusual, Miss Rooke. I have seen such upsets from a change in diet many times. We have had other shipwrecked guests and a number of them have suffered so. The results are only temporary. I assure you. And I have a good stock broth ready. Perhaps later in the day they will fancy that. There is nothing better for the return of strength. You, yourself, have had no difficulties?"

Persis shook her head. "None. I did not sleep well. There was a sound—like singing—or chanting—"

Mrs. Pryor's lips pinched together. "Yes. It is a time of some ceremony for Askra. The Captain has given her full permission to follow her own ways here. We are lucky in times of Indian troubles—and mainly because this Key and Askra make the Seminoles uneasy. They say they defeated the Old Ones, but they believe that their ghosts linger here and are reluctant to face them. Askra has been of great service in furthering that belief—which is a true one as far as she is concerned. She is a very strange person with knowledge which comes from another time and another people. And perhaps those descended from the ancient enemies of her own clan have good reason to be afraid of that knowledge."

Mrs. Pryor had always been so sensible that her present words made an even deeper impression on Persis. Perhaps there was something about this house, the mound, Lost Lady Key which could make the improbable seem possible. Persis remembered again her alarms of the night, but those were only dreams. Except—

She made some answer to Mrs. Pryor which she hoped was civil and went quickly to her own chamber.

Kneeling by the chest of drawers she searched. There it lay in truth—the fan dagger. How could Mrs. Pryor answer this appearance? Was it put there as a warning, or a threat? But why would either be aimed at her? Swiftly she pushed the petticoats back into place over it. Somehow she did not want to ask anyone here any questions concerning it. She just wanted to forget she had ever seen it at all.

But try as she would to exile the thought of it, it still intruded into her mind as she ate with Lydia and Mrs. Pryor later. They were not yet through the meal when the braying of the conch horn—which Persis had come to associate now with the sighting of a ship—broke the silence which had held the three of them. Lydia, for one, appeared half-asleep—as if she had spent no better a night than had Persis—and Mrs. Pryor was apparently deep in some problem to do with the household.

The shell horn brought Lydia in tautly alert. And Persis could not help but wonder if Ralph Grillon, knowing that Captain Leverett was confined to his chamber, would dare once more to brazenly and openly visit the Key. But Sukie came in to relay the message that it was the mail packet which had been sighted.

Now it was Persis' turn to take full notice. The mail packet—her own chance of getting on to Key West. For a moment she relished the thought of such escape. Then she remembered Molly and Shubal. Knowing the rigors of their trip from New York, she could not condemn either of the servants to a further sea voyage until they were well again and she could not venture alone.

But perhaps the visit of the very welcome ship which was a tie with civilization as she knew it would

157

be in port here long enough to make sure of their recovery— It was Mrs. Pryor who put an end to that small hope.

"They will take off some of the men of the *Arrow* if they will. Though, Captain Fosdick does not take kindly to crowding. At least he can carry news to Key West and perhaps the owners will make provision for another ship to pick them up here."

"They *will* take a letter?" Persis held on to her second hope. She had written to Mr. Hogue on the night of her uncle's burial—asked him, if possible, to recommend a lawyer in Key West—though she was not sure he would know of any trustworthy man.

"The Captain will have the mail bag; he has his own affairs concerning the *Arrow* to settle."

"And it will be long enough before he sails himself again," Lydia said. "He won't care much about having to delegate duties to others." She was smiling as if the thought of her brother's irritation pleased her in some way.

"I'll get my letter." Persis could not sit any longer waiting. Even to send the missive off to Mr. Hogue would be some small satisfaction. Also, she could certainly ask Captain Pettigrew to make inquiries for her. Perhaps if the Captain was preparing to leave she must do that first!

Excusing herself, she hurried to her chamber for the broad-brimmed bonnet which she had found was her best protection against the sun. And took from her small lap desk the letter she had written to Mr. Hogue. She could leave that with Captain Leverett and then walk down to the "hotel" and search out Captain Pettigrew.

Rapping on the chamber door confronting hers, she
158

heard a muffled voice from within giving her permission to enter. But when she came into the room she found Captain Pettigrew there also, standing beside the bed while Captain Leverett sorted through some papers the other had spread out before him.

"I'm sorry—" She was disconcerted at breaking in upon what appeared to be a business conference. But Captain Leverett was already single-handedly shuffling the papers together rather clumsily and holding them out to his companion.

"There is something I can do for you, Miss Rooke? But first I fear I have a disappointment for you. The *Annie B.* will not accept female passengers. I know Captain Fosdick and he has no accommodations for ladies on board. So I am afraid that you will have to stay with us a little while longer. Now if it had been the *Swallow*, which we were half-expecting—"

"I could not go anyway—now." Persis was so intent upon what she must do she brushed aside his explanation. "Both Molly and Shubal are ill. I would not go and leave them. But I do have a letter," she produced it as well as her netted purse in which was the small sum of money left from her last housekeeping allowance. "This must go to Uncle Augustin's lawyer—in New York. And," now she turned to Captain Pettigrew, "you are going to Key West?"

He nodded, his square-cut, gray-salted beard wagging up and down.

"Have to, Miss Rooke. Have to get in touch with the owners. We might have saved the *Arrow*—but that last blow—" He shook his head. "That nigh ripped the bottom out of her. She's only good for firewood now."

"Then if you will do me a service, sir, I shall be greatly in your debt. I am told there are reputable lawyers in the town; find me one who is reliable so that I may discover more of my uncle's affairs in the islands. I have been given to understand that I may face difficulties there."

The Captain bowed awkwardly. "That I will do surely, Miss Rooke. You'll have a message back when we send for the rest of the crew—this *Annie B.* will only ship four of us. I'm leaving Mr. Wilkinson, my mate, in charge here. He'll be glad to give you a hand if you need it—" Now he looked back at Captain Leverett. "He was on the China run a while back and knows how to handle pirates. If you have the arms, my crew will back you in any trouble with the Indians."

"Well enough," Captain Leverett said. He had taken Persis' letter and was stowing it away with others into a stained bag. "Take this out with you to the *Annie B.* The boatmen will bring back any they have for the island."

"Wait," Persis was busy freeing the ring closing her purse. "There is postage due. To go to New York—"

Captain Leverett shook his head. "We have a yearly contract with the mailboats. They come seldom enough to make a good profit—and we might as well use up all the surplus we can. Keep your money, Miss Rooke."

She could not keep on urging him. But she disliked being again beholden to him for even so small a matter. However, when she turned toward the door, he spoke again with his usual to-be-obeyed tone of voice:

"If you will wait for a moment, Miss Rooke. Well, Pettigrew, that finishes it. You can turn that claim over to the court in Key West and send the copy to your owners. I'm plagued sorry we had the second blow—we could have gotten your ship afloat if it hadn't been for that. But there's a full description of
160

what happened for the claims court, and I cannot see how you or your crew can be faulted in any way."

Captain Pettigrew sighed. "Facts are facts right enough. But to owners they don't add up sometimes high enough to match dollars and cents. You've treated us fair, Captain. It ain't your fault either that we couldn't save her after you worked her off that reef. And you're more than fair in writing it all down like you did. I'll be going now—no use keepin' the boat waiting. And you, Miss," he sketched an awkward bow to Persis. "I'll do just as you ask and get in touch with some law man for you."

"Good luck, Captain," she had just time enough to say before the door closed behind him. Then as the silence grew and Crewe Leverett made no move to explain why he had asked her to stay, just half-lay, half-sat in the huge bed, his shoulder well wedged motionless with pillows, she added nervously:

"I seem to be unable to be the proper guest, Captain—"

"How is that?" He was frowning a little once more as if, while he watched her so intently, he was trying to solve some problem of his own.

"I am unable to withdraw my presence—though I am uninvited."

"Every once in a while," he said slowly, "the sea gives more generously than it takes away. Have you ever gathered shells along the shore, Persis?"

His complete change of subject, as well as his bold use of her name startled her. Or—a spark of anger (the kind which somehow he could always awaken in her) came to life. Was he thus obliquely approaching the subject of Ralph Grillon—trying to learn whether she had kept another rendezvous with the Bahamian captain?

"No, I have not," she returned somewhat sharply.

"There are some beautiful ones—gems of the sea." His eyes were still holding hers. "Lydia has a taste for such harvesting—ask her to show you. Those who first built here used clam shells to mix with the earth to rear the mounds of their city—pave their trails. Yes, you must go shelling before you leave us, Persis, and see how generous the sea can be in its own way."

She could not understand his change of mood, nor be sure that there was not a subtle hint in his talk of shelling along the shore. Now she was at a loss as to how to reply as a short silence held between them.

"What do you think of Lost Lady Key, Persis?" again he changed the subject.

"What I have seen of it," she answered, "is at least very different from New York." Her words sounded so inane in her own ears that she thought he might well dismiss her now as a female completely lacking in brains. Of course, it was different from New York. But she was not going to go into detail about her continued uneasiness in this house, the strange dreams which had plagued her, and her fear of the sea storms.

Now he was smiling a little. And Persis guessed that his estimate of her intelligence was just what she feared. Which added a pinch of fuel to that deep-down opposition he had the power to stir within her.

"Yes—it is very different from New York," he sounded mocking. "And did you so greatly fancy New York, Persis?"

She thought back. The solid safety of life there—it *had* been solidly safe under Uncle Augustin's roof. But also—very dull. She certainly could not say the same of Lost Lady Key.

"I knew nothing else, sir," she fell back on young lady manners, "until I came here."

"And you will return to New York?" he persisted, why she could not guess. What did her future mean to him, after she was able to get away from his involuntary hospitality?

"I can tell nothing about that. Not until I learn what is to be done about the inheritance in the islands—"

"Yes," he nodded, "the inheritance in the islands. The news you got from Grillon. Just what in particular did he have to warn you about?"

Persis hesitated. She had wanted so much to turn to someone for advice. Molly—Shubal—both were loyal and they would follow where she led. They would not make suggestions. There was this, however, if Captain Leverett knew the whole tale he might be willing to somehow aid in her departure. She had been brought up in Uncle Augustin's way of silence concerning family matters, and now she could not quite understand what pushed her toward making a full story of her dilemma here and now.

"There is another heir, a new one," she cut her explanation short. "Captain Grillon knows of this and told me. My cousin—long known to be dead—left a child no one knew about—"

"Until," Crewe Leverett cut in, "there was a sizable estate to be settled, is that it? And you accept this story, Persis? Does it not seem a bit odd that such an heir comes into the open only after those most concerned are dead?"

She studied him suspiciously, half-convinced that he was indeed mocking her inexperience. Though there was no sign of that in his expression.

"I would not," he continued after a moment, "accept Ralph Grillon's word on any subject. You told me he tried to bargain with you. There is no reason to believe that this heir exists anywhere—except perhaps in his own imagination. He is—"

"Your enemy," she cut in, seething that he took her to be so stupid. "I know that. And I would take no one's word until it is all investigated. I am not," she arose, "such a ninny as you seem to think I am, Captain Leverett."

That half smile did not leave him. "So you read thoughts, too, Persis Rooke? Now that is interesting. But I fear you take your powers far too much for granted. I am merely warning you that it is best to make your own decisions on hard evidence and not on the word of a man who bears none too good a reputation. Come, now, you can't think as hardly of me as you look just now. I do have some virtues along with the usual complement of vices."

Persis hesitated. She could not read any mockery into that no matter how hard she tried. And, oddly enough she resented the fact that he seemed able to disarm her just when she thought her defenses so well organized. Now she seized wildly on a change of subject of her own, wanting to get away from that which touched her personally in a way she could not understand and did not want to.

"Captain Leverett, you asked how I liked Lost Lady. Lydia has told me some of its history—it sounds very dark and cruel."

"I suppose every piece of land has its own ghosts," he accepted her switch. "Perhaps this holds more than most. Askra's people had a city here once. Their great temple was on the mound supporting this house. Then they were hunted by the Spanish and the Seminoles turned loose to clear them from the land. And the Spanish rule was harsh in turn, being overwhelmed by a pirate attack about a hundred years ago. Has Lydia showed you the opal-eyed fan? That is a relic of the past with a very queer story—a dead pirate captain and a captive Spanish lady who disappeared.

"The Spanish came to rule once more—and then once more an Indian uprising. Finally, we came. But the sea is the last conqueror, you know. It threatens—" He moved a little on the pillows as if his shoulder hurt him.

Without thinking Persis went to the bed and settled the pile supporting him more firmly.

"You've a light hand," his face was now so close to hers that the deep blue of his eyes were like pools of the sea. A person, she thought, could be drawn into such pools. The oddity of that idea made her flush and retreat hastily. Somehow, though she had learned her deftness caring for Uncle Augustin, this was not at all like that. And she drew back to the end of the big bed as if she had fled from some danger she could not understand.

"I nursed my uncle," she tried to make her voice as matter-of-fact as she could. "One learns how to do things when one has to."

"A statement which can be applied to all our lives," Captain Leverett remarked. "And we go on learning, Persis—remember that. So you think Lost Lady is dark and cruel."

"Maybe not the land, just the stories about it." She was thankful that he returned to that. "Yes, Lydia showed me the fan—it is very strange and beautiful. But I do not think I would care to use it myself." Should she tell him of the second fan—the mock fan which concealed death within it? She wanted to, but somehow she could not find the words before she spoke.

"Perhaps you are right in that. The islanders will
165

have it that the Lost Lady is jealous of her prize possession and would not take kindly to its falling into other hands. They say she walks—but she only shows herself to those who are in danger or an islander who has angered her. So beware of our ghost, Persis!" And now he was smiling again, the mocking note back in his voice.

"Sir—" She wanted to say that such superstitions were beneath any rational mind to entertain, but knowing what lay in her chest of drawers she could not. "Sir," she began again, "I shall certainly remember your warning."

"Captain," Mrs. Pryor opened the door to look in upon them. "Nate Hawkins is here—"

Persis used the chance to escape. Escape what? She could not have said. But she did not want to think of the fan—of the Lost Lady. Nor, if she told the truth, of Crewe Leverett. Better go back to Molly and a comfortable relationship she knew so well.

12

She found the maid drowsy and inclined to sleep, saying that Mrs. Pryor had sent her a soothing draft.

"Miss Lydia brought it herself," Molly mumbled. "Most obliging she was about it."

Then her eyes closed as if she could not keep them open a second longer. And within a moment or two she was snoring a little. But Persis continued to sit on the single chair. Though her eyes were fixed on Molly's sweating and mottled face, her thoughts were busy in another direction.

If her letter was dispatched as soon as possible— even then it could be weeks before an answer reached her. And they certainly could not stay on here. Would any lawyer in Key West respond to her plea? And if so

—how long would it take for him to discover the truth? She looked down at her hands lying idly in her lap.

The purse which had been in Uncle Augustin's possession was now hers but the sum it held seemed small to her. To provide for the three of them in Key West—and perhaps pay for passage north again—would those funds suffice? Now for the first time Persis was disturbed that she knew so little about her uncle's affairs.

Slowly she got up and went to the small, single window. This room, like the Captain's chamber, overlooked the moat and the canal. Men were busy on the wharf—the *Nonpareil* had been brought in and there seemed to be a great deal of activity going forward here. Beyond lay the wreckage of the *Arrow*, driven ashore, its bow towering up so that the battered figurehead of the Indian warrior with his bowstrung arrow set to the cord now silently pointed up into the sky.

Farther out she could see the mail packet already lifting anchor, preparing to depart. In spite of her need to be about her own affairs, she was glad she was not aboard. It looked smaller and even more squalid than the *Arrow* had been.

"No—!"

Persis swung around to face the bed. Molly's face was screwed up in an expression the girl had never seen there before, one of sheer fear—though her eyes were closed. "No—" the sleeper repeated, as if to deny what she did see in some dream.

"Molly!" Remembering her own nightmares Persis moved quickly to her side, ready to shake her awake. "Molly, it is just a dream!"

"No!" There was such force in that denial that Persis grasped the plump shoulder almost fiercely. It was plain that Molly was caught in some horror.

168

"Molly! Wake up!" She shook the maid, first lightly, and then more energetically as Molly showed no signs of rousing.

Instead, the woman suddenly raised one hand and struck out at Persis.

"Let go—devil—devil!" Her mutter became a full cry now. "The knife—no!"

Persis bent over her, seized both shoulders to shake her firmly. She must break the dream which held the sleeping woman, for the grimace of fear on her face was like an ugly mask.

Molly gasped, her breath whistling between her lips. Then her eyes opened and she was staring up wildly.

"Devil—"

Consciousness came back slowly and with it bewilderment. Persis kept her hold on Molly as if to anchor the maid to the safe present.

The woman's face convulsed, and, for the first time in years, Persis saw tears gather in her eyes.

"Miss Persis!" Molly's own hands rose to snatch and grip the girl's wrists in a hold so tight her nails scored the younger woman's flesh. "Miss Persis—send her away!"

"Who, Molly?"

"The one—the one who is—" the maid's head turned on the pillow as she searched the room. "But she was here!" Beads of sweat dotted both her forehead and her upper lip. "I saw her—that witch—that Indian witch! She was goin' to kill me—with a knife—so she was! And there were a lot of others all stand' around watchin' an' jus' waitin' for her to do it! I saw her as plain as I see you right now!"

"It was a dream, Molly. I've been right here with you—there's no one else in the room."

Now the tears brimmed over in Molly's eyes and ran down her cheeks.

"I ain't never had such a dream as that before, Miss Persis. It was realer nor any dream. She—she was like a devil—wearin' that nasty false face of her an' a-comin' for me with a knife. I couldn't get away nohow—" Molly's sobs shook her stolid body. "What's the matter with me, Miss Persis? Is it true what they say, that there old witch can lay a sendin' on you an' you jus' gets sicker and sicker?"

"Nonsense!" Persis interrupted with all the authority she could summon. Let Molly begin to believe that she was cursed or some such thing and she *would* be sick. "It was a dream—just a dream."

Molly still clung to the girl. "I ain't never had no such real dream before," she repeated with some of her old stubbornness. "Seems like if it were a dream somebody made me dream it. 'Cause there was all those people—heathens wearing feathers and masks—and with burnin' torches—jus' standin' there a-watchin' what was goin' to happen to me. An' they wanted me dead!"

"But it isn't true," Persis pointed out patiently. "You're right here in your bed, and I'm here with you." Her own dream! Molly had experienced something very close to it. However, the last thing Persis would do now was to let the maid know that they had shared the same terrible vision. For she felt that if she did Molly would cling to the fact that they both might have been led to dream by another's evil will.

Could one's dreams be dictated by an outside force? It was a very strange idea. Persis exiled that quickly to the back of her mind now. The main thing was that the maid must be soothed and led to believe that her fear had no base in fact.

"I—I was—it was so real—"

"Some dreams can be, or seem to be. But this one was not real, Molly. Now, I'll stay here with you, I promise."

Molly's hold on her loosened a trifle. "If you will, Miss Persis, I'll take that kindly, 'deed I will. I feel so sleepy." Again her eyes, though she appeared to fight to keep them open, were drooping shut. "Don't let me dream like that, please, Miss Persis."

"I won't!" the girl promised stoutly, but how she might prevent it she did not know. Then sighting something resting upon the bureau gave her a new idea. She gently disengaged herself from Molly's hold and went to pick up the worn Bible which the maid, as she well knew, read each morning and night.

"See here," she held the book with its scuffed cover out so Molly could easily see it. "You're going to put this under your pillow. Do you think then any bad dream can come near you?"

"Give it here, Miss Persis. My, you're a knowin' one! That's the truth. Ain't nothing evil goin' to come nigh that. It was my mother's an' she taught me my letters out of it."

Molly smoothed the Bible with loving hands. "T'will be like havin' mother here—like when I was a small maid and afeard of somethin'."

She was her old confident self again and Persis blessed the inspiration which had made her think of that device. Or was it only a device? She had heard once, just now she could not remember where, that something on which had been centered good thoughts was indeed a barrier against evil. And if Molly believed she was safe, then her own belief might carry over into her sleep, preventing any more dreams.

The maid settled herself once more against her pillows, eyes closed. But Persis was left with a puzzle she could not solve. The bits and pieces Molly had mentioned certainly fitted in her own nightmare. Though she had not been an actual part of that as Molly apparently had been—just an onlooker. However, if the maid had been gripped by the same horror she had felt, Persis did not wonder at her terror on waking.

Did the dark history of this house, of the mound on which it squatted, indeed force itself into sleeping minds? She herself had had bad dreams in the past but never ones as clear and as barbaric as those of last night. And to have the same touch Molly—? What *did* haunt Lost Lady Key?

True to her promise she settled herself once more on the chair. But this time Molly's sleep seemed undisturbed by any visions and Persis began to feel restless. Had it not been for her promise she would have at least slipped to the next room to look in upon Shubal. As she twisted a little in her chosen seat she saw the door open quietly. A moment later Lydia came in.

"She's sleeping? Good!" Lydia moved with a swish of skirts to take up a small tray on which rested a mug. "She'll feel much better when she wakes. Mrs. Pryor's tea always settles the stomach."

"It was kind of you to bring it up," Persis murmured in a whisper.

Lydia shrugged. "No matter. Your man is better, too. But you—" She was studying Persis intently. "Do you feel feverish—have you a headache?" she asked with an emphasis which seemed almost eager.

"No." Persis was not going to go into details over her disturbed night. "I am concerned, naturally."

"What did Crewe want to see you about? Tell you

he was going to take over running things for you?" Lydia's eyes were very intent upon her now.

"No, in fact he suggested that I turn to shell hunting on the beach," Persis said, "and that I ask to see your collection."

Lydia simply stared for a long minute as if she did not believe her in the least. Then she smiled, a little unpleasantly.

"What he means, of course, is that you are to play companion so I can't see Ralph. That was not particularly clever of him. I," her chin lifted and her jawline was as firm and stubborn looking now as her brother's, "intend to do as I please in this matter. If Crewe thinks he can keep me shut up on this Key until he picks out a husband for me, that is *his* plan, not mine. And—" now the look she turned to Persis was close to hostile, "I would suggest that you mind your own business!"

With a last flirt of her full skirts she was gone, and the door closed behind her as firmly, if not as loudly, as if it were slammed.

Wearily, Persis arose and went once more to look out of the window. For some reason Lydia's visit brought back her preoccupation with the fan. It was almost as if some thought beyond her control connected the girl with that sinister find. Could Lydia have been the one who had disinterred that and put it in the chest drawer? But why?

Lydia was certainly linked with Ralph Grillon and determined to go her own way in spite of any restraint her brother tried to provide. She had been shrewd in her quick appraisal of what might lie behind his suggestion of shell hunting. Persis determined that she would play no part at all in the intrigues existing between the Bahamian and her hostess. If Crewe Leverett wanted a watchdog for his sister, let him look to his own household for such a one.

"No—"

Persis swung hastily back to the bed. Was Molly fast in another nightmare?

The maid's eyes were closed; Persis was sure she was asleep, but her hands moved back and forth across the light sheet which covered her body.

"Safe—safe—" she repeated the words as if trying to reassure herself of something. "Must have dropped it when the bed was made. But the lock—it is safe—"

Persis came again to the side of the bed. There was so much uneasiness in those gabbled words that she felt she must discover the source of this new troubling dream.

"Molly," she spoke softly, "what is safe?"

"The portfolio." To Persis' surprise the maid answered as if she were awake and fully cognizant of what she said. "It was on the floor. But now—it is safe. Must have fallen out when the bed was made—the only way—"

The portfolio! Persis had half-forgotten she had given that to Molly for safekeeping.

She slipped her hand now under the upper narrow featherbed, groping for the familiar feel of the leather. With Molly ill it was best she took it in charge again. Her fingers closed on the edge of the leather and she drew it slowly to her, taking care not to disturb the sleeper.

"Safe?" Somehow that one word held the note of a plea.

Persis clasped the portfolio tight against her. She leaned closer and said, hoping that her assurance would reach the other's mind no matter how deeply guarded by slumber:

174

"Safe, entirely safe, Molly."

The sleeper sighed, her head turned on the pillow, away from the girl. And as Persis watched her closely it was apparent that the maid was now deep asleep, as if her nightmare had so worn out her energy that she must rest to make up for what the fear had done to her. Persis began to go over the papers—the will, the letters, the depositions from the two privateersmen who witnessed the death of James Rooke in the sea battle. Everything was present. Only she could not now believe that they had not been searched for—read—

Why? To her knowledge no one under this roof, save herself, Molly, and Shubal had any interest in Uncle Augustin's affairs. Ralph Grillon's story—had some servant secretly in his employ made a report, giving him that ammunition he had used to try and force his bargain on her? That seemed very fantastic, like some strange device of a novelist. But that the papers had been perused, perhaps for a second time, Persis somehow had no doubt at all.

Where could she hide them? Or need she hide them again? If they had been inspected and left to her, there would be no reason to try to protect them now. She longed to awaken Molly fully and ask her more concerning what she had murmured about the portfolio. But she could not do that.

Persis found it hard to sit still. What she had always been told was her greatest fault of character possessed her, growing stronger by the minute—her impatience. She wanted to plunge into action, to do *something*. Only reflection kept saying, "What?" And to that she had no answer. There was no one under this roof to whom she could go with her questions, her—her imaginings. But she felt haunted by something which she

175

tried to tell herself was merely the result of her disturbed night—by the impression that just beyond the edge of her comprehension, forces were in action which vitally affected *her* but which she could not understand.

There was Crewe Leverett. Oddly her thoughts kept coming back to him. But what utter stupidity it would be to pour out to him two—no, three dreams (counting Molly's)—and the fact that she believed, without adequate proof, that her private papers had been twice rifled. And she wanted no interference from an outsider.

There had always been Uncle Augustin. Now she understood fully how much she had depended upon him. Not that she could have gone to him with any dreams or fantasies either. She could guess what his response would have been to such vaporing on her part. But the responsibility he had left her—that she would not have needed to concern herself with.

Persis had always believed most firmly in her own judgment, her own strength of character. Had she done that just because such qualities had never been put to the test before? That question left her shaken, but she would not yield to it.

She had duties—to Uncle Augustin, who at the last had trusted her, whether forced by circumstance or no—to Molly and Shubal—and last of all, to herself. She must make decisions and steer them all into the future.

Molly was sleeping now, lying quietly and without any of the distress she had shown. Persis, still holding the portfolio to her, took a quick turn up and down the room. Above all, she wanted to get this to her own chamber again. She wanted a chance to think (if she could ever control the random dart of thoughts which now struck at her calm—or what should be her calm consideration of the future).

But she had promised to stay and Persis kept her promises. What if Molly slid once more into one of those nightmares and she was not here? What if—?

There was a faint tap on the door and Persis started as if she fully expected the menace which had earlier filled the darkness for her to enter. But it was Mrs. Pryor who opened the door very quietly, moved with firm purpose to the bed and rested her hand for a brief moment on the narrow bit of forehead showing below the ruffle of Molly's nightcap. She nodded competently.

"The fever has broken, she is sleeping quite naturally," she observed. She glanced at Persis as if she wondered what the girl was doing there.

"Molly—she had a very bad dream. I promised I would stay with her—wake her if it came again."

There was very little expression on Mrs. Pryor's face. If she thought Persis oversolicitous and even rather silly, she betrayed none of that conclusion. Instead she said something which the girl found remarkable, coming as it did from such a manifestly sensible woman.

"Dreams are very odd at times. But the herb tea she took might well have been the cause. Askra told me once that her tribe in the old days took a much stronger mixture of the same properties (that is, their wise men and women did) to induce visions. Only I have never used such proportions. But—yes, dreams can be most strange. I have heard of warnings which came in dreams and because they were not heeded, the dreamer later faced misfortune."

She had not looked at Persis when she spoke. But *was* there a subtle warning in what she said? That was

177

another question Persis dared not ask now. Meanwhile, Mrs. Pryor was continuing.

"You need not worry about her dreaming again, Miss Rooke. This is a very natural and deep sleep—not the kind which gives birth to such disturbing fancies. And," for the first time she faced the girl squarely, "you look very tired. It is mainly our custom to rest during the early afternoon. I will have Sukie bring something light and tasty for you and then I would advise you to take such a rest."

"But Molly—" Persis was torn between her own fatigue and her promise.

"I shall get my darning, Miss Rooke, and sit right here. It is cool with the sea breeze coming in. And you may rest assured I shall call you if anything occurs which needs your presence."

There was such authority in that it was plainly a dismissal. To counter it might well awaken some suspicion. Reluctantly, Persis agreed. It was true that Molly seemed to be resting now without any unpleasant effects. But she stood by the bed watching her narrowly until Mrs. Pryor returned with a large drawstring bag. The housekeeper drew the chair a little closer to the window and settled herself as if perfectly willing to spend some time there.

Back in her own chamber Persis discovered that Sukie—or someone—had indeed left a covered tray on the bureau top. And after she had stowed the portfolio under her pillow, much as Molly had tucked the Bible she believed would keep her from evil, Persis lifted the napkin, realizing she was indeed very hungry.

There were some slices of cold roast chicken, cut a little thin, to be sure, but still enough. Also a plate of bread and butter with a small side dish of the jam made from some of the exotic fruit Dr. Veering
178

brought from Verde Key for Mrs. Pryor to experiment with, and a custard, firm and lightly browned on top—just the way which would satisfy the stomach. There was also a small jug from which Persis poured what seemed to be a fruit drink.

She ate hungrily, but drank more sparingly, for she found the slightly strange taste of the liquid not quite to her liking. Perhaps the sweetness of the custard made it seem a little bitter. For the rest, she finished most of what had been provided.

Though Persis was sure she could not sleep, not with her mind invaded by all those unanswered questions, she did pull the upper coverlet back on the bed, take off her dress and her slippers, and stretch out fully expecting to now be able to think things through calmly and rationally.

The bed appeared unusually soft and pleasant. She closed her eyes and relaxed without realizing until she did so how tense she had been for hours. So soft a bed—it was like resting on a cloud—a big, drifting billow of cloud—far above the earth and all its problems.

Just to rest so was wonderful—wonderful—wonder—

13

Persis awoke slowly, reluctantly. Around her the room was dusky. How long had she been asleep? Memory filtered back into her mind. At least this rest had not been plagued by dreams. Or if they had come she could not remember them—for which she was very thankful.

But—

As she sat up she was aware that her right hand was closed about something. Persis looked down. And the dim light of the room was not dull enough to hide what she held. The false fan!

She dropped it quickly as if the very touch of the carved and jewel-inlaid wood burned her fingers. Who—?

The drawer where she had hidden it was closed this

time—she could be sure of that even through the gloom. She stared back down at that—that *impossible* thing.

However this time—Persis could not understand what moved in her. She did not will the action certainly, but her hand went out, to close once more about the pseudo-fan. And also, without any conscious desire for such action, she gave the slight turn which freed the blade, drew it forth.

The distaste, even horror, she had for that eerie weapon no longer possessed her. Instead—instead she felt a desire to keep it close to her—that it was a promise of safety for her against formless, nameless evil.

Fancies—imagination—! Persis stared about the very ordinary room. There was nothing here, nothing at all to suggest danger. Yet her breath was coming faster, the palms of her hands were sticky wet; so that she put down the dagger to wipe them back and forth across the sheet.

There was an odd metalic taste in her mouth—like the lingering bite of that drink she had not completely finished. How long had she been lying there? It had not been just an afternoon nap to so hold her. Surely the hour was well into twilight.

There were—forces—

Persis looked around her, studying each portion of the shadowed room. For all her call upon sensible thinking and calm, she could not lose that feeling of impending trouble.

Now, turning a little, she thrust her hand under her pillow, seeking the portfolio. That was— Persis snatched up the two pillows, looked upon the spread of sheet. That was gone!

Pushed off on the floor during some restlessness on her part while asleep? The girl struggled off the bed to

181

look first on one side and then the other. Striking the tinderbox, she lit the candle and got down on her knees, lifting the fall of covers, draping back the netting, to see under the bed. There was nothing there.

Persis tried to think. Who knew she had taken the portfolio back from Molly? Mrs. Pryor had certainly seen her carry it from the room. But she could conceive of no interest the housekeeper would have in it. Unless she was acting for someone else—

Though the room still held the enervating and muggy heat of the day, and no breeze stirred through the open windows, Persis shivered. She was cold—cold with a chill which was born inside her and not reaching her from without.

And the house—there seemed to her an unnatural quiet in this room—as if something waited—

She wanted company, she had to have it—now!

But she moved jerkily, as if her body had less courage than her will, must be driven into action by determination. This time she was going straight to Captain Leverett. *This* was no dream, but the reality of a loss which might be bitter for her.

Setting down the candle she hastily put on her dress, thrust her feet into her slippers. Then, as if moved by something outside herself, she fitted the hidden blade back into the mock fan and that she hid away down the front of her bodice, feeling the dig of it between her stays and her skin. Never in her life had she known a need to lay hand on any weapon with the thought of protecting herself. Now—

She had done this once before—? No, she had not! But still haunting her there came a fleeting memory of such a need and that this very hidden blade had provided safety.

The cold continued to lap her around as Persis took

up the candle and went to the door. Opening that a crack, the girl listened. The utter silence which enfolded her was not natural. And this was no dream.

But it took all the will she could summon to make her open that door wider, venture into the hall, where the tiny glow of her single candle was nearly eclipsed by the growing dark. Again she paused to listen. Not even those creaks which were a part of the house sounded now. It was far too quiet.

She pushed away from the wall, crossed the strip of carpet to Captain Leverett's door. Again it required a vast amount of will to raise her hand, rap on the surface. While that rap seemed to echo and re-echo hollowly up and down.

Persis bit down on her lower lip. She—she had to see, to talk to someone! She had to!

Turning her head toward the stairs she could perceive no glimmer of light below. Though at this hour the lamp in the hall, other candles and lamps should have been, according to routine, burning enough to make the stairway clearly visible.

Once more she rapped. But there was not a single murmur of voice from within. Because she could not stand this eerie feeling of disaster any longer, Persis tried the latch. That gave easily under her hand, the door itself swung open as if in invitation.

But the chamber beyond was utterly dark. Which was wrong. Even if Captain Leverett had been asleep there should have been a well-shaded nightlight such as had burned all through his illness. With a catch of breath Persis took one step and then another, holding out her candle to illumine the bed.

She blinked; it took her a second or two to realize that was empty. The curtains of net were pushed back on one side; she could still see the impression of a body

183

against the heaped pillows which had kept the injured shoulder protected. But—Crewe Leverett was gone!

Persis was sure of that before she made the rounds of the room. And she believed that only some dire emergency would have taken him from his bed. Dr. Veering had warned him, in her own hearing, against any exertion which might again throw out the shoulder.

She turned and ran. Lydia's room was next. She pounded on that door. The very force of her fist against those panels sent it flying open as if it had never been latched at all. There was no one there. Somehow she had not really expected to find the other girl.

The feeling that danger crept in this house so tightened her throat Persis could not have cried out any name no matter how much she wanted to. As she moved she felt giddy, so she had to stand with one hand braced against the wall for a moment or two to steady herself.

Molly—and Mrs. Pryor!

Back she went, wavering a little, to the second staircase. She climbed, not as fast as she wanted to, but as swiftly as her increasing light-headedness would allow, holding the candle with one hand and the narrow banister with the other.

This time she did not rap at the door she sought. She dreaded the sound of that hollow noise, just as she tried to hold up her full skirts so that they would not brush the carpet and betray her passing. Betray her to who—or *what*?

Once more she looked into darkness, but this time she heard heavy breathing. Her relief was so great she could have cried out, save that same inner need for silence kept her gagged.

Molly lay on the bed. And apparently the maid still slept. But—Persis' candle revealed something else. Mrs. Pryor still sat in the chair. Only her capped head had fallen forward so that her full chin rested on her breast, and she was snoring also. A stocking with a needle still thrust into it lay under one hand. The other had fallen limply to her side. As Molly's, her face was flushed, her mouth a little open to let the breath whistle in and out.

"Mrs. Pryor!" Persis hurried to the housekeeper's side, dropping her hand on the woman's shoulder. As she had done to awaken Molly out of the nightmare, she shook her gently. But somehow she already knew that Mrs. Pryor was in no natural sleep.

And, when the stout body nearly toppled from the chair, Persis was forced to set down the candle and re-settle the housekeeper as comfortably as she could. Her charge did not even mutter in answer, and Persis had no idea as to how to rouse her.

She went to Molly. Again unconsciousness defeated her. While the coldness within her grew. This was no illness, the girl began to believe—rather it was planned. Had they been drugged? That queer taste of the drink which still lingered somehow in her own mouth—but she had swallowed very little of that. She looked around for any evidence that Mrs. Pryor or Molly had been served such—but there was nothing but water in the carafe on the bed table.

Shubal—Without much hope, Persis went to the next chamber. She was not surprised to find the old man sleeping as heavily as the other two. But why—?

She could find no answer to what seemed to her the strangest happening in this house. Lydia and the Captain were gone, these three so deeply asleep she could not hope to rouse them. What had happened?

It took all her courage to move toward the staircase once more. Every few steps she paused to listen. The silence was like the dark, it fed her imagination—too well. She dared not lose control, she dared not!

Step by hesitant step she went down into the hall onto which her own chamber opened. The doors of both the Captain's and Lydia's rooms were wide open as she had left them, and she hurried by what seemed like caverns of darkness, to descend once more.

The outer door onto the veranda was closed and there was no light—not anywhere. Irresolute, Persis paused—she needed more than just a single candle which flickered now and then to threaten her with complete dark. She lit the lamp standing on the table in the front hallway. It was more awkward to carry, but the wider glow from it was heartening.

Now hesitatingly she began a systematic search of the rooms, only to discover dark emptiness. The drawing room with its wealth of salvaged luxury, the dining room—its table bare of any sign that anyone had eaten here—the small room which she knew Captain Leverett kept as his office.

It was when she stood in the doorway of that, holding the lamp high enough so that the light would reach as far as possible, that she saw what fed her fear.

There was a strongbox pulled to the middle of the floor, its lid thrown open on emptiness. And on the desk, papers had been swept from pigeonholes so that some had shifted to the floor. Robbery!

But such a suggestion did not fit somehow, or at least she was missing some important fact. Robbery on an island controlled by Captain Leverett—with no escape possible—that would be the act of a madman. But—where was Captain Leverett? Her heart gave a quick, hard beat.

Suppose he had heard—suppose in his one-armed condition, weakened by his ordeal, he had struggled out of bed and confronted the invader? What would—? Persis refused to allow her imagination looser rein.

Robbery here—and the portfolio gone—the drugging of the household—or those she had so far found—someone had known a great deal—had dared much. And only one person came to mind—Ralph Grillon!

With Lydia also gone—

But how *could* she have agreed to the despoiling of her own brother? Lydia might be angry with Crewe for his interference in her life, but Persis could not readily believe that a sister could so betray a brother. Unless Ralph had far more influence over her than they had even guessed. But why then had he tried to use her, Persis, to reach Lydia?

She closed the door of the office firmly and moved toward the kitchen quarters. Mam Rose, Sukie, the other maids—if none of them were there—then she must find her way to the hotel and rouse the men there. Even to be able to plan that act heartened her.

Persis pushed open the kitchen door. Here there was light, for a fire burned low. But no sign of those she sought. Except—

The girl froze. Something moved on the hearth, uncoiling as might a serpent. A head was raised and eyes caught and held hers in a straight gaze.

Askra!

The Indian woman was not wearing her mask. But she moved deliberately as if she knew that her will would keep Persis exactly where she was.

Slowly Askra raised an arm which was nearly stick thin, the fingers at the end of it seeming like roots pulled unwillingly from the soil. She made a gesture between them, not beckoning Persis to her, but rather as if some ritual existed in their night meeting.

187

Then Askra spoke.

"The old ways—what think you of the old ways, white skin?" She held her head a little to one side as if she were indeed a bird of prey, her heavy nose a beak poised to strike.

"What old ways?" Somehow Persis was able to summon up her courage to the point she could ask that question. But within she understood—that dream! Only how could this old woman know what she had dreamed?

Askra did not even answer that question. Her contemptuous eyes said Persis knew, that she would force the girl to admit that knowledge.

"Sacred place, a long time the gods breathed here," Askra continued. "Then the gods turned away their faces; they sent wild ones who were not of the People. And those slew until the blood colored the ground, the sea. But no good came to them of that killing—for the gods looked not to them afterward. Those answered only to us—us of the People!" She balled her fist to strike at her flat chest. "I can still call the gods and those eaters of snakes know it! I can summon up the call. When I so do those who have eyes and ears open in their dreams—they can see and hear. Even as you did."

Now she advanced a step or two. "You have that in you which answers to old troubles, ancient ways. Were you of the blood—then I would open the knowledge to you. But you are not of the People—therefore that which should be a gift for you is rather a burden heavy to bear. You shall dream, but that dreaming you cannot control."

"I will not—!" Again Persis pushed her courage to
188

what seemed to her to be the highest point she could reach.

"You cannot stop it." There was malicious satisfaction in the old woman's eyes, the girl thought. As if Askra could and would use terrifying dreams as weapons against those of that other race who had supplanted her people. But Persis needed information, not warnings.

"Where are they all—the Captain—Lydia—?" She was surprised, pleased that she could insert such a fierce note into her demand.

Askra's deep-set eyes no longer held her pinned; rather it was as if the Indian woman herself was momentarily at a loss.

"There has been evil walking here." Again she made one of those gestures which had meaning for her if not for Persis. "I heard—I came—He who has been a friend is in danger."

Inspiration moved the girl to a quick question:

"Captain Leverett?"

The Indian witch produced from within her blouse a small bag of leather thonged together, from which dangled the stubs of worn feathers, a loop of small shells pierced into beads. This she held between palms pressed closely together, raised level to her mouth as she blew upon it, and murmured in so low a whisper that Persis could make out only the faintest of sounds.

"What has happened to Captain Leverett?" Persis demanded again—louder, in an attempt to break through the other's preoccupation, get some sensible answer.

Askra eyed her over that bag. But any emotion in her dark eyes was unreadable. Then she said:

"He will die."

189

The words were so baldly spoken and with such finality that, for a long second, they did not even make an impression on Persis. Then the lamp wavered in her hand.

"What do you mean!" She advanced threateningly on the woman as she would not have done a moment or so earlier. It was plain Askra knew something. "What has happened here?"

"His enemy came and found doors opened for him. There are always those who believe lies, because they desire to do so. They have taken him because they want what he has—"

"Indians!" Persis remembered the warnings from the cutter. But surely Indians would not have left them—she, Mrs. Pryor, the servants sleeping—they would not—

"Those!" Askra's return was scornful. "They do not dare to beach their canoes on this land. They know that I have the calling of the Old Ones and that even now I can bring their ending. No, it is among his own household that he should have searched for danger. Yet to it he was as blind as the Great Chief long ago when he was warned that the younger wife, taken from the outlanders—the evil ones—had not been cleansed of *their* darkness. Even as she betrayed her lord, so has the Captain been betrayed."

Askra's words fell into a sing-song pattern and she swayed back and forth, the bag now clasped tightly against her breasts. "Ahhh—men are ever foolish when they look upon a woman, deeming that because she has perhaps less strength of arm than they possess she is not to be feared. The Great Chief died of his folly and after him, there was death here again, and by a woman's hand, so that those who took this land held no profit from it. You carry death—it lies now between your breasts. I, Askra, can smell it. Old death, old blood. And that would not have come into your hand had you not summoned it."

Persis shrank back until one of her heels scraped against the bottom of the three steps leading to the kitchen. She was fast losing any command of the situation she might have once had. This old woman with her compelling eyes, her measured speech, was such a potent force as made even the awe-inspiring dignity of Uncle Augustin seem the strutting of some schoolboy.

Death between her breasts—the fan? Had Askra crept above then to plant the noxious thing between her hand as she slept?

"She was strong, was the Spanish woman," the Indian continued, "strong in her hate—in that she might have been one of the Old Ones. We knew how to hate—how to use cunning against our enemies. Aye—we knew—until we were betrayed and the gods turned their faces from us because we had become such weak tools for their use. But she—perhaps the gods looked upon her and made her again their hands and feet upon the earth. The captain of the sea sharks she destroyed, shedding blood on this sacred mount, even as was proper. Then the sea she sought herself. But with their chief dead those others were easy meat for the avengers. Yes, *she* knew. And you know—white skin. If you had not a fraction of the true sight you would not stand here now, her treasure warm against your body. The pattern changes in years reckoned by men, not the gods, to whom the seasons are but beads they slip easily between their fingers, letting this and that one fall when they tire of it. Now it is time for the pattern to change again.

"I am Askra." She held her head proud and high. "Once those of my blood spoke to chiefs saying do this, do that. And what we ordered and desired was so done. For we had the power of the gods warm and rich in us. The white men came, slaying, breaking down our sacred place—putting slave chains on those who did not cleanly die. And those who escaped, who kept the old gods in their hearts and minds, fled—became wanderers and outcasts.

"But it was given to me that I should return and what small power remained here, that I can summon—if only in dreams. You have dreamed, daughter of strangers—" She came forward until her face was only inches away from Persis. "There is that in you which entered into my dream, just as there is that in you which summoned the knife of vengeance. You cannot escape either—for that is the way of your inner spirit. Is that not so?"

Persis opened her lips to deny vehemently what she only half-understood. But it was as if another within her had taken command, a hidden self she had never realized shared her body, and who was now moving into the open.

"It—it is so—!" The denial she longed to give she could not utter.

Askra nodded. "This is not of my gods, white woman. Therefore, it cannot by my undertaking. What you do now you must do for yourself. There is evil to be faced, and perhaps the death shadow lies at the end of it. But if you seek him in truth, then the road is open to you."

Persis moistened her lips. She could only sort out of this weird harangue that Askra did know where Crewe Leverett was and that he also lay in danger. She owed him her life—yet that was not entirely why she must act to aid him if she could. There was the warmth of the fan against her body; it seemed to build in her a
192

desperate resolution she never realized she possessed—at least to this degree. She returned to her first question:

"Where is Captain Leverett?"

Askra moved back, toward the hearth, leaving the floor before her clear.

"They have taken him down," she detached one hand from her bag and pointed, the nail on her forefinger long and near black, toward the floor under their feet.

The cistern! Slowly Persis moved forward, setting the lamp on the long table, stooping to jerk away the rug which usually covered the trapdoor. What was she going to do? It would be better to rouse the men at the hotel—have them handle this.

As she leaned forward without consciously making any decision, her hand curled about the ring to raise that barrier. The light suddenly went out. Startled, she looked over her hunched shoulder. The Indian woman, her figure only partly revealed by the fire light, had blown out the candle flame.

"Would you," she asked in what sounded to Persis like a superior tone she was quick to resent, "allow them to know that you've come?" Then she moved to join Persis, gathering up the braided strip of carpet and making of it a screen to be held between the dying light of the fire and the trapdoor.

Reaching out with her other hand, she twitched at the girl's full skirt, the petticoats under it.

"These are not good in water, white woman. Best you shed them first."

Persis fumbled at buttons and ties, stepping out of muslin skirt, of the two petticoats under. Now she wore only drawers, her chemise, stays, for she laid aside, too, the waist with all its bows, laces, and ruffles.

Feeling outrageously bare of body, she lifted the trap-door, straining at its weight, for Askra made no move to help her. Why she was doing this unbelievable thing she could not have said, it was as if she were caught in another dream and there was no way out—she must endure it until the end.

14

It was not entirely dark below. For, when her eyes adjusted after the extinguishing of the lamp, Persis could see a faint radiance on the waters. Also there came the murmur of voices. She crouched on her knees. The visibility was strictly limited from where she now was, but she had no intent of descending recklessly until she could better know what was going on in this dark, smelling of the wash of lapping water.

Though Persis strained her ears she could not catch a single clear word, only the rise and fall of a voice which she thought was that of a man. Narrowly she surveyed the waters below. They washed a little upon that ledge where trails of moisture showed higher reach of the flood. But she was certain that the lamp or lantern which gave so faint a light did not rest on that.

How much could she believe Askra? Suppose she was to venture down into this watery cavern, only to have the Indian witch slam the trapdoor on her, trapping her. Persis' hands twitched. She doubted her own courage at this moment. To be down there in the dark —with no one but Askra knowing where she was—

Still that same resolve which did not seem a part of the Persis Rooke she thought she knew—that entered into her from the fan dagger. She was conscious of that strange weapon with every move she made, as it impressed its weight and shape, not only physically, but emotionally, against her.

The sound of the voice continued; it might have been a distorted echo from a greater distance. Persis struggled to remember what she had seen on her one trip below—the bathing place. Beyond it the cistern, and also the strange escape tunnel, leading, alongside the turtle pen, out into the canal.

Believing that she was utterly foolish in what she was about to do, but somehow compelled to act, Persis raised her head and once more looked directly at Askra.

"There are the men at the hotel," she said. "If we call them—"

Askra's mouth spread into a wide, malicious grin. With one long-nailed finger she drew a line across her own scraggy throat.

"And before they reach here—what if death comes first? Does white skin live with fear so close to her that it is a cloak she cannot shed?"

She held her head a little on one side, watching Persis with those compelling eyes. "The gods do not

196

try to govern time—it means nothing to them. Only men live by its bindings."

Persis drew upon all her resolution. She wondered why Askra herself had done nothing to help Crewe Leverett, if the Captain was indeed in danger.

"I serve only the gods—" The Indian woman straightened to her full height. "Only by their commands must I act. They care nothing for a white skin. Such overthrew their temples, drove forth those who believed in them. If I stepped aside from the appointed path, then would I be powerless—"

That the woman believed in what she said Persis understood. But Askra was continuing:

"What I could do, that I have done. Are you not here? For in all this house you were the only one to answer such summoning as I might use." Once more she raised her hands to sketch a deliberate gesture in the air, one which Persis could not understand. "You have seen, you feel. Those who have gone can, in a little, work through you. But that is all I can give you, white skin."

Persis realized that she was nodding as if in agreement. Common sense meant going for help. But she was committed, she realized now, to something the common sense in which she had been drilled all her life could neither answer nor understand. She was forced to do this— and, at the back of her mind, lurked always that strange and eerie feeling that she was under some command, just as Askra averred she herself was. There was no escape now.

The girl swung onto the ladder, the wood under her hands felt wet and beslimed, so she hated the touch of it. But she continued to descend step by hesitating step. When she reached the ledge and faced around she saw that the light came from the left, glimmering dimly from the old escape tunnel.

There was no one in sight and Persis quickly moved back against the wall, so her shoulder scraped along it as that compulsion sent her stumbling ahead toward the tunnel entrance.

"—snug as a weevil in a biscuit."

The words came out of nowhere loud enough for her to distinguish them at last. While the tone was one of malicious amusement.

"Don't fret yourself about him, m'dear. We've got what we need, and before they wake up and start hunting we shall be safe. Look at him now—the great Captain Leverett tied up like a prime hog on the way to market!"

"Please, Ralph—we should leave—I don't know how long they'll sleep—"

Lydia! Much of the habitual assurance was gone out of the girl's voice. She sounded on the verge of tears.

"Oh, they'll take a time even after they wake to find their lord and master. And what we've got right here, girl, will end all our problems. I did not think Leverett was such a fool to keep so much cash in hand. But once we're safely married, m'dear, he daren't raise any squeak about it, now can he—seeing as how this we can claim as your marriage portion."

"But that other thing—the portfolio?"

"Don't you fret yourself 'bout that either, m'dear. That's maybe worth more than what we found in the strongbox—to the right people. We might go to Paris, love—what would you say to that? You've been talking how you want to see the world—well, we've got the key to do that right here now."

"But Persis—"

"Persis Rooke, m'dear, hasn't the faintest hope of getting what that old fool dragged himself down here to grab. A silly woman made a silly will. And the breaking of that, aided by the disappearance of these papers, that is as easy as dipping your hand in this water and flipping off the drops. Kind of him—and her—to keep it all in hand, making the lifting so easy. It's a duty really, an honest duty to see that will broken. These high and mighty Rookes had it in for Amos. But, you'll notice, they weren't so high and mighty that they did not come nosing around for what was never theirs in the first place!"

There was no amusement in his voice now. Instinctively Persis' hand went to the fan case. Light as Ralph Grillon's tone remained, there was that in it which added to the cold gnawing in her ever since she had awakened in that seemingly deserted house.

"All right, girl, we're heading out. Rest well, friend—" There was a faint splashing sound and then Lydia cried out:

"Don't, Ralph, you nearly upset the canoe then! Stop it!"

"Did you ever think, Lydia, what might happen if this brother of yours was to die? You'd be a pretty important heiress, wouldn't you? Here—what are you doing, you little fool!"

"You needn't try to grab me, Ralph. I know you're only funning. But you leave Crewe alone. We got what we want—stop playing games, I don't like it!"

Ralph Grillon laughed. "All right, m'love, you have the saying of it. I'm not a greedy man, leastways not *too* greedy. We've done well enough over this night's work. Get along into the other dugout now and mind you keep well down. I'll take us out. Wearing this hat and all they'll think me that old red witch Crewe makes a house pet of. We'll be able to get to the south of the island and set up the flares then."

"What if those are seen, Ralph?"

"They won't be. I found a place where the rocks cut off the light except seaward. Now—move!"

"What if they find Crewe before your boat comes?"

"No chance of that. I've planned this well, m'dear, very well. It's my big chance—yours, too, of course. Think about Paris, Lydia, and lie still, and all is going to be just as I promised."

Persis heard noises which she thought came from paddles slipped into the water and out again. The light dimmed and went out. She pushed one fist hard to her mouth. The ledge ended here except for a narrow ridge which in the dark she could not see. To venture along that, slime encrusted as it was, single footed—she could not. But she had to!

In the end she felt her way by inches, hunching along rather in a froglike position, sweeping one guiding hand in the water. She had guessed from Ralph's words that Crewe had been left helpless in a dugout. But was that moored, or was it drifting free away from her?

Then she barked her knuckles against wood so hard that the blow made her gasp with pain. She felt along what she had discovered—the edge of a canoe, side against the very narrow ledge on which she crouched. But—there was water inside it, too!

With horror Persis plunged her throbbing hand deeper, felt sodden cloth, a body under it. Ralph—Ralph must have known that the dugout would fill—that his victim had been left to drown!

With her other hand the girl jerked free the blade of the false fan, feeling along the wet body with her right. Her fingers met a tangle of wet rope. Not knowing how much time she had, she sawed away at that with the dagger edge. Was Crewe's head underwater—could he have already drowned?

The body was quiet, cold. But suddenly there was movement, an upflung arm nearly sent her spinning from her perch.

"Please," she found her voice at that sign of life, "lie still until I can get you free."

But the arm moved away from her and a moment later there came a hoarse, croaked whisper as if from a throat which had not been recently in use.

"This craft is going to settle in a minute. Get me a handhold—"

Persis waved her hand through the dark, found and caught at a well-muscled forearm which she drew toward her.

"The ridge here—it's very narrow—" she cautioned.

"I know. But just let me hold on. I think that I can kick off the rope now."

Splashing sounds suggested that he was doing just that. Then she heard what could only be a sigh of relief.

"That's done. But with this shoulder I can't pull myself up—we'll have to go out the canal entrance."

"I can get back—find help—" Persis resheathed the dagger, and got to her feet.

"I'm afraid," though there was no note of fear in his voice when he answered her, "that I can't hold out that long. If we can swing the dugout over, it may float and support me down to the outside. Only trouble is that I do not think Grillon will be ready to leave until he has made very sure of me."

"But Lydia would never let him—" Persis began in protest.

The sound out of the dark which answered that

might have been a laugh but it was far from expressing any amusement.

"Lydia will soon discover that she is nothing whatever to Ralph Grillon once she has served his purpose. He may make some pretense of a plausible story to appease her, say that the dugout had a leak he did not realize. But he wants me dead just as much as if he faced me with a primed pistol in his hand!"

Persis knew, with a growing fear, that she could not hope to support Crewe in any climb out of the water. She simply did not have the strength. Guiding his good hand to the edge, she could feel the tension of the grip as his fingers closed upon the slippery stone there.

"Now if you can turn over the dugout," he ordered. His tone was as even as if he had asked her to draw a curtain or light a candle. Persis knelt, her hands running along the side of the rough native craft. It was hardly above water now. Obediently she jerked and exerted what strength she might from such a cramped position. The wood of the side she held was slippery so she could not get a good continuing hold on it, but still she tugged almost wildly.

The splashing her efforts caused sounded very loud to her. She could only hope that Ralph was well enough away not to hear them.

"He won't trust entirely to this little trap," Crewe spoke out of the dark in that same meditative fashion, as if he were an onlooker and not the victim of this attempt at long-distance murder. "He can't be sure he has succeeded until he knows I *am* dead."

Persis felt a rising anger, not at Ralph Grillon, not yet, nor at Crewe, but at the unwieldy craft which stubbornly resisted her efforts to master it. She gave a last fierce tug, unmindful of her own precarious perch, and, by some miracle, the edge of the waterlogged craft she pulled moved at last. There was a great splash. At the price of two torn nails and a hand scraped raw she had made the dugout turn bottom up. Her fingers touched two holes in the wet surface bobbing there.

"It's over," she said, with a catch of her breath. "But won't it sink now anyway? There are two holes—at least—cut in it."

"Perhaps." Crewe Leverett did not sound alarmed. "But I think it will support me to the turtle pen. There are the stakes set upright there, a better chance to wedge somehow with my head above water—unless the tide—"

Persis nursed her scraped hand against her breast. "The tide!" She had not thought of that. And the very mention of the turtle pen made her flesh crawl.

"Why can't you hold on to the dugout and let me pull that back to the house pool? Then I can get the men—"

Again Crewe laughed until she hated the hollow echo of that sound.

"Do not underrate Grillon," he returned. "He will have the house watched. Do you think that you would be allowed to reach the quarters?"

"Askra is there—in the kitchen. She was the one who told me they were doing this thing—"

"Askra will not lift a hand to help. Why should she? To her all our race are interlopers and murderers. She lives in a past which is hers alone and will not be dragged out of it. And I cannot climb that ladder with one hand."

"Then how did you get down?" Persis was reluctant to surrender what she believed was the most sensible solution to their difficulties.

"Oh, they lowered me by ropes, I think. I'm not too

clear-minded about that. Seems that Lydia was very busy today. Concocting a potion which reduced everyone to a state in which they could be easily handled if the need arose. The little fool! I ought to let her go, she'll discover soon enough that Grillon is not the hero she dreams of. He's filled her with his own version of affairs and promised her the moon, with all the nearer stars thrown in. And she's weakminded enough to believe him!" That was bitter.

"She would not let him hurt you," Persis protested. "I heard her—"

"Just showing a trace of squeamishness when it is too late to matter," Crewe returned. "But now—if you can edge the canoe nearer—"

"It's slippery, you can't hold on to it! Wait—"

Before she had time to fear what she knew must be done Persis lowered her own body from the ridge, throwing her left arm across the upturned canoe. The dugout bobbed and sank, spattering water into her face. But it did not go entirely to the bottom, and she found that it did offer support enough so that her head and the top of her shoulders were above water.

"What are you doing?" Crewe Leverett demanded harshly.

"Hold on." She began to kick her feet slowly, edge the damaged craft along so she could hear it grate against the side of the wall. Then, to her surprise and growing confidence, she discovered her clumsy efforts did work! She could force the nearly waterlogged boat closer to where she knew the Captain clung.

"I'm moving the canoe toward you," she explained. "And you're right, it will support us—"

"*Us!*" The word broke from him with the urgency of a pistol shot.

"Us," she repeated firmly. "You cannot manage

with one arm—it is foolish to even think of trying so. Now—tell me when—"

Then came a bump and a bitten-off exclamation. Either the bow or the stern of the dugout had struck him.

"Can you get your good arm across it now?"

She heard splashing, mutters, and then the dugout sank deeper into the water, so that wavelets washed about her neck. But at least her head was still above water.

"Are you all right?" she cried out with foreboding.

"Well enough. But you—get out of this!"

"No." All Persis' stubborn determination built into that one-word denial. "You can't manage alone and you know it. How far is the turtle pen?"

"Not too far." He at least made no more open protests. They advanced at a snail's pace. By a slightly swifter motion of the unwieldy support under them Persis judged that the Captain was also using his feet to help propel the half-sunken craft along the way. Suddenly Persis felt a self-confidence she had seldom tasted in her life. *She* had done this—she was succeeding. She spat out water which washed unexpectedly into her face, concentrated on keeping their support moving, nudging its way along the wall of the tunnel.

Then she felt a difference in the obstruction which had been their guide so far. Daring to loose one hand from a desperate hold across the dugout, she felt out, to discover that there were stakes here, between which the water flowed in and out.

The pen! She tried not to think of those creatures moving sluggishly beyond that barrier. A moment later Crewe spoke.

"You've found it."

But Persis, exploring farther by touch, was afraid.

205

The stakes, stout as they were, were also slimed. Certainly Crewe could not hold on here for any length of time and the openings between were too narrow to allow him, she was certain, to squeeze himself amongst them for support. Not with his broken shoulder.

"You can't hold on here," she said flatly. "Any more than you could back there."

"I don't intend to," he answered coolly. "We shall have to go through the pen—"

"Through it!" She felt like shuddering, but feared that even such a slight reaction would jeopardize their frail support.

"If Ralph has left any guards, and I do not think he is stupid enough to overlook that, they will expect us in the canal where the escape route comes out. Our only chance is to go through the pen and hope to reach the mound to the north."

Persis set her teeth. She had no idea of what one of the giant turtles she had seen might do to a soft-skinned invader of their prison. But if this was their only chance—

"Feel along the stake wall. It has been over a year since that was renewed," Crewe continued. "There ought to be at least one stake which is rotting. I have had to replace two or three such every season since this was built."

Persis moved very cautiously, keeping one hand on the dugout. The fingers of the other she ran around the stakes at a little below water level. To her they all seemed iron fast and completely firm. One—two—three—four—five—at the sixth she could not be sure. Had her now-broken nails scraped wood which was a little spongy? She tried to keep her mind entirely off what lay beyond. If Crewe said this was the only way, then it was. At that moment she was not even aware that she was accepting his pronouncement without question.

"Find one?" He did not even sound impatient, yet there was a note in his voice which bothered her. She began to wonder if he was tiring she *must* find the way out! If Crewe collapsed here—with all her strength and determination she could not help him then.

Persis felt for the fan dagger. Using only the one hand she drove it point deep, gouging again and again at the stake which had seemed the least resistant. And, after an initial resistance, the wood was giving!

She dug away at it feverishly. The water was washing more and more into her face so she had to strain her neck muscles in order to be able to breathe. Still she battled on. Then holding the dagger in her other hand she explored what she had done. The stake *was* whittled down.

"One of them—I cut at it—" she said.

But there still remained a tough core she could not break.

"Hold very still," Crewe's voice was somehow heartening. "I am going to move up, so you move back. I will go one small space at a time. One—"

Persis had sheathed the dagger again. Now she edged a short distance down the dugout. A moment later that heaved under her. She held on with both hands praying that it was not going to completely sink and fail them. Crewe was moving up its length toward the stakes.

"Two—" Again at this count Persis changed position, steadied herself against the resulting bobbing as Crewe advanced. They had then to wait between such changes of position before they dared to try again.

"Three—" Persis spat out the water which washed suddenly against her lips. And this time she was sure that Crewe's countermove would sink their own support.

She heard a grunt through the dark and at first envisioned one of the turtles waiting just beyond. Then the canoe rocked perilously again. Her hands slipped so that she nearly screamed aloud in her horror of being flung off that very precarious support. There was another sound, a cracking, and then Crewe's voice:

"It's open. But we can't get the dugout through!"

"Then how—? She could not swim, nor, she was sure, could Crewe, not with his shoulder encased in the heaviest bandages Dr. Veering could devise and his left arm strapped to his chest.

"Work your way back to me." She almost resented that he sounded so controlled, so sure of himself. "Then hold on to the stakes. The pool is not too deep—and we have no choice."

So once more, inch by inch, she drew herself along the length of the dugout. Only this time it rode higher and she guessed that Crewe had taken to the stakes for support. Then, reaching out, her hand closed once more on sodden cloth with strong, well-muscled flesh under it.

"Good enough. The stakes are here." She groped out blindly with one hand, her other one still clinging to Crewe as if not even death now could drag her from that hold. And he was somehow moving ahead, drawing her with him.

The turtles! In her mind she cringed, waited for some paralyzing snap upon arm or leg. But, though she could pick up some odd splashing sounds, those
208

were not near. Perhaps their own presence frightened the sea monsters as badly as they did her.

She floundered in the water and there was a thick, unpleasant smell in the place. But ahead—yes there was a lighting of the heavy darkness which had encased them since Grillon and Lydia had left. Did that mean they were near the outer world at last?

"Along the wall," Crewe's voice, still calm and quiet, steadied her. Once more her outflung hand hit hard against what could be a rocky surface. But there were fingerholds there; she could catch them.

"You—your shoulder—"

"With three good hands we can manage. It is not far. Keep moving!"

Persis obeyed, heading for that lighter strip in the dark.

15

Crewe had said it was not far; to Persis the distance stretched through time and space like a full-day's journey. Her whole body ached with the effort she put out. At each advance, drawing herself along that inner wall of the pen, she paused to reach back and tighten her hold on her companion. She could hear the whistle of his breath, as if he were straining his own powers to the uppermost. Yet they did not speak, saving all their energy for what must be done.

Once she nearly screamed, feeling the touch of something else swimming free—certainly one of the captive turtles. But her heart quieted its frantic beat, for the creature must have sheared off again instead of pressing the attack she had feared from the first. Somehow they did continue, though at times her hands slipped vainly down a slimed wall and she had to search for the smallest hold.

Then—

There were more stakes here and beyond them grayish light. She pressed her face against the stakes and caught a glimpse of moon-touched water.

"There is a gate here." Crewe's voice was as measured as ever, but weaker, she was sure of that. "The latch is on the outside. To your left—can you reach it?"

Persis pulled herself from one stake to the next until she could thrust her bruised and scraped arm nearly to the shoulder between two of the stakes. She felt up and down the outside frame of this door until she did indeed find the fastening Crewe mentioned. A pin was wedged in to hold it shut—and the water must have swollen that for her tugging did not move it in the least. Finally she felt once more for the dagger, drew that and chopped at the wedge which might well have been of steel so fixed was it.

Just as she had gouged away at the stake which had let them into the pen, so now did she hack awkwardly at the wedge, prying at it with a spurt of energy which was largely rooted in despair. She needed no warning from Crewe—his strength must have been so tried by the ill usage he had suffered that he could not possibly hold on one-handed for much longer, though his shoulder now rubbed against hers and she knew he gripped one of the door stakes determinedly.

Finally the dagger struck deep into the upper part of the wedge and Persis pulled, with much of her remaining strength. It came free so suddenly that the door of their cage swung open spilling them out into the small lake which washed the mound on three

211

sides. And she clung to the door as her only hope of support.

"Crewe!" Water swirled up into her face, half-smothering her call.

When he did not answer she felt out along the open door. Her hand caught at sodden clothes. He was down! His head was underwater! Why had she never learned to swim? Her shoulders were racked with pain as she tried to lift him. He was giving her no help at all and his dead weight in the water was too much!

In the moonlight she could see the side of the mound not too far away. She had to reach that, drag him with her—she must!

She heard a gasp—and then felt him move a little.

"Crewe—the mound!"

He did not answer but out of the water his head raised, he reached his good hand and she caught at it. There were the rest of the stakes of the pen—they reached to the foot of the mound—if she could work along them—

"Float—" the word was hardly distinguishable. "Turn on back—float—"

He was moving with weak purpose against her hold. And it took her a minute or two to realize what he meant. Then she did not release her grip on his body but, even as she had striven to overturn the dugout, so she fought to get him on his back.

Once that was done she slipped her free arm about his throat, trying to make sure that his head was above water enough for him to breathe, and turned back to the grim task of dragging them both from stave to stave toward land.

Again that seemed an endless task. Her breath came in short gusts which never quite filled her laboring lungs. And she hoped for only one thing, the feel of the thick earth and shells beneath her hands again.

So worn was she with the battle that when her knees struck the shelving of the mound under the water she could not believe at once she had made it. But her hand came down hard against what could only be one of the shells worked into the earth there, and the pain aroused her better than a shout might have done.

Persis turned her head. To the left was the short landing where long ago she had seen Askra moor her dugout (it seemed years ago now), and she knew that she did not have strength enough to climb out of the water onto that refuge. On the other hand, rough as the surface of the mound seemed to be, she had no hope of clambering up that—not with Crewe. But she pushed her head and shoulders up against the earth in spite of the bite of broken shells and pulled Crewe around so his head was well out of water.

What now?

There was that faint path she had seen Askra use on her first coming to Lost Lady. But the steps of that were hardly more than niches gouged out of the earth. Perhaps, after she rested she could attempt to climb those. But she was sure Crewe could not make it. And, were she to leave him here, with the tide rising, it would be the easiest thing in the world for the water to lift him from the mound—give him the death that Ralph Grillon had planned.

"So you are still alive, white skin—"

The wharf was shadowed by the bulk of the mound and the house. Persis could not see anyone crouching there and the sibilance of the voice could almost make one believe that one of the captive turtles had spoken.

"Still—alive—Caller of the Dead—" Crewe's voice,

213

hardly above a whisper, answered while Persis was still bemused with shock.

"The dead do not answer, unless there is reason. Ask your woman what reason they would have."

Persis found her voice, but it was a ragged one. "We don't need riddles. Askra—get us help!"

She heard a low chuckle. "Help? The only help you'll find abroad this night, white skin, is that which will spill the life out of you."

"And you—" Crewe's words were more steady this time, with some of his old authority behind them. "I have dealt with you fairly, Askra—"

"I do not bargain," the unseen witch or priestess replied. "I am Askra, and the gods I serve are far away and long ago."

"Perhaps. But *your* powers are here and now," Crewe continued. "And even in this place and time you are not one without weapons or resources—"

Again came that chuckle. "Because you have opened your house to me, Captain, that does not mean that I am to be commanded by you. There are powers even I cannot summon. But ask your woman—she *knows*! White skin powers are different—"

"I ask nothing of your powers then. But only aid in getting to such footing where I can use my own."

For a long moment (so long a moment that Persis wondered if Askra had slipped away in the gloom), there came no answer to that.

"I do not bargain!" There was a haughty arrogance in that. "The moon calls across the waters and I should be one with my gods. Standing here is an insult to them— But—this much I will do. And make the most of it. Only do I do this because you have not spoken ill of my gods nor forbidden my seeking. And before this night closes you may well wish that I had not helped at all!"

Something flew through the air, fell across both Persis and Crewe as they rested at the foot of the mound. Persis put out her hand to close about a rope.

"For your aid—" Crewe began, but the woman in the dark interrupted him swiftly.

"I do not aid. See me," and her speech changed into a guttural rhythm Persis did not understand. But Crewe had already pulled taut the rope.

"Hold tight, pull up out of the water," he gave orders now, and Persis obeyed, not knowing just how she found that last small thrust of strength. With the rope she could move along the edge of the mound, three quarters of her body now out of the water. Then she came to the small wharf and climbed up on that.

There was no sign of Askra, though she had hoped that the Indian woman would still be there, ready to lend her strength to getting Crewe up also. Persis took a turn around one of the posts with the slack of the rope and began to pull with all the energy she could summon.

When Crewe's head appeared above the edge of the landing she could hardly believe they had done it. But with him at last on the waterwashed boards she collapsed. His outline against the moonlit canal and pond was misshapen because of his tightly bandaged shoulder. And she saw his bare legs protruding beneath the calf-length of his sodden nightshirt. Which made her aware of her own lack of clothing.

"You are all right?" As it had been when he talked with Askra, the Captain's voice had taken on a new authority and assurance. "We're not out of trouble yet, you must understand. Grillon, if he has the sense of a half-wit—and he is a good lot more than that—

may have left a guard here. He certainly was not stupid enough to come ashore alone to carry out this raid, even with Lydia's help—"

Persis tried to listen. But all she could hear now was the swell and ebb of the water about them, punctuated by her own labored breathing.

"Your men—the hotel—" she hazarded a whisper since they were so close together.

"Be sure we'd have trouble reaching either." He did not try to soften anything for her. "Both the big wharf and the hotel must be well watched. When Grillon broke into my strongbox, he had taken the final step that put him outside the law. With me dead he can make a play to take over Lost Lady."

"They took Uncle Augustin's portfolio, too." Persis rested her forehead on her drawn-up knees.

"Its loss would cause a legal tangle, yes, but with the papers your claim would, or should, have a better than even chance." Crewe rose to his knees slowly, as if he must save every fraction of strength.

"But if I don't have them, then what?" Persis asked. She was so tired that she hardly cared one way or another anymore.

She was not even aware at the moment of her partial nudity—her drawers were plastered so tightly to her legs they could well form a second skin, and her chemise was both wet and torn so that only her stays held it in place. But such things did not seem to matter. That the two of them had won alive out of that underground nightmare of waters still had the power to vaguely astound her.

The girl simply huddled where she was, too worn out to try to think even one second ahead. But through that stupor Crewe's voice came again.

"They will be expecting us on the big wharf—"

Persis turned her head a little. The lantern which had always marked that at night was out. In the moon lines were sharply black and white and nothing moved among the barrels and cases piled there.

"Also the warehouse will be guarded—" He could be thinking aloud. "We've got to reach Johnny Mason's—"

The name meant nothing to her. To be out of the water was all that mattered and she was exhausted by the struggle just past. But his hand fell now on her shoulder, warm on her bare skin where one of the rents in the chemise had given freedom to her flesh.

"Can you walk?" The decisiveness had come back to his voice.

Persis swallowed. Certainly Crewe Leverett must be in far worse case than she, yet, now that he was ashore, all his seemingly impatient decisiveness was back in his voice.

"We cannot stay here," he continued. "We must make it up to the servants' quarters."

"How can we?" Her great weariness kept her voice to a whisper.

"There is a path up the mound side—then we skirt the back of the house. I need only rouse Mason—"

Persis made no move. "Go—if you can—"

"No." The grip which had been but a light touch on her shoulder tightened. "Ralph was never so foolhardy as to venture in with only Lydia as his aid. I know he spoke of signaling his ship, but that he does not have others here already, that I do not believe. We must both get under cover—in safety."

"I can't," she returned flatly. Sure of that.

"You can!" he answered with equal determination. "Luckily the moon does not reach here and few use

217

Askra's path. "We'll get up if we have to crawl by inches."

And his pull on her was such that she gave a small, weak moan but somehow tottered to her feet. It seemed that the master of Lost Lady needed no guide whether it was night or not. For he drew her down the wharf toward the rise of the mound. She staggered and wavered, but somehow kept moving, thought she wanted to cry out bitterly as her bare feet now and then pressed the edges of broken shells.

"About here—" Crewe had loosed his hold on her and was feeling the mound where the small wharf ended. "Yes!" There was a quickening in his voice, "There it is. Climb on hands and knees if you will—but keep going. If Grillon's men find you now," he continued with what might have been calculated brutality, "a knock on the head and a toss in the canal will neatly solve all their problems."

Persis could believe him, but even fear was dulled as she felt for those half-lost niches in the wall of the mound. And she went very slowly, marveling a little that he was able to not only locate them in the dark, but drag upon some reserve of strength to pull himself up, one handed as he was.

The house stood, a black blot against the sky, shutting out the moon, offering not the least gleam of a candle or lamp. But they did not climb to the veranda. Instead Crewe lurched to the right, setting a course around the mound. They passed a second corner of the building and found themselves in that wider space at the back where Mrs. Pryor had overseen the stretching of the lines to dry Persis' clothing.

"Just along the causeway now," Crewe murmured. "Mason's cabin is the first in the line of the quarters.

He's canny enough to play scout for us and find out just what is happening."

"Crewe—" Persis fell rather than leaned against a bush. "Crewe—listen!"

In the water-filled ways below she had been always aware of the wavelets, listening in true terror for the splashing of the turtles. Here she could hear the sounds of insects, once or twice a call which might have been that of a night hunting bird.

But suddenly all was still—far too still. As if all the small life natural to this island now crouched hidden, also listening. Her companion *must* be conscious of the same sudden change in the dark world about them.

Then—cold—a chill which had nothing to do with the ordeal she had just been through but one she had experienced before, one which formed inside her to reach outward, gripped her.

There *was* a sound now. One Persis would swear was born of no wind, no rustle of grass, for it continued evenly through the dark. Now she looked for what she knew she would see—those glittering points of light which fluttered back and forth in regular pattern. There was a presence here. Was it as aware of them as they were of it?

Persis stuffed the end of one bruised and torn fist in her mouth to keep from crying out. Between her breasts the sheathed dagger seemed to gather an extra degree of icy power.

Swish—unseen skirts—stiff, wide—proudly worn, moved before them. The flutter of the sparks did not alter rhythm, as if stern pride kept that to the same back and forth movement. Yet—there was no one there—no one Persis could see with her eyes.

She closed them as she had before, and now her other hand tugged frantically to jerk the fan dagger

219

from its hiding place. Was this what that *other* sought—had been seeking for a long, long time?

In her mind, a thought which had never been her own intruded swiftly, easily, claiming kinship in spite of her repulsion. There walked in a half world which was not theirs a dark woman, but one whose skin was white. About her, pride was wrapped like a great cloak or an armor which no ill could force.

She had been a force herself, had that woman. In her way she was as great as Askra. Though she depended upon her natural powers, not upon gods long fled. And she had seen in the end that death was the only price to be paid for some indignities of soul and body. But death not only for herself.

Persis opened her eyes. In her hand the sheathed dagger fan was like a piece of ice, cold, cruel, no longer of her world.

There was no longer any swish of skirts to be heard. But the flutter of the lights continued, back and forth, slowly, languidly, as if to ensorcel those who watched.

Persis took one step forward, her whole being crying out against what she must do but the action forced upon her. She was no longer even aware of Crewe's presence. This was between her and that *other*—that other who had been tied here so long.

Murder—red death had come from what she held. And afterward perhaps, self-murder. A high price, but the one she believed now led them had been willing to pay.

"What's the matter with you?" Crewe's demand came impatiently.

Could not he see—did not he feel—anything? The girl tensed. What was happening to her? Some illusion born from all she had been through? But that answer could not satisfy her. She wet her lips with the tip of
220

her tongue, tasted the salt the water had encrusted there.

"Can't you see her?" Persis wanted so much his reassurance that she had not totally taken leave of her senses.

"See who?"

Again she wet her lips and forced out the words she felt would only make him sure she had lost command of herself.

"The Spanish lady—"

For *she* was still there. Even though she could not be seen except perhaps by the eyes of an overexcited mind. All that hung in the air were the slow, now-languid flutterings of those sparks of light. Of course—the jewels on the fan! That fan which should be safely in Lydia's chest, brought out only as a queer and eerie treasure to show visitors.

She expected Crewe to flare out at her, even to tell her that she was caught by delusion. But, to her bewilderment, his voice was quite even and controlled as he asked:

"Where?"

Somehow Persis was able to raise her arm, only a shadowy movement in this dark, but the whiteness of her flesh made it more visible. She pointed to the sparks of ever changing light.

"She is right there."

"You can see her?" his voice was still undisturbed.

"Not—not really. Not until I close my eyes. But the fan—she's holding the fan! Those little dancing lights —Can't you see them?"

She was so hungry for some collaboration, needed to know that her mind *was* clear and not overcast by this night's work.

"I cannot see her—"

Persis felt as if she were shriveling inside. So this is how it felt to lose one's mind—to—to go mad!

"But then she has never appeared to a man."

For a moment Persis could not take in what he meant. He—he sounded as if he believed her! But how could he? Such superstitions were only born of unsteady and hysterical minds. She laughed and that laughter grew more wildly loud, until an open palm met her cheek with bruising force, choking off the laughter, returning her with the shock to some manner of control.

"I'm—I'm not insane—" She did not know whether that was a question or a statement.

Crewe Leverett made no comment in answer to her half plea. Instead, still holding to Persis with his one usable hand, he asked with that old ring of authority in his voice, a shadow out of her past to draw the truth out of her:

"Where is she?"

"Just ahead, by the corner of the house."

"Does she face us or away?"

Persis could not understand his reasons for accepting what surely must be a hallucination as a truth of some consequence to them.

"She passed us. Now she is—she is moving on!" For it seemed that that strange whisper of wide skirts again filled the air, the fan was fluttering a little faster.

"Good—then we follow—"

"Why—? There is nothing there—there can't be anything!"

Persis struggled to free herself from his grip. If he had been weakened by the exertions of this night he seemed to have recovered much of his strength again, for the girl discovered she could not twist free.

222

"We follow," was all he said. And because Persis was too weak herself to fight him, she obeyed. However they both wavered and staggered as they went. And she cried out twice as her bare feet scraped on broken shells. But she did not try anymore to reason with her companion. The kitchen doorway lay not too far ahead. She fastened her eyes on the dim wall and the break in it which marked that opening. If she could only get in the house— in spite of all which had happened this night, the thick walls promised safety.

But when she would have broken free from her companion, turned in that direction, his grip tightened even more until she could have cried out at the pressure on her upper arm. It would seem that the last thing in the world Crewe Leverett intended to do was enter his own house. Instead he forced her along as the swish of invisible skirts could still be heard. And always she saw the glinting of the jeweled fan. They were both mad, Persis decided at last, with an unnatural calmness spreading over her exacerbated nerves— that was the only possible answer.

16

They limped over the causeway toward that part of the Key beyond the mound where the cabins of the islanders straggled along. And there was the brightness of moonlight in the full, so that Crewe drew her back into what small shadow might protect them. They had passed the house which appeared to Persis the only refuge she could trust. In this black-and-white night anything might be stealing on them.

Then—*it* was gone!

The chill of the air passed; there was no more fluttering of the jewel-sparked fan, no faint swish of skirts unseen. Just ahead was the first of the cabins.

"She's gone—" Persis somehow got out the two words in a voice which was near a whimper.

Beside her Crewe wavered and almost fell. Persis

drew his good arm around her nearly bare shoulders, supporting him. They staggered on together until they reached the first of the huts.

Crewe's voice came in a breathy rasp. "Pound on the door—now!"

She was so near exhaustion that it was hard to raise her free hand, obey his order.

There was no light showing behind the windows of the cabin where matting was tied down. But as Persis' fist arose weakly and fell again on the door there came a muttering and finally someone who must have been standing very close to the door, or crept there during her assault, said:

"Who be you?"

"Mason—" There was a muffled exclamation from within. Persis heard a bar thud away from its hoops. Now the door opened inward—though they still looked into the dark.

"Cap'n! It be you?"

"What is left of me." Again Crewe's voice strengthened as it had when he had asked for help from Askra at the landing. "Let me in, man, and be quick about it!"

"Truly will, Cap'n."

As they tottered forward stronger arms caught Crewe, drew him along. Persis freed from his weight had to catch at the side of that doorway or she might have slipped to the ground. Then a hold was on her also and she was pulled within, to have the door slammed, and hear, through the dark, the bar thud back into place once more.

"Cap'n—what's been happenin'?"

"Grillon's ashore, with I don't know how many of his bully boys. Can you scout out our men—those at

225

the hotel? He thinks I'm dead—or maybe just hopes it."

"Cap'n—! Here you, Carrie—light up the dish light— T'ain't much, Cap'n, but it's better than a lantern."

There was a tiny flicker in the dark, the sound of a tinderbox, and then indeed a light so faint it reached hardly beyond the border of the crude bowl in which a twist of fiber was awash with oil from which came a very strong smell of fish. So strong Persis' stomach near heaved.

She was sitting on a stool where she had been pushed, her battered and bleeding hands lying limply on her knees, every bruise she had met with that night adding to the ache of her body.

"Carrie," she heard Crewe's voice now as if it had come from a much farther distance. Her head was so light that when she tried to look at anything it spun in a slow but dizzy whirl. "Carrie, take care of the lady."

A shape moved forward between her and that tiny wisp of light and she found herself once more on her feet, being guided over to the far side of the hut and there settled on a pallet while a woman's voice murmured in the thick dialect of the islanders which Persis could not understand. She closed her eyes to fight that terrible giddiness and lapsed into a darkness more complete than that of the night outside.

If dreams pursued her in that dark, none of them lingered when she again roused. For several moments as she looked about her, she was dully amazed. This was not her bed—her room—It was as if she had awakened into another world.

The walls about her were rough stone fitted together as if they had been quarried of broken pieces. The spaces for two windows had irregular edging, just stones left out from the wall. Over her head was a framework of palm fronds based on timbers. There were two stools, a table rough-made but scrubbed clean. And, on the far wall, a rack in which rested two of those heavy swordlike knives the islanders used to cut away fast-growing underbrush. The mats which had closed both windows at night were now pushed out and held so by sticks braced against the wall.

This was—this was the cabin to which they had won their way last night. But she was alone in it. Persis struggled to sit up, the rags of her chemise, her stays, and her torn drawers had been taken from her. She was glad to find she was decently covered by a kind of loose robe which had a neck opening wide enough to slip over her head. Her hands hurt when she tried to move her fingers and she saw that they had been liberally smeared with a thick substance which had dried and which carried a pungent odor, some sort of herbal remedy she decided.

The giddiness, which had struck at her in the last moments of consciousness she could remember, was still enough to make her lean quickly back against the wall. But she was listening intently. There came the usual sounds of birds and insects from outside. And in addition, from not too far away, the sound of several voices rising and falling in the island dialect which Lydia had informed her very few not of native blood could hope to understand. A mixture it was of Indian, African, and a few Spanish words—reflecting those who had in turn subdued the Key and held it for a space.

Lydia! And Grillon! And Crewe!

All Persis' anxieties flooded back and she got to her knees on the pallet. It was then her eyes fell on what must have been carefully laid beside her head as she slept—the false fan with its hidden steel. This time she had no compunction in picking it up, even though the curling of her fingers around the hilt made her wince with pain. It had served them well last night. There was no place in this robe she could hide it, but keep it with her she would!

The door was unbarred, she saw now, partially ajar. And as a figure appeared in that gap, Persis held tightly to the dagger hilt. But the dark-faced woman who entered was one she remembered vaguely having seen in the washhouse conventionally employed in sudsing clothes. She wore a loose blouse of cotton which must have once been sun-bright yellow but was now faded in uneven streaks. And her skirt was full, though above ankle-length, patterned with a border of colored thread in a strange design.

She carried a bowl in both hands, steam arising from it. Seeing Persis awake she smiled widely, displaying two gaps in her front teeth. Her frizzled hair was caught up under a bright red kerchief, save for a fringe across her forehead. And certainly there was nothing more alarming about her than there had been in Mam Rose or Sukie, though she was clearly not a house-servant.

"Missie feel good?" She set the bowl down on the table, produced from a box a carved wooden spoon she dropped into it and then brought it to Persis. "Eat— eat—good—give strength—" She hesitated between words as if she needed to translate from her own speech into one Persis could understand.

"Captain Leverett—where is he?" Persis accepted the bowl, laying the fan dagger down beside her. She was instantly aware that the woman's eyes had flickered quickly to it and away again as if it were something she refused to acknowledge had any existence in her world.

228

"Th' Cap'n—he be doin' what needful—" The woman watched Persis spoon up the stew. To the girl's taste it was overseasoned, too peppery, but once she had started to eat she discovered that she was hungry, hungry enough to even relish this. And when she had emptied the bowl her turbaned hostess produced some fruit, the coolness of which relieved her mouth and throat.

She wondered what was "needful" for Captain Leverett. Surely to take care of his shoulder which might well have been reinjured during their activities of the night. But that she had any influence over him, or even over this woman, she doubted.

That she had not been returned to the house both puzzled and alarmed her. Now that she tried to remember those scraps of conversation she had overheard before Ralph Grillon left Crewe to what he believed a certain death, she wondered if the Bahamian had not after all ever planned to leave Lost Lady, but rather, with Lydia very much under his control, had seen a good chance to take over the whole operation. He could well have landed men (just as Crewe kept insisting through the night) and perhaps more than just Mrs. Pryor, Molly, and Shubal had had doctored food or drink served them, keeping them helpless while Grillon had moved in.

Molly! If the maid had recovered and discovered her own absence Persis imagined what an outburst there had been. Were the three she had seen sleeping in the house now under guard? And what of the remainder of the *Arrow's* men, and those from the Dutch ship—as well as Dr. Veering and the islanders?

How much could Crewe depend upon the latter? They were a mixture of races whose ancestors had seen many masters here and a new one might philosophically be accepted. While perhaps the rescued seafarers at the hotel might be persuaded that this was no fight of theirs, only a personal quarrel between two wreckers.

But where was Crewe—and what could he be doing?

The woman took away the second bowl she had offered when Persis signaled that she could eat no more. However, just as she placed it on the table, she turned sharply toward the doorway. And her attitude was such that Persis put out her hand once more to close on the fan dagger.

The man who ducked his head a little to enter was not an islander and Persis got to her feet quickly.

"Dr. Veering—! What is happening? Where is Captain Leverett? And—?"

He held up one hand defensively. "Not so fast, Miss Rooke. Though I can well understand your present bewilderment. Captain Leverett has sent me with a message—as well as to report upon how you fared after your ordeal. For reasons he himself shall later explain to you, he wishes you to keep out of sight. However, as soon as it grows dusk, Carrie here will get you into the house. If you will then at once go to your own chamber and dress as if for a regular dinner and then wait—"

"I don't understand—"

Dr. Veering had come up to her and had taken her hands, seeming more intent on inspecting the damage now hidden by Carrie's treatment than he was upon her beginning protest.

"Yes, yes, excellent. You may wash this off when you reach the house, Miss Rooke. I shall see some healing salve is there ready for you. Then I would suggest that you wear gloves upon your appearance. As for what Crewe Leverett plans—well, I left him growling like a veritable tiger because I would not let him undertake the first of it himself. Luckily he did *not* put out that shoulder again. No thanks to the strain with which he used it last night—"

"He might have died!" Persis said hotly.

"So he told me, very much to the point I must say. And how you, a slight female as you are and unable to swim, managed—" The doctor shook his head, "Though I have long ago learned that with females a man may never judge by appearance. The most fragile of ladies can on occasion develop the toughness of sword steel. Anyway—I would suggest that you rest all you can. The news I can give you is limited, for the simple fact that success depends on a number of 'ifs,' 'ands,' and 'buts'—and had anyone but Crewe mapped out such a piece of recklessness I would not have given a fig for its chances.

"Briefly, he has rounded up a force of volunteers—most of his own men on shore had been drugged and locked into the warehouse. Thanks to the help of Mason they are out, with the door still locked behind them and a group of island boys left inside to hammer and yell at intervals. With his crew, six from the *Arrow* and two of the Dutchmen, they have taken off to intercept the *Stormy Luck*—with Lan Harvery in command—much to Crewe's disgust. Though he had finally to admit that a willing spirit cannot induce a broken body only half-healed to do its best."

"And Grillon—Lydia—?" Persis wanted to know.

"Grillon is patrolling the south beach and Miss Lydia has been, shall we say, persuaded, to return to the house. She believes Grillon will come for her. There is a guard of his men, but those have been judiciously whittled down by the islanders. If Crewe's
231

force can board and take the *Stormy Luck,* then Grillon is bottled up here—in a manner marooned. And by evening we shall know one way or the other."

"But Captain Leverett is all right?" Persis returned to the question uppermost in her mind. That time they had spent in the water-filled darkness beneath the house had somehow lengthened in her own thoughts to such a space that she would never think of Crewe Leverett again as a stranger. It was as if their shared danger had somehow tied them together whether they would have originally willed it or no.

"Good enough," Dr. Veering assured her. "He has an amazingly strong constitution and I can't find that he has done anything to disturb the knitting of the broken bones. Had I had my way, of course, he would be in bed and asleep, if I had to pour a potion down his throat to assure that state. But with matters as they now are I cannot argue with him. You can help him best now by doing exactly as he asks—remain here in concealment until Carrie can get you into the house—"

"Molly, Mrs. Pryor—Shubal—?" she made a question of their names.

"They have all recovered from an amazing sleep. I had good reason to visit your man Shubal and so looked in upon the others. Mrs. Pryor is well aware of the situation and of what Captain Leverett intends. Your maid, after the manner of these island fevers, has again a temperature and so I gave her a soothing draft."

Persis looked down at her glazed and discolored hands. "Dr. Veering, will the plan be a success?"

He shrugged. "I am no gambler, Miss Rooke. I know the men Crewe Leverett has chosen and if anything can be accomplished—they are the ones to do so. It is no more foolhardy than other ventures they have tried in the past. But we can only possess our souls in patience and hope for the best. And—"

His attention had shifted from Persis to the dagger fan lying beside her on the pallet.

"The opal-eyed fan—but how—why?"

The girl shook her head. "It is not that one—the one Lydia keeps. Look," with ease of practice she slid the blade out of the mock fan.

"But where—?"

Dr. Veering was a man of science, a believer in the possible as ranked against those impossible things which had been happening. He might consider her bereft of part of her wits, but Persis needed his shrewd common sense to back her in her own belief that she was not under some disillusion.

She made her tale brief, of her finding the box after the second storm, of the strange way the fan had returned to her keeping even after she had repudiated it.

"But I was wrong in hating it," she added now. "Had I not had it with me last night Captain Leverett might well have been drowned—or even both of us ended dead."

Dr. Veering picked it up almost as if his hand moved against his will. He drew forth the dagger, sent it plunging back into its sheath again with a quick smack of his palm against its pommel. Then he inspected carefully the carving of the cats with their narrowed opal eyes which appeared to return his gaze with a knowingness that no artifact could have.

"Two fans—" he said slowly. "And one a weapon. It is a deadly trinket—I wonder who first devised such a deceit. But I think we can know now how the Lost Lady escaped her captor. It is very old, I think, and deadly—"

233

"Not always—it helped me," Persis said soberly. "And the lady—" She hesitated. Though Dr. Veering had displayed no sign of incredulity over her story of the discovery of the fan, the fact she had returned it to the ground, and then it had appeared again—oddly when, in spite of her repulsion, there was a need for it. The other tale of the "impression" must certainly place her in his mind as one of those hysterical females credulous to the point of silliness.

"Miss Rooke," he drew one of the stools away from the table and sat down, his expression one of serious consideration, "you have probably heard some of my past history. I have lived among native peoples—people who have beliefs—and, yes, talents—which our world would scoff at. I have seen, half-smothered by the jungle, parts of an unknown city, stone built, carved with forgotten beasts—or maybe gods—which has endured against the push of nature perhaps as long as the stones of that Rome, which our historians so revere, have been planted one on another.

"I have witnessed rites performed by those the outsider would term 'naked savages' which produced results our most learned doctors cannot begin to achieve. There is more in this world than we in our blind arrogance of race, we of the North, have been taught. Sometimes a fate or power beyond our conceiving moves and we are caught in that move—to play a part we do not even understand.

"This island has known many different peoples—and each has had their own beliefs. Did you ever think that belief in itself is a very powerful thing? It has caused men, yes, and women, too, to die painful deaths, by fire, wild beasts, hanging—even torture—because it was so much a part of their lives that they could not deny it. When I was very young Fox's *Book of Martyrs* was a favorite reading for Sunday. I am afraid that my youthful reaction to the heroes and heroines held up to the admiration of the reader in that dark chronicle of fanaticism was that they were stupidly self-righteous. Now I wonder if they were not possessed by beliefs they could not make the uninitiated really understand.

"There are many strange and wonderful things to be discovered yet. We are, I think, on the edge of a new age in which man is going to set forth exploring—not only land, but within himself—I know the story of the Lost Lady, of course. I also have spoken with three people who do faithfully believe that they have seen her. A land so soaked in blood and tears and violence as this island, may well project to the sensitive some fragment of the past— not what the ignorant term 'ghosts' but rather 'memories' or dreams of an emotion so overriding that time means nothing to what is netted in it."

Persis blinked. She could see he was in earnest—that his belief in his own explanation was perhaps as strong as that of the martyrs who had suffered for their fate generations ago.

"I saw her—twice—" she said slowly and this time did not expect derision from him in return. "No, not saw, perhaps—but there was a presence." And now she dared to tell of that meeting in the upper hall, and again of what had walked before them last night on the mound. "But that still does not explain how this," she gestured to the fan dagger, "returned to my keeping when I had buried it."

"No, But it served you well. And it served her in its time, did it not? It could be that your own uneasiness and fears made a path or thread of communication

235

between you and this 'presence.' She had great determination and courage of her own. Maybe that is the thread which united you. Now, Miss Rooke, put out of your mind that you have been visited by fantasies which suggest a weakness of intellect. Rather rest your thought upon the fact that had it not been for that," he pointed to the fan he had once more put down within her reach, "one, or perhaps two, worthwhile and needful lives might have come to an end last night. I would advise you now to rest. And when Carrie comes for you do just as I have suggested—get to your chamber, dress yourself in your best frock—come down to dinner as if nothing has happened. I do not know what play Crewe would set in action, but it is of utmost importance to his own plans for putting an end to this, that I can assure you."

He arose with a bow and left, giving Persis much to think over. But the languid heat of the afternoon did not aid thinking. She drowsed before she knew it and awakened to Carrie's soft shaking of her shoulder. Slipping behind the island woman, she crossed the open, sure at any moment in spite of the dusk, to be sharply challenged out of the shadows.

Then they came into the kitchen, a kitchen so much as usual that Persis could almost believe the happenings of the past twenty-four hours had been a complete nightmare. For Mam Rose was busy at her usual tasks, and both Sukie and her younger companion working well under her eyes.

But Persis, herself, might have been invisible. None of them looked up or appeared to notice her and, before she could thank Carrie properly for the shelter and tending the other had given her, she too, was gone. Dr. Veering's instructions, or rather Crewe's delivered through the doctor, carried her on, into the back of the
236

lower hall, up that much narrower and steeper staircase used by the servants.

Only there were lamps in the rooms tonight and a different feeling in the house. It was alive and—expectant—somehow that word came into Persis' mind as she gathered up the loose robe with both hands and hurried up the staircase, seeking the chamber which had been assigned her, ridden somehow by the need for haste.

She had been expected, that was very sure she saw as she entered for there was a hip bath filled and waiting behind a screen, towels laid out to her hand. Only Molly was missing.

Shedding the robe, she washed, reveling in the soft herb scent of the soap. There would be no time to deal with her hair, except to work it into the most possible coiffure, rather more severe than her usual one. And only time could fade the bruises showing black and ugly on her skin. Some had been spread with Carrie's ointment and that she washed off, making use of a box of salve left well in sight on the wash stand.

Persis deliberately selected one of her brighter dresses—a rose with satin stripes and rather more lace than usual about the shoulder bertha. It seemed to lend color to her face, and in a way that kind of courage a woman gains when she knows she is well and fittingly clad for some occasion.

Her hair was the hardest to handle. Carrie must have dried it and gotten some of the saltwater out of it. But there was no way Persis could produce the fashionable side curls. She braided and rebraided twice until she got top loops which looked at least smooth and then defiantly fronted them with her coral-topped comb, adding the coral earrings, which were a part of the same set, to offset the lack of ear curls.

Studying her reflection in the gold-edged mirror Persis was not entirely satisfied. But at least she presented the most proper appearance within her ability to achieve. She gathered up a handkerchief, folding it into a small drawstring bag of rose satin, just as the gong which had always heralded dinner sounded from the lower floor.

Looking herself straight in the eyes of her mirrored reflection, Persis raised her chin a fraction. But, before she moved to the door of the chamber she hesitated and made one more choice. Her hand closed on the false fan. Carried this way no one might guess that it was not real—and she felt safer with it for protection.

17

Persis reached the head of the stairs as the mellow tones of the gong sounded a second time. Pausing, she summoned all her courage. What game Crewe Leverett would play she could not guess. But, a little to her amazement, she discovered that her confidence in him was as great as once had been her acceptance of Uncle Augustin's complete command of any situation.

There was no one she could see below, but there came the murmur of voices through the high-ceilinged rooms and she descended step by step composedly. Her hands were covered with mitts of white silk thread she herself had skillfully knitted, and in the left she gripped the dagger fan. Though that she needed any such weapon she doubted.

"Miss Rooke—"

The voice from below was low, clear, and unmistakable. Persis felt a wave of relief as she looked down at the man who had moved into the brightest pool of lamplight. Most of his figure was muffled in a dressing gown of green and gold, such a robe as a king might envy him. And the bulky bunching of the material on one shoulder, the flapping sleeve, told her that he had probably chosen this garb because his injuries could not allow him a coat. But she could also see as he moved the cream-white trousers of Southern evening dress, and his hair was carefully arranged, his face, in spite of a bruise or two, impassive.

"Should you—" she tripped a little faster down those remaining stairs between them, "not be resting?"

There was an odd light in his sea-blue eyes. "Rest for the weary, eh? Veering would have me in bed again, eating slops and half-mad with my own worries. No, Persis," he had dropped his first formal salutation. "There shall be time enough for rest later. One deals with a snake before it can truly strike. Now, they are awaiting us— though they do not know it. Play up, my girl, give them your haughtiest stare and your grandest manner."

He bowed a fraction and held out his good arm. Making herself smile, Persis curtsied and laid her fingertips on the heavy brocade covering his forearm near his wrist. She longed for him to give her some clue as to what was about to happen, but there seemed to be no time, for already he was urging her on toward the entrance to the dining room.

More than the light of a single lamp beamed out through that door and Persis heard the sound of voices growing louder, but at that moment she was too flustered to make much sense of the words. Then—Crewe took a step into the full beam of that light as if he would first face any trouble, but she was only a step behind.

The long table had been covered with the whitest of fine linen and spaced along it were five candelabra, which seemed to Persis to light the room with a steady glare not far from the fullest reach of the sun. She was so dazzled for a second or two that it was difficult to sort out the company gathered around the table.

But the moment of instant silence, which had followed their entrance, in its way steadied her. And though her face felt frozen in expression, she hoped it expressed only polite acceptance of the fact that dinner was served.

A chair grated on the floor as the man at the end of the table pushed that back and rose to his feet. Her own companion broke the silence first:

"Lydia, my dear, you are looking well tonight—"

The blonde girl's breath hissed. Her dress, an elaborate one of lace ruffles and bows in a delicate blue, was in sharp contrast to her face. That was a mask of fear, her usually full lips flattened against her teeth, her eyes very wide and staring.

"One would begin to think," Crewe Leverett glanced about the table, his eyes catching each who sat there for an instant of meeting, "that this was indeed a festive occasion. May we be allowed to share the secret also?"

Persis' momentary bedazzlement was gone, she could identify some of those gathered here. Others were strangers. And in that company Lydia was the only woman—sitting on the right of the man who had arisen so suddenly.

The girl had seen Ralph Grillon in his working clothes, as master of a ship of which he was manifestly

241

proud. Now he wore a super-fine cloth jacket of dark blue, a ruffled shirt and complicated cravat, trousers of black strapped under shoes never meant to tread the deck of a working wrecker.

His handsome face was not flushed, and if he had paled under his tan, it was not visible in the softer light of the many candles. But his eyes—Persis might have shuddered at the look of them earlier—now she seemed armored against any threat from the Bahamian captain.

There was Dr. Veering, twirling the stem of a half-filled wine glass between his fingers, his glance turning from Crewe to those at the table, back again—although he showed no expression. But was rather as one who watched a play.

Three other men sat along the board—one wearing a captain's jacket, its insignia dimmed from the breath of the sea.

"Yes," Crewe continued, "a festive occasion. Captain Van Horne," he nodded to the stranger who arose and made a rather awkward bow, "and naturally Julio Valdez—"

The man on the other side of Grillon showed his teeth in what might have been meant to be a smile, but his eyes were very cold and calculating.

"It's been a long time, Valdez," Crewe continued, "though, of course, I knew that our account was not yet completed."

"Account?" The man's dark eyebrows lifted. "If one deals with thieves, Captain Leverett, one can only expect trouble to come of it."

"How correct you are in that prediction, Valdez. 'Deal with thieves.' But why do you not follow your own wisdom?"

"Halden had no right to Lost Lady!" Valdez put
242

palms down on the table, leaned forward, angry animation in his narrow face. "Mariana Valdez had no right to sell what was ours since we cleaned this isle of the rabble of Indians who infested it. I am Julio Valdez; there was a Valdez ruling here before your country even had a name to call itself by."

"Granted," Crewe commented. "But Martin Valdez was, there is no doubting, the heir-in-law. When he died his property passed to his wife and she sold it to Halden. I believe your offer, complete with threats if I am not mistaken, was thrown out of court and you were warned off. If Halden then chose to sell to me it was a perfectly correct transaction with not a hint of illegality about it—no matter how hard you have since tried to prove that true. Times have changed since the days of Satin-shirt Jack—"

The dark-faced man drew in his breath with a hiss which made Persis think of a threatening snake. Dr. Veering still kept his expression of lazy watchfulness, and the Dutch captain looked merely as if he were at a complete loss. Persis expected Crewe next to carry battle to Ralph Grillon himself, but instead he looked to Lydia.

"Is this occasion of your devising, my dear?"

Persis hoped that never would anyone use such a tone of voice to her. But Lydia had recovered quickly from any surprise she might have felt at her brother's sudden appearance.

"It is an occasion, yes," she returned in a voice as cool as his, but edged with defiance. "I am the betrothed wife of Captain Grillon."

"How very interesting," was Crewe's comment. "Has he yet explained how he intends to rid himself of the present Madam Grillon? Though I cannot but believe that he has already planned some highly ingenious method—not that such are always successful. My own appearance here is proof of that."

Lydia rose from her seat, her face contorted into an ugliness which was near that of the strange mask Askra had worn.

"Liar! Liar!" She beat both small fists upon the table. Her wine glass trembled and went over, discharging its contents, like newly shed blood, across the white linen. "Ralph *will* marry me—"

"Since bigamy is a crime, both here and in the islands, that presents a problem," Crewe continued his even, considered speech. "He does have a wife—oh, it is true enough," now he had a faintly contemptuous tone. "Do you think I am too dim-witted to check on any young buck who comes paying his addresses to my sister? But the present situation must task even *his* abilities. How do you balance the situation, Grillon? Is it Lost Lady and what you can gain here, against that which might or might not fall to your hands through Caroline Rooke?"

Persis started. Who was Caroline Rooke? In a second or two her mind leaped forward in a guess. Ralph Grillon had talked of a missing heir. She had always accepted that the child of James was a man—but what if the opposite were true and her rival for the Rooke fortune was a woman? Was that why Grillon knew so much and in such detail as to taunt her?

"If you were a whole man—" for the first time Ralph Grillon spoke, "I'd call you out—"

Crewe shook his head, an odd half smile on his face. "Do not try to play the gentleman here, Grillon."

"No!" Both Lydia's hands were at her lips now, half-muffling what she had to say. "You can't keep me here with your lies! Ralph loves me—we're to be married—"

"Where?" asked her brother. "In the islands—or in Key West?"

"It doesn't matter. He'll take me away—he—" Suddenly her voice was gone. Persis saw that the younger girl's eyes were fixed not on her brother but on that seemingly closed fan she herself had brought with her.

"*No!*" Lydia backed away and her long skirts pushed against the chair behind her, sending it crashing to the floor, the noise so startling that Persis herself shook for a moment. But her brother seemingly had no interest in the fan.

"You little fool," he said with a kind of weariness which made Persis uneasy. So far he had held them all, and more than half of these gathered here must be his enemies. "He wants Lost Lady—thanks to providence and the courage of this lady he did not succeed in his first attempt. It was a mistake, Grillon, to leave the sea to do your ill work for you; it is always capricious as you should know by now."

"You were in no harm!" Lydia cried out. "Just left for a space so Ralph could—could—"

"Make sure of me." Crewe was brutally direct now, as if his weariness was increasing so he felt he must make a swift end to this confrontation. Persis saw Dr. Veering move unobtrusively up the table, come to stand at Crewe's other side, and that action added to her worry. "Yes, Lydia. I was left well bound, in a dugout which had been holed—death was already lapping at me when you left."

She shrank even farther away and now her eyes went to Grillon.

"That is a lie—you would say anything to—"

But some slight change on the Bahamian's face must have broken her last defense against the truth. "But why, Ralph, why?"

"I have already said it—Lost Lady—" Crewe returned. "Once he no longer needed your help—another accident—" He tried to shrug and winced. Dr. Veering put a hand gently on the well-swathed shoulder.

Persis saw a deathly pallor spread across Lydia's face.

"To—to—kill—" the younger girl said as if it required all the possible effort left in her to bring out the words.

"Just so," Ralph Grillon spoke for the second time. He, too, had taken several steps away from the table and with him moved the man who called himself Julio Valdez and three of the others who had remained silent during this exchange. "And since I am now master of the Key—" There was a pistol in his hand now, deadly, and steady. And the others held them also.

Lydia had hidden her face in her hands and was crying —fast becoming hysterical.

"Since I do hold the Key," Grillon continued, "it would seem that the game is not yet played out."

There was a queer dizzy feeling in Persis' head for a moment or two. It was as if she had seen, or been a part of this same scene before. Only for a second rift out of time other faces, hard, brutal, fitted like masks of smoke across the faces of those in this room. She dropped her hand from Crewe's arm, fumbled with the false fan until its inner deadly steel core appeared. They would be killed—these monsters from the sea— she was—

A sound, strident, carrying, drew her back into herself. She was once more Persis Rooke and not another who had looked upon death as a welcome door to another kind of safety.

Ralph Grillon threw back his head and laughed like a boy.

"Done in, by Neptune himself!"

"Wait and see—"

Persis was sure that Dr. Veering was lending Crewe more support than it looked. Yet his voice remained steady.

"There is nothing to wait for—that's the *Stormy Luck*!" Ralph was exultant. "With your men safely housed I'll have what I came for and be away. Though it was a pity you did not play the part you were set, Captain." He shook his head, the old reckless mockery plain on his face. "It would have been so much more convenient all around. I could have done very well as master here. Now, m'dear," he bowed to Lydia, "this time I fear I shall have to say good-bye in earnest. Though I have much to thank you for—"

Her face was blotched, tear-reddened. She looked like a child who had been slapped by a trusted hand.

"But I'm to go—"

"Your big brother is infernally right. Dear Caroline would hardly welcome you; she will only welcome me because I am a source of future wealth for her now— thanks to your clever little fingers and your ability to concoct interesting drinks."

"Then—then it's true?"

"That I am married to Caroline Rooke; yes, that is the truth—though I had another claim, y'know. It would not have held in court, of course, but it was enough to send me prying into old secrets. Amos had more than one son on the wrong side of the blanket. Though he was only really sure of James. My father was born out of a shorter entanglement, one he found easy to forget. So dear Caroline was my cousin. Thus we joined forces as soon as we knew there were pickings to be had. Not that I fancied Caroline particularly. She has a hag's own temper and I can think about her more happily when there's a goodly portion of the sea between us. But we were both Rookes, you see, and we weren't going to let Amos' hoard go to anyone else.

"Now that I can destroy the papers, I am sorry, Cousin Persis," he made a mock bow in Persis' direction, "to say that you have had a very fatiguing and fruitless journey —"

For the second time the conch trumpet sounded.

"I would suggest," Crewe said evenly as the last of that braying, mournful sound echoed around the well-lighted room, "that you do not count on calm seas yet a while."

"With the *Luck* coming into the wharf and no one but you to say me 'no'—?"

But one of the silent men who had backed him had stepped to the window which was open to the night save for the netting which kept the insects out. Ralph Grillon jerked a quick glance in his direction.

"What's to do, Grimes?"

"There's trouble—down on the wharf. And your double lantern ain't ridin' on the bowsprit neither!"

Ralph backed to the window. "Cover them," he ordered. Only when the Bahamian saw Crewe caught fully in the sights of his companion's boarding pistol did he turn his own head to look.

And they could hear now—more than the moan of the conch trumpet heralding the arrival of a sail.— There were shouts and the roar of at least one pistol. Grillon's lips grew thin in a grimace.

"The *Luck*?" He looked directly at Crewe.

"A prize crew," the other returned as calmly as ever.

"Damn you to hell! But how—" Then Grillon caught at his self-command with a speed Persis would not have thought native to one of his temperament. "So—and now what do we do?" But he did not lower the pistol and the look in his eyes brought back to the
248

girl a flash of strange and terrible memory—of a mound torch lit and a sacrifice delivered to masked priests. So might those have looked upon their prey.

"We do nothing." Crewe moved forward to the nearest chair and lowered himself into it, keeping his bandaged shoulder well from the back so that he leaned forward as if about to pour himself a glass of wine. "It is what you will do, Grillon. By rights I could have you before the courts for conspiracy, attempted murder, perhaps even piracy and certainly for theft."

"But you have an alternative, of course. A desperate man might even take a few desperate measures, were he driven too far," Grillon cut in. His pistol's deadly mouth was again held steadily level, and now it seemed to Persis to be sighted on Crewe's head.

"I have an alternative. But not for any fear of that armament you are so keenly trusting to. You are a liar, a cheat, and a would-be murderer," Crewe spoke with the deliberation of a justice pronouncing sentence. "However, you will return what you have stolen and you will sail from here—with your men. Mainly because my sister is a fool. I will not have her stand in any court to be smeared as you would gladly smear her to save your own skin."

Ralph Grillon suddenly laughed, and then dropping his pistol to his side, he gave Lydia a deep bow.

"By all means—a lady's name is above—"

"Close your mouth!" For the first time Crewe raised his voice, and Persis saw the anger which must have seethed within him for hours rise to the surface. "Do not try my patience too far."

As the pistol disappeared beneath his coat, Ralph Grillon gave him a half salute.

"You are really the fool, you know," he said frankly. "To let me go so."

"Yes, I should have you killed, should I not?" Once more Crewe had obtained command of himself. "But I hunt my own snakes, Grillon; I give no orders to another to do that. Now you will tell Dr. Veering exactly where you put the gold and papers taken from my strongbox, plus those which belong to Miss Rooke. When those papers are returned, you shall be free to go—"

There was a sound at the door behind them. Persis glanced around. Mr. Harvery stood there, and behind him crowded the bosun of the *Nonpareil*, two of her crew.

Again Grillon bowed. "Your forces have arrived, I see. Very well, Veering. You will find what the Captain wishes in a rock crevice just above tide level out on the point. The rock which guards it is the highest one in sight."

The doctor left the room, taking from the bosun as he passed a lantern the man carried in one hand, as a balance perhaps for the unsheathed cutlass in the other.

Persis came to the table, pulled to her an empty glass and splashed into it, with no regard for the drops which flew out to stain the napery further, a good portion of wine. She pushed it into Crewe's hand. Almost absentmindedly he raised it to his lips and drank. She watched that pinched look about his lips. How long could he hold out? He should be in his bed right now, not trying his fading strength further and further. Yet she knew instinctively that no one would ever stop him until he was ready.

Lydia's loud sobs had died away to sniffles. Her face was blotched and she kept her eyes down, huddling into the chair where she had sat earlier with such an assumption of pride of place.

"Cousin," Grillon broke the short silence, "if I have you to thank for taking a hand in this matter—"

But it was not Crewe who interrupted him, but Lydia. She pulled herself erect and pointed with a shaking hand.

"Don't you see it!" her voice near shrilled into another scream. "Look at what she holds! She—the Lady—"

Persis had near forgotten the blade. Now she stared down at it and allowed it to fall from her hand onto the table where its black hilt was dull, but where the narrowed jeweled eyes of the watching cats glittering in the light, coldly, removed from all which was real and of this time and place.

"It—it was in a fan—a false fan which would not open," she said. "Yet the fan looked the same."

"Even the ghosts," Lydia wailed, "don't you see—even the ghosts were against us!"

Persis expected either Grillon or Crewe to refute such folly. But when she looked from the face of one man to the other, she saw that instead their attention was riveted upon the fan as if it were some strange and unexplainable omen.

"The ghosts—" Grillon's voice was lower, far less assured now than he had ever heard it before. "Maybe you are right, m'dear—" Then he turned to Crewe:

"The greatest folly of all—"

"And that being?" Crewe asked as if Grillon's half sentence made some sense to him.

"That of always choosing the wrong woman. Dona Isabelle had that in her which put an end to her worst enemy—is that not so, Valdez—?"

Now the dark man who had claimed the Key, was staring also wide-eyed at the false fan. He gave a visible shudder.

"They told tales of her once," he said. "She knew too much, they claimed, of things better forgotten. The fan was part of her dowry; she was never without it about her. But that there were two fans—that there is no history of. Only—it was also said that she had such courage as a man might envy."

"She was not alone in that," Crewe returned. He reached over the sharp blade which the false fan had hidden, and before Persis knew what he was about his fingers caught and held hers in a warming, demanding hold against which she discovered she had no will nor need to struggle.

"As I said," Grillon seemed determined to have the last word, "always the wrong woman, Leverett. Your infernal luck has not failed you yet."

"And it never will," Crewe answered with the same firmness as the grip of that hand holding hers. For once in her life Persis Rooke found she could believe anything at all—provided a wrecker captain chose to say it.

W0105-W

Dorothy Eden

One of today's outstanding novelists writes tales about love, intrigue, wealth, power—and, of course, romance. Here are romantic novels of suspense at their best.

☐ AN AFTERNOON WALK	23072-4	$1.75
☐ DARKWATER	23544-0	$1.95
☐ THE HOUSE ON HAY HILL	23789-3	$1.95
☐ LADY OF MALLOW	23167-4	$1.75
☐ THE MARRIAGE CHEST	23032-5	$1.50
☐ MELBURY SQUARE	22973-4	$1.75
☐ THE MILLIONAIRE'S DAUGHTER	23186-0	$1.95
☐ NEVER CALL IT LOVING	23143-7	$1.95
☐ RAVENSCROFT	23760-5	$1.75
☐ THE SALAMANCA DRUM	23548-9	$1.95
☐ THE SHADOW WIFE	23699-4	$1.75
☐ SIEGE IN THE SUN	23884-9	$1.95
☐ SLEEP IN THE WOODS	23706-0	$1.95
☐ SPEAK TO ME OF LOVE	22735-9	$1.75
☐ THE TIME OF THE DRAGON	23059-7	$1.95
☐ THE VINES OF YARRABEE	23184-4	$1.95
☐ WAITING FOR WILLA	23187-9	$1.50
☐ WINTERWOOD	23185-2	$1.75

Buy them at your local bookstores or use this handy coupon for ordering:

B14

John D. MacDonald Travis McGee Series

Follow the quests of Travis McGee, amiable and incurable tilter at conformity, boat-bum Quixote, hopeless sucker for starving kittens, women in distress, and large, loose sums of money.

"McGee is top-notch MacDonald."
—Chicago Tribune

Historical Romance

Sparkling novels of love and conquest against the colorful background of historical England. Here are books you will savor word by word, page by spellbinding page.

☐ AFTER THE STORM—Williams	23081-3	$1.50
☐ ALTHEA—Robins	23268-9	$1.50
☐ AMETHYST LOVE—Danton	23400-2	$1.50
☐ AN AFFAIR OF THE HEART Smith	23092-9	$1.50
☐ AUNT SOPHIE'S DIAMONDS Smith	23378-2	$1.50
☐ A BANBURY TALE—MacKeever	23174-7	$1.50
☐ CLARISSA—Arnett	22893-2	$1.50
☐ DEVIL'S BRIDE—Edwards	23176-3	$1.50
☐ ESCAPADE—Smith	23232-8	$1.50
☐ A FAMILY AFFAIR—Mellow	22967-X	$1.50
☐ THE FORTUNE SEEKER Greenlea	23301-4	$1.50
☐ THE FINE AND HANDSOME CAPTAIN—Lynch	23269-7	$1.50
☐ FIRE OPALS—Danton	23112-7	$1.50
☐ THE FORTUNATE MARRIAGE Trevor	23137-2	$1.50
☐ THE GLASS PALACE—Gibbs	23063-5	$1.50
☐ GRANBOROUGH'S FILLY Blanshard	23210-7	$1.50
☐ HARRIET—Mellows	23209-3	$1.50
☐ HORATIA—Gibbs	23175-5	$1.50

Buy them at your local bookstores or use this handy coupon for ordering:

FAWCETT BOOKS GROUP
P.O. Box C730, 524 Myrtle Ave., Pratt Station, Brooklyn, N.Y. 11205

Please send me the books I have checked above. Orders for less than 5 books must include 75¢ for the first book and 25¢ for each additional book to cover mailing and handling. I enclose $_____ in check or money order.

Name_____
Address_____
City_____State/Zip_____
Please allow 4 to 5 weeks for delivery.
